*The*
# WEKA–FEATHER CLOAK

# THE WEKA-FEATHER CLOAK

## A New Zealand Fantasy

# LEO MADIGAN

BETHLEHEM BOOKS • IGNATIUS PRESS
BATHGATE, N.D.        SAN FRANCISCO

*For the benefit of our many young American readers,*
*we have used American spelling rather than the British*
*form used by most other English-speaking countries.*

Text © 2002 Leo Madigan

Front cover art © 2002 David Hohn
Interior and back cover art by Roseanne Sharpe © 2002 Bethlehem Books
Cover design by Davin Carlson

First Printing, March 2002

ISBN 1-883937-68-X
Library of Congress Catalog Number: 2002102850

Bethlehem Books • Ignatius Press
10194 Garfield Street South
Bathgate, ND 58216
www.bethlehembooks.com

Printed in the United States on acid free paper

*For Carol Murphy*
*of Hamilton, New Zealand*

# Contents

# 1

## A Plane Crash

THE OCEANIA Airways flight 313, its tail ablaze, burst out of the night sky like a meteor. All Wellington to the south, and the Hutt Valley to the north, saw the fiery monster hit the harbor and skid on its fuselage across the surface of the water. Hissing and spluttering like a steam iron, it came to a standstill with its nose against the low, bush-covered cliffs of Somes Island.

The city, suspending breath and movement, was tensed for an explosion. But it never came. Instead the great machine belched like a sleeping elephant and settled itself a half a meter onto the shallow seabed.

Straightaway sirens started up, searchlights drowned out the moon and an armada of launches and helicopters sped off towards the island.

On a television screen in a shop window in Lower Hutt High Street, Danny Mago caught a glimpse of the survivors being brought ashore. Women clutched at salvaged purses, children at sorry-looking toys. The men were nonplussed. All were disheveled and wet and their eyes were frightened.

Danny pulled up his bicycle and wheeled it onto the pavement. There was something ghoulish about watching people who had suffered a tragedy, but something compelling too. Danny was vaguely wishing there was something he could do to alleviate the shock and devastation these people were under-going when the screen suddenly switched to a helicopter land-ing with survivors.

Among those who emerged was a blond-haired young man in a white shirt, still so wet that it clung to his skin. His trousers were torn so that they looked stereotyped, Robinson Crusoe trousers, and he had bare feet. Yet he moved like a prince. A Red Cross nurse placed a blanket around his shoulders, which he wore like an ermine cope. He smiled as he passed the cam-era, just as a prince might smile.

Danny had the oddest sensation that he had seen him before. Or maybe it was just an even odder presentiment that he would see him again.

When Year 10 crowded into the Art Room much of the working space was taken up by the project that Year 9 had left. What was it? Year 10 asked. What was it supposed to be?

"A pyramid of death," Mr. Grundy explained. "Year 9 con-ceived, designed and constructed it all by themselves. They got no help from me."

"Very wise of you to disown it, Mr. Grundy. An art teacher could lose his job if it got about that he had been promoting rubbish like that."

"The word 'rubbish' in this context, Duffy, reflects the dis-order in your own mind. Year 9 was asked . . ."

"It's just black crepe paper wound around a bamboo frame, Sir. It's not a pyramid. No self-respecting Pharaoh would be seen dead in that. It's a wigwam."

"Year 9 were very disturbed by the plane crash in the har-bor on the weekend. They got together and decided to express their concept of death in some tangible form."

"Sir?"

Mr. Grundy was an Englishman. He looked like an English-man. He spoke like an Englishman. His Englishness prompted the extrovert element of Year 10, born and bred Kiwis who wouldn't normally address a knight of the realm as "Sir", to come over all *Tom Brown's Schooldays* in Mr. Grundy's class.

"Sir?" Pascal the Handsome, who never got less than 90% for Geometry, made two, maybe three, questioning syllables out of the word. "How can a polyhedron with a polygonal base and triangular faces meeting in a common vertex represent death?"

"How indeed, Pascal. How indeed! When you know that you will understand the Poetry of Art, and the Art of Poetry. We live in a world of representation as a fish lives in a world of water. What is this?" Mr. Grundy took a ten dollar bill from his pocket and waved it above his head.

"A ten dollar note."

"That's mine, Sir. I dropped it earlier. Honest!"

"If I was starving," said Mr. Grundy, "could this keep me alive for another few days? Don't bother with smart answers. It could. Or rather its buying power could. We all know that. However, were we to turn the clocks back two hundred years and I was standing in this same spot would this ten dollar note avail me any?"

"No, Sir!"

"The Maori would have eaten you before you could spend it, Sir."

"There were no dollars then, Sir, and none of us pakeha."

"The Maori had eaten them all . . ."

"Yeah! And not paid the bill. We should mass together and demand payment for our eaten ancestors. . . ."

"It's like refusing to pay the tab in a restaurant, only on a global scale . . ."

"Too right! We demand compensation . . ."

"The United Nations . . ."

"It's traumatized my life, I can tell you . . ."

"Settle down, now! Settle down!" Mr. Grundy summoned placidity into the room by patting the air with his hand. "Now I want to go over your term papers with each of you individually. While I'm doing this I want you to design what you think would be an artistic representation of death AND . . . listen for it . . . Pascal, sit down. Libby Wright, over here where I can see you . . . AND I want you to write why this represents death for you. I don't want a plate of spaghetti and then some airy spiel about how it could be poisoned spaghetti. Paper there, pencils there. Each student to work individually. No need for discussion."

"Please, Sir, Mago's cheating already. He deserves a beating, Sir. Will you thrash him?"

"I will not. Settle down now, will you, and give this project some thought."

"There's nothing to stop me from thrashing him, Sir. Shall I do it? I could put the boot in, Sir. Or maybe garrote him." This was Myers. Myers was adept with words. "Oh, do let me garrote him."

"Cut the cackle, Myers. Get on with your work."

"Sir, I need a model for death. Do let me use the Maggot, Sir. He's a very insignificant maggot. No one would miss him."

Mr. Grundy said, "Danny Mago's got more artistic potential than all of this school put together, and that includes the teaching faculty."

This was greeted by a rising groundswell of OOOhhhs! Thin, plain, timid Danny Mago bent low over his desk as the blood burned his cheeks.

"I think he's hemorrhaging, Sir. Shall I finish him off? Please let me finish him off."

Sister Eileen, the Deputy Headmistress, entered the art room from the corridor and within an instant the class was absorbed in work. She wore a long white gown and around her hair was a thin blue veil. A silver crucifix hung from her neck on a silver chain. All the students admired Sister Eileen, who had the knack of making each feel that she was his, or her, Guardian Angel. But you didn't fool in Sister Eileen's classes. You didn't fool if she was anywhere on the horizon.

Sister Eileen smiled briefly at the class and conferred quietly with Mr. Grundy. Occasionally they would look out over the sea of heads and then both nodded in agreement. Sister Eileen walked to the door. Before stepping into the corridor she said, "Danny Mago, I'd like to see you in my office after school."

The door had barely closed behind the Deputy when the whispering started: The Maggot was in for it. The Maggot was in deep trouble. He'd been found out, the miserable little Maggot, whatever it was he'd done. He'd probably get the death sentence.

"Sir, let me put him out of his agony. A quick chop in the nape of the neck, thus . . ." Myers had jumped up from his seat and was standing over Danny Mago demonstrating his karate movements when Sister Eileen stepped back into the room. She said, "I'm sorry, Danny, if I made that sound like a summons. I want to ask a favor of you, that is all. Do forgive me if I alarmed you. Or gave anyone else the wrong impression." She smiled sweetly at Colin Myers, who was still standing over Danny Mago's desk as if, like Lot's wife, he'd been turned into a pillar of salt.

# Fifteen Dollars
# an Hour

THAT NIGHT, over dinner at the kitchen table, Danny told his mother, "I've got a job after school and on weekends, Mum." He leaned across and began to cut up the pieces of meat on his sister's plate. Sometimes she could do it herself. At other times she had no control over her hands. They would twist in the air like the hands of a wizard casting some complicated spell. Angela was 17, but there were times when she had to be looked after like a seven-year-old, and at other times she was as knowledgeable as a person of seventy. It was a strange, mysterious gift having such a sister.

"A job, Danny, how nice. Good experience for you, and some pocket money," said his mother without proper attention and then, as the implications dawned on her she said, "After school and on the weekends! But I rely on you at those times to be with Angela. I really can't work at Kirkaldies all day and then come home and start all over again, Danny."

"I told Sister Eileen that, Mum, but she said the Sisters could include that in the job description. Angela can stay on at the Nazareth Center free."

"Sister Eileen? Free?" Brigid Mago laid down the newspaper she had been leafing through and gave her full attention to her son. "Better start again, Son. Slowly."

"I've got a job—J.O.B. Roustabout at the convent at Aniwaniwa. That's where the Sisters live. The Sisters run the Center too. *Ergo*—E.R.G.O. that's Latin for therefore—they are willing to let Angela stay on at the center while I'm working. And in the meantime they are going to pay me too. Money. M.O.N.E.Y. Honest!"

Danny's mother's expression mixed surprise with incredulity. Then she turned her attention to her invalid daughter. "And what does Angela have to say?"

Angela's face twisted into what her family knew was whole-hearted confirmation. Then she knocked her fists together and revolved her hands. This was a question. She was asking Danny to be more precise about what this new job entailed.

"I've got to look after the conservatory, sweep the paths, do odd jobs—and help Mother Madeleine when she needs me. There was mention of her helping me to paint, or me helping her. That part's still a bit vague."

Brigid Mago sort of gulped. "Mother Madeleine! Your father would be over the moon. He always claimed she was the greatest artist in the world." She picked up her newspaper, then promptly replaced it on her lap. "Are you sure you mean *the* Mother Madeleine. I'd heard she'd died."

"Oh, come off it Mum. She was on a stamp only last month." He cut up another slice of meat on Angela's plate.

Angela managed to tap the back of Danny's hand with her spoon. It looked like an accident of her strange gyrations but in fact it was an affectionate tap, which said: *That's enough, thanks! I can manage now.* You had to know the body language to interpret it.

Danny said, "Sister Eileen is going to contact you."

His mother considered for a moment. "How much did you say they were going to pay you?"

"I didn't say, but as you ask it's fifteen dollars an hour."

Danny's mother echoed the sum and sat with her mouth open, waiting for him to revise it. "Fifteen . . .?"

"Fifteen big ones. I swear! It's nothing to them. Mother Madeleine probably makes a million dollars for the convent with every painting she does."

Angela thumped her legs with her hands and made a vibrating sound with her tongue between her teeth.

"Well, there's no arguing with you this time, Ange. It really is the bees' knees."

## *Meeting Mother Madeleine*

THE NEXT afternoon Danny cycled to the Convent. He timed the journey. It took eight minutes to the entrance with the sign, *St. Martin de Porres' Convent, Aniwaniwa* painted on a wooden arch above it. A half a minute along a drive between boxwood hedges and across a bridge that straddled the Waiwhetu Stream. At that point he had to stop pedaling and wheel the bicycle up a steep driveway cut into the side of the hill, a very cool, very dark driveway like a great cathedral with cataracts of light spilling through the leafy windows high above. That took three minutes and then, suddenly, the convent itself.

It was a cheerful building. There was no immediate reason why, but it made one want to smile. It was decorative in an old fashioned, almost Gothic, way and the rosy stone that it was built with had clearly absorbed the sun of well over a hundred summers.

Danny leaned the bike against one of the half dozen columns that held up the portico and climbed the steps. The door was three times as tall as he was and twice as wide. The panels on the side were stained glass showing scenes of trees and vines and nymphs not wearing much at all. There was a bell-pull set into a niche with a cross above it. Danny jerked it and a mighty clanging was set up inside.

9

Through the stained glass he could see a figure approaching. The bell was still clanging when the door opened, though it stopped in time for him to say, "I'm Danny Mago from Holy Trinity. Sister Eileen told me to ask for Sister Paula."

The nun was dressed in the same sort of white habit and blue veil that Sister Eileen always wore, but she also had a black apron strapped around her waist and her sleeves were rolled up to the elbow. "That's me," she said. Danny thought she was very young, for a nun. She had one of those faces that always intrigued him, innocent, practical, amused. It was a face that gave a boy confidence, and demanded respect. It was a Joan of Arc sort of face. "Come!" she said, smiling cheerily, "I'll give you the grand tour and show you what's to be done. Then I'll take you to meet Mother Madeleine. She'll put the fear of God into you, I'll wager. Let's go down to the conservatory first."

The conservatory was reached by an elegant stone stairway,—100 steps, Sister Paula pointed out, 10 flights of ten steps each—that zigzagged down through the native bush to where posts in the water showed where a footbridge had once crossed this stretch of the Waiwhetu Stream. The area around, apparently, had formerly been called the Lower House. Now it simply consisted of paths and steps and walls with rusted doors and gardens run to seed between the crumbling walls of abandoned buildings.

The conservatory itself—Sister Paula called it a greenhouse—was almost as big as the railway station in Lower Hutt. Much of it was overgrown with weeds and moss, and green slime covered the panes of glass that weren't broken. One corner, though, was well tended. Rows of dahlia and carnation and iris and chrysanthemum stood in pots along serried tiers of planking while spring clematis and passion flower and bold bougainvillea ran up the walls and across the ceiling wires, spilling out colors like an empress' jewel box.

"Originally we had a Boy's Preparatory School down here," Sister Paula said, pushing back some exotic red-petalled blooms to peer behind a statue of Diana the Huntress as if some urchins might still be lurking there. "In those days all the land beyond the stream, several hundred acres of it, was the Convent Farm. But times change, times change. Most of our Sisters are too old now. The few younger ones go out to teach or run the Nazareth Center. I daresay we'll be selling the place before long and setting up somewhere more practical. The Order is really only keeping it till the older Sisters move on. As you can see, there is plenty of clearing up work to do."

Back at the Top House Sister Paula took him through corridors where calm, unhurried nuns, in white with blue veils, moved as though they were on castors. She showed him the Green Room with its chandelier like a forest carved from crystal and the Blue Room with its S-shaped chair, which Sister Paula said, was for lovers to sit and gaze into each other's eyes. "Not much in use these days," she commented dryly.

Carved monkeys held up the banisters of the staircase and the porcelain of the sink basins had been painted with flowers and leaves before being glazed. The chapel was small but magnificent, built all of dark wood, kohekohe for the walls and ceiling and towai for the nun's choir stalls, except for the sanctuary where the wood was a creamy kahikatea, polished to look like ivory. Back at the front door the sunlight shone through the stained glass nymphs, provoking Danny into thinking that the decoration wasn't quite what he expected of a convent. Sister Paula, as if reading his mind, commented laconically, "The house was built in the early days by a wealthy family. We've only had it since 1889."

"Ah!" said Danny. "Then these nymphs are not saints?"

"Not to my knowledge," Sister Paula replied.

As they left the house by the front portico a wide graveled

area spread before them. To their left it disappeared around the side of the house and became the drive that lead back down to the road. Directly in front of them were the 100 ornate steps that led to the Lower House. To the left was a rectangular building standing by itself. It had six large sash windows on the side wall and, at the end separated from the main building by an arch, which led into a courtyard, a plain door up four steps. "Mother Madeleine's studio," said Sister Paula. They crossed the gravel. "Originally it was the billiard room. None of the Sisters played billiards, so Mother Madeleine appropriated it. Are you ready?" She knocked briefly, then opened the door into the vast, airy studio.

Canvases, large and small, were stacked against walls while tables with paints and brushes and odd props were placed around the room, apparently without design. Near the door, propped on the ledge of a huge mirror in a gilt frame, was a blackboard. On it was written, *November 2, All Souls Day.*

Mother Madeleine had been working behind an easel at the far end of the room, but she stepped out when Sister Paula called. She was a large Maori lady, like a balloon that has been blown up till its skin is squeaky taut, and her forehead was as thick with perspiration as a windscreen in the rain. Danny and Sister Paula walked forward. Mother Madeleine was very old but her eyes were young. And her smile was young. As they reached her she held out her veined brown hand. For a moment Danny didn't register that he was supposed to shake hands with this legend of a woman. It wasn't that he found her intimidating. On the contrary—he felt he had known her for as long as he could remember. If he was momentarily stunned it was because he experienced an overwhelming urge to paint her. Indeed, it was more than an urge, it was a compulsion. Human converse, food, could wait; rational life itself could be suspended—he must paint her. If he was staring at her, somewhat agape, it was because his eyes were pho-tographing and storing her every detail.

Mother Madeleine waited a short while, then picked up Danny's right hand as if it were a knot at the end of a bell rope; she tugged at it perfunctorily, saying as she did so that she would see him in the morning. Then she addressed Sister Paula, "Tomorrow's St. Martin de Porres, Sister—November 3rd. Don't forget the cloak."

Still dazed, Danny followed Sister Paula across the studio and through a doorway on the far side. It led into another goodly-sized room the most compelling feature of which was an enor-mous mirror, freckled in parts with age, but splendid and commanding. It reached from the floor almost to the ceiling and must have measured two meters across. The frame was rich, oiled kohekohe, carved all over with Maori symbols, like canoe prows and weaving pegs, all rolling spirals, unaunahi and tikis.

Sister Paula opened a cupboard in the wall, which ran at right angles to the wall that featured the mirror. Gripping a pump handle that stood there, she began to jerk it backwards and forwards. "Now you will learn some of our little secrets," she said.

Suddenly she stopped. "What am I breaking my back here for?" she exclaimed. "This is the sort of thing we have imported your young muscles for. Get to it." Danny took over the handle and slowly, as he pumped, the mirror swung back as a door. "It's hydraulic," Sister Paula explained in her mat-ter-of-fact fashion.

The room inside was about the size of an ordinary bedroom. A small window of opaque glass bricks high up to the right admitted a little light. The walls were paneled in white tawa. A knob was fixed to the left wall, and an old clothes brush dan-gled from it by a length of twine. Apart from that the room was empty except for a tailor's dummy in the center. And encircling the tailor's dummy was a splendid object—an ancient and regal weka-feather cloak, the ceremonial garment of the Maori chiefs, held around the shoulders by a clasp of woven flax.

Sister Paula removed it from the dummy and gave it to Danny to carry. It was heavy. The brown feathers of the weka bird were as smooth as silk and the black lining was cold, almost wet. "Eel-skin," Sister Paula said. "This cloak belonged to the Chiefs of Mother Madeleine's Te Ati Awa tribe for generations and by a strange coincidence we inherited it with the house. It had been lost, or stolen, or sold long before Mother Madeleine was born. You saw the statue of St. Martin de Porres in the chapel, the young black Dominican? Well, every year on his feast we clothe it with the cloak. Also the statue of Our Lady of Fatima on the 13th of May. These are little devotions we have grown to love."

They walked back through the studio. Danny was still carrying the cloak over his arm. Mother Madeleine called, "Guard that with your life, Big Boy! That cloak and me are all that's left of the Te Ati Awa, and I won't be around much longer, hey!"

His fingers itched for a pen and a sketchpad.

That night Danny didn't go to bed till very late. His mind was full of conservatories and chapels and ladies in white with blue veils who moved without any fuss whatever.

And dominating all was the compelling figure of the great Maori nun. There was no point in even trying to sleep. That would be like being cured of blindness and then being told to shut one's eyes. Once he had said goodnight to his mother and sister he went straight to the desk in his room and turned on the lamp and started to draw Mother Madeleine.

The problems seemed insurmountable. She was old but she had a quality of youthfulness that had nothing to do with the

number of years she'd lived. But how could he draw that? He
could net it in his mind's eye but there was no way he could
fix it on paper. Perhaps in oils if he studied her more closely.
Sometimes that sort of thing crept into oil work. No amount
of trying would do it. It would just happen. Mr. Grundy said
it was a sliver of the soul of the sitter. Two artists could put the
same dab of paint in the same spot and one would net the sliver
of soul and the other wouldn't. It was a mystery, a mystery of
art. The artist had to be very humble, and to work very hard.

Danny worked on sketch after sketch of Mother Madeleine.
He worked until that hour when the last train had passed on
the line beyond his window and there was no more traffic on
the roads. In some vague way it seemed that if he could pin
her down he could borrow from her genius and experience
because, come what may, Danny was determined to be a
painter, to strive for perfection, to be worthy of his father.

# 4

## *Aotearoa—*
## *God's Signature*

 ON SATURDAY, November 3, St. Martin de Porres, Danny spent most of the morning cleaning out the greenhouse under Sister Paula's direction. When she left him it was with instructions to report to Mother Madeleine in her studio at eleven o'clock. In the meantime he was to cut back the undergrowth that had sealed off the path between the greenhouse and the footbridge. The rubbish was to be taken to the incinerator ready for burning. It was while he was hacking away at the tangle of rushes and ivies by the side of the deep, swift-flowing Waiwhetu stream, that Danny disturbed an opossum. It had darted up among the undergrowth with an agility that didn't seem possible, given the thick and knotted nature of the growth.

Hacking away in the direction the opossum had taken, he discovered a flight of stone stairs cutting up into an old stone supporting wall, or revetment. In all there were six steps, spacious, with a balustrade and classical urns on the top and bottom uprights. The bush had reclaimed much of the surface of the steps. A heavy pine had fallen across the paved space that the steps gave onto, but beyond that was the open mouth of what looked like a tunnel. It had stone arch work and a large oil-lamp hanging from an iron support directly beneath the apex.

16

He looked at his watch. It was five minutes to eleven. His sense of duty and fascination with Mother Madeleine and her studio outweighed his curiosity about the tunnel. And, anyway, it would still be there the next time he came to work at the conservatory.

He was walking away when a flash like lightning burned the air behind him for a moment and knocked him to the ground. Dazed and fumbling among the leaves he managed to turn his head. A being, like a young man not much older than himself but of a different order, vastly superior, was standing there in the mouth of the cave. He was so bright and so beautiful that Danny couldn't focus on his face for more than a second or two without hurting his eyes.

"Are you God?" Danny asked.

The being ignored the question. Instead he somehow hit Danny, quite stunned him for a moment. He hadn't actually raised a fist, if he had one, and taken a swing. It was more a matter of will and although it was humbling, it was also a wonderful contact, and Danny thought he would be content spending eternity being stunned by this being and would never tire of it.

Nevertheless he said, "What did you do that for?"

The being didn't deign to answer. Danny tried to lever himself off the pavement, but the pavement wasn't there. Then he realized that he was in a world quite at variance with anything experience or imagination had prepared him for. It was as if his whole essence had been caught up into the life of the being as into a tornado, a tornado beautiful and magnetic, as strict as it was mighty.

With new-found eyes, Danny gazed at what he realized must be an angel. His eyes seemed to see without looking, taking in everything, everywhere, quite without effort.

And round about there were other angels, all individual, all splendid beings, equal and greater, each a living city, each an ocean that touched no shore.

Shortly he was aware that he was moving very high and very fast above the earth. His body was with him but he wasn't in it. It was not dead; it was trailing him like a shadow, like a wispy vapor, and he knew that he must return to it when he had been to where the angel was taking him.

"Where are we going?" Danny asked. An answer came, but not in words, yet had Danny been constrained to verbalize the angel's answer, he'd have said that he was being given a glimpse of New Zealand, which he was to absorb and reproduce.

To absorb the quintessential New Zealand and later to paint it. That was his brief, but why or how remained a mystery.

He could see the curve of the earth like a great tire, blue and gold, swirls of cloud around Europe and Russia, like cream finding its way in coffee. As they circled the globe, the angel hinted, in his wordless way, that these vast continents with their mountains, deserts and rain forests, were a letter written by the Creator to mankind, a letter which told of his tender good-will, of his greatness and of his capacity to be little, of all his infinite variety of shade and color and light and impenetrability, it said everything mankind needed to know about him until he was ready to tell more. And there, at the end of the letter, in the lower corner, when he rested and saw the world was good, the Creator's Guarantee, his two islands, containing in themselves the marrow of all that went before, his Name, his Seal, his Signature—Aotearoa, New Zealand.

The dawn brought the islands of the Pacific into relief, setting fire to the ocean, engulfing atolls and emblazoning archipelagos. As the oncoming light neared the shores that arched from Siberia to the Antarctic the angel dropped down at an incredible speed to join the advance guard of it, a new day's light that swept along as if on the crest of a thundering surf.

Danny had the sensation of speed but none of the discomfort. He might have been wrapped snugly in a papoose and gliding on a snowflake as they skimmed over the Three Kings Islands, which were, in fact, eight, and ahead to the lighthouse on the cliffs of the northernmost tip of the country behind which stretched a peninsula of dune and forest like a long narrow runway for approaching craft.

Danny said to the angel, "They tell us at school that the Maori believe that when they die their souls travel up here and pass over the cliffs and into the spirit world of Hawaiiki."

The angel, after his manner, told him that was precisely what they did, which gave Danny matter to puzzle over, but not now, later, because now he was intent on the singular experience as they moved from the sea to the land, flying, not as a bird does on currents of air and vapor spirals but direct, cutting through the ether like the point of a javelin thrust by a giant with a long arm.

As they flew Danny became aware of heightened faculties. He could hear a leaf falling from a tree, the sounds of diverse conversations with none imposing on the other; all distinct and fully absorbed.

This multiple attention caused him no surprise. The surprise was that, locked in a body, the mind was limited to attending to only one thing at any one time. It was that norm of everyday life that seemed, from this vantage, a crippling restriction.

Even the layers of time—time past, not future—were visible. There is no describing the phenomenon but it was as if each passing moment dropped a veil over the moment before to hide it from mortals. History only had meaning when it was refocused in the present. Each generation was like a mountaineer roped to the one before and the one behind on a sheer escarpment. There was no action, not even the lifting of a little finger of a Cro-Magnon drop-out, that didn't effect the entire thread of humanity—

From the endless surf of the peninsular beaches to the single northern fjord and the Sea of Islands, iridescent in the pearl and rose of dawn, on over the great kauri forests and ferned hills and shorelines as straight as pencils which suddenly ran to a riot of coves and inlets where the sea had found an undefended fort.

First above isolated jumbles of houses, and then in urban areas up and down and across the land, pools of intense light marked the landscape. Although they occupied very little space they seemed to dominate and support the whole. They were like brilliant flowers, just budding, with centers too bright to look upon. Most of the people were unaware of the light in their midst, which seemed a very curious fault in communication from Danny's perspective. Some people, who were active enough, nevertheless appeared dead and buried in the darkness of their own shadows.

"Remember what you see," said the angel, his communication now shaped more like spoken words. "Print it on your mind and in your heart." They seemed to have left the land and were speeding through glorious nothingness. "You must know the land of your birth as a fantail knows its nest."

"Why did you hit me?" Danny asked. "Don't Myers and Pascal and Duffy and those jokers do a good enough job on me?"

"With them it is like poking the elephant. They sense that you are more gifted than they and taunt you because you won't fight back."

"So are you telling me I should?"

"I wouldn't, if I were you. Your superiority is artistic and moral—not physical. To attack them would give them the victory, and an excuse to thwack you."

"It's all pretty loaded against me isn't it? If you're a . . . you know . . . superior being . . . angel or whatever, could you do something for my sister Angela? She's got . . ."

"I know what she's got. I'm not authorized to make bargains. And anyway, you don't keep yours. What did you promise your father as he lay dying?"

"To go to morning Mass."

"And . . . ?"

"To say the rosary."

"Do you do that?"

"Some days," Danny answered weakly.

"Every day from now on. Every day. You have a great work to do. You must train for it, train like an athlete trains to win the gold."

"What are you on about—great work? Don't talk angel talk with me, I don't understand it. Talk Kiwi." But there was a swirl like sliding down a shoot in the sky and Danny was back in the bush behind the conservatory. His hands were smeared with damp soil and his dark hair, which was usually brushed back, was now flopping onto his forehead. In front of him was the mouth of the tunnel as silent and as lifeless as a cave in the morning of pre-history.

He shook his head as if to jostle errant ideas into manageable formation. Had he been sleeping? Had flying with the angel been a dream? He looked at his watch. It was still five minutes to eleven. He felt stupendously peaceful, yet energetic and active at the same time. He looked at his watch. Curious! It was much the same time as it had been before the appearance of the angel. Yet he seemed to have been away for hours. He'd figure that out later. Now he must clean up and attend to Mother Madeleine in her studio. He'd explore the tunnel the next time he came to work at the conservatory.

# 5

## *To the Crystal Cathedral*

THE STUDIO door was open. Danny stepped into the room while rapping his knuckles on the jamb. Mother Madeleine was seated at her desk beneath the far window, which overlooked the valley. Her back was to the door but she raised a hand above her shoulder and flapped it as a sign to come in. The hand continued to flap as Danny walked the length of the room. When he reached the desk it stopped flapping, the forefinger stood erect, swiveled, then pointed at a series of large boxes on the floor nearby.

"Do you understand this gadgetry?" asked Mother Madeleine without turning. She had trouble breathing yet her voice was deep and clear, with a roguish humor tiptoeing around in the shadows of it.

Danny looked at the boxes. The label disclosed a computer, monitor, scanner, printer and various ancillary gadgets. Danny said that he took Computer Studies at school.

"The manufacturers have given this to me as a gift. Isn't it ridiculous! Eighty-nine years old with my grave dug and my coffin varnished and they give me a computer. Do you know why?"

"No, Mother."

"So that they can photograph me alongside it, then use the

22

photograph in their advertisements. But we'll trick them, shall we? We'll think of some way to trick them. In the meantime perhaps you can get it going and we'll investigate its marvels." Mother Madeleine sponged her forehead with a piece of towelling and took several deep breaths. "But not today. Today is reserved for a little pilgrimage. In fact I think I hear the taxi."

Sister Paula stepped into the studio to announce that the taxi was waiting. She pulled Danny back as he was following Mother Madeleine out the door and pressed an envelope into his hand. "There's 100 dollars there," she said. "That's more than you'll need. I want an account of every cent when you return, and the change. See that Mother doesn't get flustered. Her blood pressure won't take it."

Mother Madeleine took the back seat saying that there was too much of her to fit in the front. Even then it was a squeeze getting her settled. "You'd never believe I was Miss Paekakariki Beach of 1937, would you?" she said to the taxi driver. "Well, believe it, son, believe it! And I've gone on to greater and greater things, hey! Take us to the site of the new Holy Face Cathedral in Wellington." Danny slipped into the front seat.

"The Glass House?" guffawed the driver.

"Hey! None of your lip, fella!" said Mother Madeleine. "Just take us there." She could be quite Olympian when circumstances called for it.

They criss-crossed the suburban streets of the valley and at Petone joined up with the motorway which, in tandem with the railway line, followed the contours of the hills where they met the 'eye of the fish' that was Wellington Harbor. There was much activity on Somes Island where contractors were removing the evidence of the recent plane crash. But Mother Madeleine paid more attention to the railway line.

"When I was a girl," she said as an electric locomotive zoomed past like a comet in the opposite direction, "there were

steam trains on this line. Like great ogres, they were, relentless. We used to put the big old pennies on the track and the
great wheels would crunch them, flatten them so that they
looked like the coins of the Caesars. Each summer we went
on holiday to the King Country. They'd never seen trains in
the King Country so we used to sell our mangled pennies for
twopence each. Quite a nifty little business my brothers and I
had going. If we could convince buyers that the coins actually came from the vaults of Croseus we charged threepence."

The city, when they reached it, was quiet. Only the bars and
eating-houses and betting shops were open. The taxi pulled up
in front of the new Cathedral, much of which was still encased
in scaffolding. Getting Mother Madeleine from the back seat
was like extracting a paua from its shell but eventually she was
standing upright on the pavement. Danny paid the driver the
25 dollars he asked and quashed a desire to feel a sense of self-
importance as he did so. Nonetheless, he wouldn't have
minded if some of those kids at school could have seen him
flip the notes out of the envelope and replace it nonchalantly
in his pocket.

Architecturally the new Cathedral was to be a stunning
affair—a phenomenon of contemporary design, some said, or,
others objected, a man-made morass. It was constructed
entirely of glass and durable plastics so that it looked like nothing more than a rock of quartz prisms, blunt crystal logs thrown
haphazard as in a game of children's pick-up-sticks. Critics
were already calling it a spacecraft from an alternative universe.

It was only a few yards up an incline to the door of the
Cathedral but to Mother Madeleine it must have seemed like
climbing Mt. Cook, Danny thought, as she shuffled one enormous leg in front of the other and balanced herself with one
hand on her stick and the other on Danny's shoulder. The bold
NO VISITORS ON SITE notice didn't apply to Mother

Madeleine. The workmen recognized her and greeted her with the deference of affection and respect. Once inside the emerging shell of the building the nun blessed herself from a holy water font that wasn't there yet and knelt, rather nimbly, considering, for a few moments. Then she sat on a plasterer's bench and beckoned Danny to sit beside her. They sat for a long time in silence and then she leaned across to him.

"This church," she whispered, "is to be our new Cathedral when it's finished and dedicated in less than two months time. It has taken three years already and cost more money than it would cost to launch the space ship they say it looks like. In a way it is a space ship to minds fueled by faith, but we'll let that pass. Something is missing, though. What would you say is missing? What would you say is needed to make the building complete, eh?"

Danny looked about. It wasn't like any building he had ever imagined. In fact it wasn't like a building at all. It was more like a cave, a cave of light, an enormous chamber of light. Light came from everywhere, from all angles, even corners and crevices admitted light or reflected light or played with light like bubbles in a bath. It sure was modern, but not soulless, Supreme-Soviet-Council-Chamber modern. It was modern in that it defied all preconceptions of building.

Glass grottos around the sides gave onto side altars. Above these grottos a balcony ran around the upper level of the church. Built as it was into the side of the hill this balcony had two entrances from the street behind, called, unimaginatively, Hill Street. This meant that above the main altar was a vast, vacant space, not of glass but of rendered stone and mortar, almost the size of a tennis court.

Danny felt that this localized void probably symbolized something, though he couldn't think what. Like his father before him he had a passion for art. Even the sight of a paintbrush, or words like *ochre* or *madder* or *burnt sienna* would excite his imagination and make him itch to create. But he was only happy with creating what was recognizable, or at least recognizable as a symbol of something recognizable. If the blank space was supposed to represent infinity, or divine perfection, or an abyss of mercy, Danny felt that it should carry a tag announcing *Infinity,* or *Divine Perfection,* or *Abyss of Mercy.*

But, of course, he couldn't say so. And certainly not to Mother Madeleine.

"I don't know," he said. Then, feeling the answer was rather uninspired, added, "An organ?"

"No! There will be an organ behind us. Many of its pipes will be part of the façade.

"Look—it's that space on the wall at the back of the altar. It needs something . . . hey! Something . . . celestial, don't you think?"

That was exactly what he had thought! If only he'd said so!

"Nothing anyone has suggested seems appropriate. It's a majestic site and requires a majestic composition. So the Diocese has decided to launch a competition for the most suitable piece of original art to occupy the space. That's why we're here. The Cardinal is holding a press conference this afternoon to get the thing off the ground. There is a prize of fifty thousand dollars for the winning entry. A brewing company has put up the money. That's a lot of schooners of beer. I'm sure the public would prefer to see the price of ale drop rather than spend the profits on decorating a church, especially *this* church, but it would be churlish to refuse the offer on that count, wouldn't you say?" She chuckled in her throaty way, then took his shoulder and said, "Come on. We're having lunch with the Cardinal and then you can witness all the pomp and machinery of the art world when it gets a sniff of money, hey!"

Danny moved through the afternoon as if he was caught up

in the pages of a glossy magazine. Lunch with the Cardinal had been simple and the Cardinal himself had even joked with him as if they'd met before and were on the best of terms. Perhaps His Eminence was mistaking him for some other schoolboy, Danny thought. He supposed all schoolboys looked much the same to Cardinals.

In a hall alongside the old Cathedral he'd sat up on the dais with Mother Madeleine and the Cardinal and another Bishop and some priests and businessmen facing the television cameras and light bulbs. These dignitaries on the dais had answered questions from a variety of men and women, mostly blasé Kiwis, but foreigners too, as was evident from the smorgasbord of accents. There had been a film of the new Cathedral, which had intrigued him because computer-graphics had been used to impose various art forms on the sheer wall above the altar.

There was a giant 5th century iron cross with the Alpha and Omega letters hanging from the crossbars—Too stark; the comment was audible around the hall. There was Blake's etching of *Albion and the Crucified Christ* magnified a hundred times.—"Impressive" was the verdict, but the nakedness of the figures distracted from the devotional content. Stanley Spencer's *Resurrection* was even more impressive but here again the nudity interfered with the message. Graham Sutherland's *Crucifixion* looked too much like a butcher's shop (general laughter) and Emil Nolde's *Last Supper* would give children nightmares. Gauguin's *Yellow Christ* was considered too amateur and Rossetti's *Annunciation* looked like a tribute to anorexia. Sculptures, carvings, tapestries, glasswork, Old Masters, New Masters, abstracts, montages, every feasible medium was shown as worthy to be considered for the competition. Entrants had *two* months to submit designs. Ten finalists would be selected and their submissions exhibited and given the widest possible publicity. The winner would be chosen by ballot among a committee chaired by Mother Madeleine on December 31st, the last day of the year.

The competition was to be known as the *Reredos Lampadephoria.*

"The what?" asked the Press.

"The *Reredos Lampadephoria.*"

"What on earth is that?"

"We are using the word Reredos very liberally," said a spokesman. "Just think of it as referring to the wall behind the altar."

"And what about the . . . ?"

"*Lampadephoria!*"

"Yeah! How do you spell that?"

The spokesman enunciated the letters of the word. "A *lampadephoria,* as you doubtless know, was a competition, a race run by the ancient Greeks. The runners held a burning lamp aloft and the first to the finishing line, with flame unextinguished, won the prize."

"Why not just call it an art competition?"

"Thank you, members of the press, ladies, gentlemen, all. Thank you. Drinks and a buffet are now being served in the reception room through that door to your right. Thank you."

As they walked off the rostrum Danny heard the spokesman say, "Blasted embarrassing, *Reredos Lampadephoria.* It's the Brewery's idea. They are going to call one of their beers after it. No one will remember it, of course, but the initials will double for Real Lager and any sot can remember that."

Very little had been said in the taxi back to the convent, and once there, Danny gave the left-over money to Sister Paula and rode his bicycle back to Hinau Street. His mother was ironing in the kitchen while Angela, quite subdued and smiling that evening, was shelling broad beans at the table and getting a goodly number of them into the bowl, too.

"How did the job go, Danny? Did you have a good day at the convent?" his mother asked as he walked in from the back porch after parking his bike in the washhouse.

"OK," he said vaguely. He sat down at the table to help his sister with the beans. "I was actually inside the Glass House in Wellington."

"That iceberg!" said his mother.

That night his dreams had nothing to do with the glittering world of Prelates and the Press, of Rembrandt and Rich Brewers. He dreamed of mighty, magnificent angels, and of a revetment buried behind undergrowth with the mouth of a tunnel, silent and darkly alluring in the center.

## *Half a World Away*

ODO VON Blumenkohl was rich, but that was incidental. Wealth accumulated by a sort of osmosis, as a by-product, a bonus in the vitally serious business of controlling money. The World Markets were the orchestra and Odo von Blumenkohl was the conductor. He carried every note of every symphony in his shiny bald head and required a perfect rendition from each of his musicians.

Odo von Blumenkohl was ruthless for harmony.

Born into the German middle class, he immigrated with his family to the United States at the age of 7. With an initial investment of four dollars, a grandmother's indulgence, he made his first million, quietly, in his elementary school in Vermont. This was expanded and consolidated during his secondary education. He was to have attended Harrow, an English Public School, but his father, who was in marine insurance, lost heavily in a series of mammoth claims, was constrained to economize, and sent him to the local high school. In the tenth grade Odo bought Belgian Tea, in eleventh, Mirlees Zinc. U.S. Asian Rolling was the major acquisition of his senior year dealings. U.S. Asian Rolling controlled a third of the world's butter and this imbued him with an almost paternal interest in New Zealand.

At the age of 19 Odo von Blumenkohl broke his spine. He was in New York at the time, meeting with a junket of Brazilian financiers on neutral ground. The subject was diamond mining in Namibia. The potential assets were staggering, even by the standards of the major banking houses. Secrecy was vital. The scene was a Wall Street conference room, lead-lined, constantly debugged, and as guarded as Fort Knox. Odo, punctual to the second, marched into the room with the confidence of money-backed power, threw his portfolio on the table, greeted the Brazilian consortium with a smile as lavish and as all-embracing as it was insincere. Then, with a determination, which was to establish the serious tone of the negotiations, he sat down. Unfortunately the chair wasn't there.

Odo was hospitalized for two years with the minimum use of his body. A more passive man might have resigned himself to his fate, but not Odo. He bought the hospital (it was in Maine), selected the medical staff and introduced electronic gadgetry which kept the World Markets and political fluctuations under his unsleeping surveillance. He later described those years as the happiest of his life.

When he was 26, and fully back on his feet, the Generalissimo (he had somehow acquired this nickname in The Odo von Blumenkohl Clinic for Medical Progress; he had liked it, so it had stuck) married. Nothing was ever known about this nuptial partner except what was written on the marriage certificate—N° 278004, State of Maine. The Generalissimo never spoke of her or introduced her into company.

Of this union a child was born who was immediately named Claude. Claude was surrounded by every possible convenience from the moment of entering this world, and even before he threw his first tantrum, Claude was officially named the sole heir to the considerable assets of Odo von Blumenkohl.

The local enthusiasm created by the *Lampadephoria* contest

for the new Cathedral wouldn't normally have entered the Generalissimo's sphere of interests except that Claude, now 19 himself, and always the rebel, had asserted his independence and had gone off to study art in the *Académie Parisienne de l'Art (est. 1998), 13 Rue de la Supérieure,* (Bottom bell, ring twice) *14ᵉ Arrondissement.* It was the only thing he had ever wanted to do, he told his father, and he was going to do it.

It had taken no longer than a spider takes to spin its web for the bombastic, ignorant, manipulative, incredibly egoistic, financially shrewd, cigar-smoking Generalissimo to come to a series of decisions.

First he would buy the *Académie.* It was always an insurance, when playing the tables, to own the Casino.

Next he would praise Claude for his stance. If the enemy was climbing a ladder, knock out the rungs behind him. It made backtracking impossible.

Then arrange for Claude to enter and win this New Zealand *Reredos Lampadephoria* thing he had heard about. One of his brewing companies out there had put up some money for an art competition. After a quick check, Odo decided it was the most prestigious competition of its kind in the current art world. If you wanted to get anywhere, start at the top. It had always been Odo's motto and he would make sure it was his son's. There was no substitute for money and a reputation for talent if you wanted to be noticed. It was unfortunate that this New Zealand thing wanted a religious subject. Nonetheless, whatever design of medieval cant Claude entered could be neutralized later.

Lastly, add a million or two to the prize money. Anonymously. Anonymity was a close cousin of fame and prestige. Anonymity's big advantage was that she never left a clue at the scene of any undertaking.

The Generalissimo had a contact, what was his name? A

Syrian, or was he a Turk, who knew about these things? Lectured at one of the Universities. Harvard? Cambridge? Or was it that French place? Abu Kyed. That was it! The Generalissimo pressed a button and voiced through some instructions to his secretarial center. He'd have a dinner with Kyed. Make it top priority. Fly him anywhere convenient. He'd always felt an affinity for the Turk, or was he a Syrian? It was unspoken, but they had an understanding. He swung his managerial chair towards a row of onyx and platinum phones.

# 7

## *Zelia*

 IT WAS A school day like any other. During chemistry the teacher had gone to the door to attend to something and the slagging started. It was a bit more intense than usual because Danny had been seen on the television at the press inauguration of the *Reredos Lampadephoria*. Envy poured extra acid into the taunting.

"Mago, you worthless piece of fish bait, I hear you sniveled your way onto the box on Saturday."

"Did he? Was it one of those Slugs and Polyps documentaries, all slime and goo?"

"A horror film, more likely. *The Maggot from Outer Space.*"

"Sitting up there as important as you like with a fat old Maori nun and all the big wigs, talking about art."

"Art! The miserable little bludger. Only wilting violets talk about art. That's why he isn't in the rugby team."

"Only wilting violets play soccer."

"He's not even in the soccer team."

"A depraved, degenerate, arty wilting violet. I think this calls for drastic measures, don't you, Myers?"

"I think it calls for torture, Pascal. I think it calls for disembowelment, at the very least."

At that point the chemistry teacher walked back into the class with a new student. It was a girl, dressed in tan skirt and blue blazer. Danny looked up from his desk and decided she had the most beautiful face he had ever seen. He thought she had the most beautiful face he could imagine.

Her skin was dark, but not like a Polynesian's skin was dark. This girl's skin was like polished leather, like kauri gum, but soft and smooth and glowing with vitality. The whites of her eyes were as clear as flawless opals and her lips were sometimes mauve and sometimes purple. Her complexion, so fresh, so startling, so vivid, touched only by soap and water, made the rouged and lipsticked faces of the other girls look like first efforts in crayon in the Bo Peep Coloring Book.

She was introduced to the class as Zelia Mazloum. The reaction was subdued but audible.

"Piquant!" said Myers.

"Toothsome!" said Pascal.

"Spiffing!" said Duffy—spotted Duffy—but if the new girl heard these encomiums her demeanor didn't betray it. The expression on her beautiful face registered zero on the "*Rictus* Scale"(the former class had been Latin). Her eye seemed set to disdain itself—a facility peculiar to teenaged girls, and quite effective in discouraging unwanted attentions. Indeed Zelia Mazloum was such a master of the art that she seemed to fold in on herself like a piece of origami. Five minutes after she had taken her seat, her beauty had become a thing so foreign as to be mistaken for plainness.

Only Danny still noticed that she was there. In Chemistry alone he made 32 sketches of her without anyone knowing. The sketches didn't come anywhere near to capturing that elusive *something* about her that he wanted to encompass. Indeed, this enigmatic quality would vanish altogether in the effort to ensnare it on paper. But, Danny was beginning to learn, that was art—especially when drawing women, he suspected—yet the paradox didn't thwart or frustrate him. On the contrary, seizing the challenge and deploying one's wits to meet it was the greatest art of all.

The last period of the afternoon was Mr. Grundy's, and without any scheming on Danny's part he found himself sitting next to Zelia. He was psyching himself up to speak to her when Myers and Company started their usual routine.

"Mr. Grundy, Sir, the Maggot has inveigled himself onto the television. Shouldn't he be thrashed, Sir?"

"Inveigled, Myers! What sort of word is that?"

"Inveigling, Sir, insinuating, Sir, crawling on its gut like a worm, Sir, like the lowest of reptiles, Sir. Like the horrible Mago, Sir."

"I know what it means, Myers, I'm just surprised at your using it."

"Sir, as a representative of authority could you please forbid the Maggot from appearing on television. His appearance is undermining the national morale, Sir, and the school's morale, Sir. Many parents are talking of removing their sons and daughters from Holy Trinity, Sir. They don't want us to be associated with a ghastly little vermin, Sir. Thank you, Sir. That is all, Sir."

"He's sitting next to the new girl, Sir. He's giving her a bad impression of Kiwis. She'll think we're all maggots too, Sir. We mustn't allow it, Mr. Grundy. Let's slay him."

Danny no longer felt like making himself known to the beautiful Zelia. Indeed he endeavored to look even more submissive than usual in the hope that she might think they were talking about someone else, somebody on the other side of her, perhaps.

# 8

## *The Figure in the Cage*

 ON DANNY'S next day at the Convent, the studio blackboard said *Wednesday November 7, St. Deodatus, Pope.* Mother Madeleine was engrossed in a canvas. She smiled at him. He had hoped he might try to put the computer together, but Mother Madeleine's smile, though warm, didn't invite him to stay there while she was working. A sister with an Australian accent told him that Sister Paula was in the chapel, so Danny decided to carry on cleaning the paths around the conservatory. He might see the angel again—indeed, if he hadn't simply imagined that he'd seen it in the first place—and explore the tunnel at the top of the steps.

He made his way down the grand stairway whose ten flights zigzagged to the river where, at one time, a bridge had crossed. Beyond the riverside greenery, a maze of clean streets and modern houses all stood proud in their quarter-acre sections. Only the conservatory and the old Lower House still belonged to the convent, here on this, the wooded, the hillside bank.

In the conservatory Danny took the machete to cut the undergrowth and the wooden rake to collect it and, as an after-thought, the old battery torch which hung from a peg by the door. He approached the tunnel cautiously. No angel appeared. After cutting and clearing his way up the six steps he directed the weak beam into the gloom. The darkness revealed noth-

37

ing. It seemed to eat torchlight. Danny moved slowly into the tunnel, feeling for spider webs. The surface beneath his feet was something like bitumen and cluttered with animal droppings and damp fern. Glazed dark blue tiles lined the walls and arched ceiling. In a rather croaky voice he called, "Hello there!" and then felt quite stupid when he reflected that had he received an answer, he would probably have had a heart attack. But it seemed that his voice hit a wall not far ahead. A few more steps and the torchlight was bouncing back at him off a reflective surface behind a criss-cross of what appeared to be metal bars.

When he was close enough he put his hand out to explore. It was metal all right, rusted damp but metal. He shook the bars. A flurry and squealing started up from the ceiling above and for a few moments Danny thought he was being hit about the head by a crazed mob of open umbrellas. He threw his arms up to protect himself, and the light from the torch, though dim, revealed a half a dozen frightened short-tailed bats who immediately darted along the tunnel towards the opening.

Because his blood circulation and breathing had speeded up, Danny paused, closed his eyes and concentrated his mind on returning to calm. When he opened his eyes he shook the bars again. It was some sort of cage. He pointed the torch beam inside, but its light was faint and getting fainter. He could make out a wooden floor and what was probably a mirror, or a sheet of shiny metal a meter or so beyond the grille. He could see the bulb of the torch, which was little more than a tiny glowing arc, and the outline of his own body.

The mirror, if it was a mirror, was so dusty that Danny felt he was peering through a fog. He put his hand with the torch through the bars in an endeavor to see more. Straightaway strong, cold, bony fingers clutched his wrist like an iron handcuff.

Danny dropped the torch. As it hit the ground the light went out altogether but in the instant before it did he saw the face of a figure inside the cage. It was partially hidden behind a hood and the body was draped in a long cloak or gown. The visage was real, and alive. Ghastly, fiery eyes held Danny's, locked with them, and would not release them even when plunged into a darkness as dense and as dreadful as the eternal pit.

⟨⟨⟨⟨⟨⟨⟨⟨⟨⟨⟨⟩⟩ ◉ ⟨⟨⟨⟨⟨⟨⟨⟨⟨⟨⟩⟩

Even when Zelia let the letter slide into the box outside the Post Shop in Lower Hutt High Street she thought of a dozen things she could have said, but hadn't. She had written of the flight from Ankara to Karachi, from Karachi to Singapore, from Singapore to Sydney and from Sydney to Wellington. The Mamoulian cousins had met her at the airport and taken her to their home. They had shown her around, introduced her to people and enrolled her in the local Catholic School as had been agreed. Now, as tactfully as she could, Zelia was telling her parents that she had decided not to stay with the Mamoulians but had rented a tiny furnished house near the school and hence, the new address at the top of the letter.

What she didn't say was that the Mamoulian cousins seemed to drink too much beer and fight among themselves and that the Mamoulian boys were slobs. She had itched to write that they had left any respect they had for their race and religion and family traditions behind in Urfa, but in the end didn't. It wasn't fitting for a girl of her age to comment on her elders. But her parents trusted her enough to come on this mission, and she hoped this move wouldn't upset them.

In the park Zelia ran over the last lines of the letter again in her mind: "And so, my dear parents, the whereabouts of the Mandylion is as much a mystery as it ever was . . . our cousins have no new information, and not much interest outside of their own affairs. I sometimes think that we will never get any nearer to knowing the whereabouts of our great heirloom; it would seem that in spite of all his efforts, Great, Great Uncle Zeki took the secret of the hiding place to the tomb with him when he died here in 1891. Pray for me, that I won't altogether abandon hope!"

"Hey Lady!" a voice broke into her reverie. Zelia clutched her purse tighter and looked around for the speaker. It was a rather shabbily dressed blond young man with bare feet, with an artboard underneath one arm. "Do you know the way to St. Martin de Porres Convent?" His educated voice was balanced by his cheerful grin.

"I am sorry," said Zelia, "I am new here myself. Perhaps at that store . . ."

"Sure, sure," the young man didn't sound too worried about Zelia's lack of knowledge. He was looking her up and down in a manner that she should have found rude, but somehow that grin canceled out any offence that might have lurked in the glance.

"Hey," he said, "You'd make a great artist's model, you know that? The Muse of Poetry or something. Something Greek, with fountains. Here, let me get a quick sketch." He started to bring out a pencil from his shirt's pocket.

As Zelia made a movement to walk away, the young man laughed, and put the pencil away. "All right, some other time, maybe, here's my card." He pushed a rectangle of paper into the girl's startled hand, and strolled off whistling.

The card read: *Raphael da Vinci, Artist. Commissions Accepted.* There was no other information. Zelia wondered how on earth the strange young man could accept commissions if people couldn't find him. *Couldn't find* . . . The words brought back to her the immensity of her own problem, and she lapsed again into the frustration she was having with her own helplessness as she walked back to her house. How could she, a schoolgirl of sixteen, ever find the Mandylion after it had been missing for so many years? How could she even start looking for it?

If only she had a friend.

# 9

## *Boiling Venom*

 AFTER WHAT seemed an age of blood-freezing and inexplicable terror, Danny heard a voice, which spluttered like mud, like boiling venom, saying, "Away! Away! Keep off this place. THE FACE WILL NEVER BE SEEN! Away!" The grip on Danny's hand was released. The figure had gone; Danny didn't need the light to know that. It was as if a great magnetic force had been switched off and he could breath again. But his nerves were shaken; the leeches of fear still clung to his mind, his heart, his entrails and drained him of courage.

He ran as swift as a hare to the tunnel entrance and along the riverbank. He took the steps three at a time and was racing across the driveway in front of the convent entrance when he collided with Sister Paula. In trying to avoid knocking her completely over, Danny hurtled onto the gravel himself. After a stunned moment the nun chuckled at the absurdity of one winded nun and a sprawled out hired hand. She stretched out her hand to help Danny up. His hand was scratched and bleeding freely and she insisted on taking him into a small dispensary, which she called her lazaretto. Here, as she washed and dressed the abrasions she said, "You seem very nervous, Daniel. Has something frightened you?"

Danny managed to shake his head unconvincingly.

"Mother M. wants you to try to do something with this

new computer, but first the community says the rosary in the chapel. I suggest you come in and sit at the back and rest, and afterwards Mother Madeleine will take you in tow."

Danny sat at the back of the chapel and joined the nuns in saying the rosary. In the sanctuary the statue of St. Martin was still clad in the magnificent Maori cloak. As the prayer progressed, Danny found his fear seeping away like water at the seashore disappears into sand. By the time they came to the fifth mystery, where the boy Jesus was discovered confounding the stuffed shirts in the temple with his candor and simplicity and knowledge of things invisible, Danny had not only shed his fear but was feeling somewhat indignant. Whatever the presence behind the metal bars in the tunnel was, man, monster, myth or mirage, it certainly represented evil. While he couldn't help being alarmed at evil, he wasn't going to let it intimidate him.

Why had it told him to go away? If evil wished him evil, it would want to attract him to a place in order to ensnare him. Not even the most perverse of fantasists pretended that the devil stood at the gates of hell warning passers-by of danger and shooing them away. No, now that he could think clearly, Danny perceived that the *thing*, whatever it was, wanted to prevent him from discovering something in the tunnel, something opposed to evil. "Keep off this place—away, away! The face will never be seen!" The words circled in his head as if blown about by a great wind.

He would go back there and confront the evil. He found a strength in himself which surprised him. Wherever the strength came from, it was everything he needed, armor and arms, courage and spirit.

He wondered abstractedly, as the rosary came to an end, where the angel had been when that thing grabbed him? He must have known what was going on even if he was pottering around at the other end of the universe. Perhaps the angel thought it was enough just to supply this new surge of confidence.

Yes, that must be it because he never felt boosted by that sort of confidence when taunted by Myers, and Spotted Duffy, and Pascal the Handsome, and that gang at school. He never said a word or even got angry in the face of their bullying. But that wasn't evil. It was only verbal. They never hurt him. Once, at an inter-school sports day when some kids from Petone High took to insulting him because he seemed an easy target, it was Myers and company who had rounded on the Petone kids and almost come to blows.

Mother Madeleine took him to the spacious annex at the back of her studio and suggested that he set up the computer in there. He set to work with enthusiasm but a compartment of his mind was focused on the tunnel and on angels and devils. Somewhere between loading the operating system and testing the scanner he resolved to come to St. Martin de Porres straight from school the following day equipped with the halogen torch from the garage at home and, furthermore, to take the machete and a crucifix with him into the tunnel.

He was so amazed at his own audacity that before he realized it, he had the computer linked up and working without a single hitch.

⦿

When Danny arrived home that evening his mother and Angela were both at the table in the annex. His mother was deep in the newspaper. Danny glanced at Angela and raised his left eyebrow. Angela raised her wrist to her chin. Danny's eyebrow meant, "What sort of mood is she in?" and Angela's answer was, "Calm as a kitten."

Danny said, "I've got full use of a new computer that some–

one gave to Mother Madeleine as a bribe. It's the latest thing in technology."

Brigid Mago peered up at her son from over the rim of the broadsheet. "That's nice Danny!" she said. Then, returning to the newspaper she remarked, "What a weird name, Odo Von Blumenkohl. I wonder what he does for a living."

"O, come on Mum. He's the richest man in the world."

"What! With a name like that? Anyway, it says here that his son Claude has disappeared. Last seen in Paris." She lowered the paper onto her lap for a moment and looked at Danny, "If you disappeared, Danny, would that make world news?"

"I'm not heir to a quarter of the world's wealth, Mum."

"And you've your father to thank for that, too," she said airily as she raised the broadsheet to lose herself once more among its pages.

Later, when his mother had gone into the living room and Danny was doing the dishes, he said to his sister, "Have you ever seen anyone whose eyes change color, Ange? There's this new girl at school, Syrian or Armenian or Turk or something, and her eyes change color, honest. I've been studying her. I'll show you drawings. Normally her eyes are a soft, comfortable brown, then if she's worked up about something her face doesn't show it at all, only her eyes. They go violet. When she's amused, which isn't too often, they're a sort of hazel-grey and yesterday I saw her laugh, when Myers was telling that silly joke from his granddad, and they were rose colored, a beautiful, beautiful rose color. They made her whole face look like a rose."

Angela broke into an animated series of contortions, which made up her own private semaphore. Danny answered, "You think I'm getting soft on her, eh! That would be tough on me. She doesn't even know I exist."

# 10

## *Theseus Bold*

 THE NEXT morning as he cycled to school with the halogen lamp in his shoulder bag along with an ivory crucifix from the wall above his bed, Danny wasn't quite as confident as he had been the night before. After he'd helped Angela to bed—normally he'd have told her about the evil thing, but she had one of her periodic bad spells after dinner and couldn't absorb information—he had stayed up at his desk sketching. He had worked a while on some simple New Zealand landscapes—his father had loved doing that sort of thing and Danny was trying to put down some of his impressions from his "Angel Flight"—but after a while he had turned to his original ideas for Mother Madeleine. What his pencil drew on paper didn't come anywhere near resembling the nun as she stood in his head. If only he could observe her for half an hour without her knowing, or even take some photographs and draw from them. The same was true of the sketches of the new girl. At least he could observe her in class and work on the curve of her forehead and her chin between Keats and adverbial clauses, to get the angle of the cheekbone in relation to the nose (quite the most perfect nose in the history of creation) among the spider prints of algebraic equations.

And then he had found himself drawing the *thing* in the tunnel. He hadn't seen much—at odd moments he wondered if he'd seen anything, if it wasn't all in his imagination—but the preliminary drawings weren't too bad. The long black cloak that made the figure taller than any man. And the hand like a lobster's claw emerging from the folds. And the head that wasn't really a head, more of a skull with fire behind the eye sockets. He drew the figure not as he had seen it, but from the ground looking up, which accentuated the ghostly, ghastly, effect. At last with a shudder he had torn the picture up and gone to bed.

As the schoolday progressed his confidence drained drop by drop away until there was almost none left. Then during the last period, PE, he found himself paired off with the new girl on the crossbars. As they were waiting for their turn on the rungs she asked, quite simply, "Your name is Danny Mago, yes?" Her voice had a strange accent, but beautiful, like music, and she made him feel that she really and truly did want to make his acquaintance.

"Y-yes," he managed to say.

She seemed to expect him to continue. He didn't, he just continued to look at her so she said, "Mine is Zelia Mazloum."

"Zelia, eh?" said Danny. "That's cool!"

"Wow, you're *coo-oo-ool!*" mimicked Duffy, behind them, waddling his voice like a pregnant duck. "You fainthearted ferret, Mago."

Danny laughed in defiance. Then his confidence soared. Zelia's eyes had turned a pastel rose. She was laughing, but with him, not at him, so Duffy didn't matter. There was no further communication between them just then, but for Danny the rest of the PE period passed in a haze of mellow content.

After school, he left his bike against the convent wall and took the halogen lamp and the crucifix from his shoulder bag. He didn't report to Sister Paula but went directly down to the greenhouse to collect the machete. With the lamp in his right hand, the machete in his left and the crucifix hanging on its cord around his neck, Danny took the path, which led to the tunnel. On one level Danny felt as bold and as valiant as any crusading knight, as any Theseus entering any labyrinth. He felt that the steel that forged swords ran in his blood and that St. George was his mentor. On another level he wished he were tucked up snug in bed.

The tunnel looked very different in the light of the halogen lamp. The blue tiles on the walls and vaulted ceiling, where they weren't covered with grime and mould, reflected the light, and made the place look like the entrance to a run-down nightclub, or the chambers of a cut-price lawyer. From the mouth of the tunnel it was also clear that the metal "cage," as Danny had thought of it, was quite empty, and closer inspection showed it to be a very old open-style elevator.

Ducking as the bats again flew past his head, Danny walked the length of the tunnel. His confidence grew with every step until, when the metal gates folded back easily like a concertina, he was almost wondering if he hadn't imagined the spook in the black cloak with eyes like fire. He stepped inside and looked around the elevator. The back wall, as he had noted the day before, was a very dirty mirror. The ceiling was of cracked plaster, and there was what appeared to be a manhole in the center of it. A panel with a knob like a large ball bearing on a moveable indicator was set in the wall to the right of the door. The only other outstanding feature was a casing, like the telegraph on a ship's bridge, with a lever like a truncheon.

Danny felt for the crucifix around his neck. It was still there. He pushed the lever forward. It moved with ease, which was fortuitous considering the years that it must have been sitting stationary. He pulled it back to the central point. Was it his imagination, or was there a sucking, gurgling sound rising from below the floorboards of the elevator? He pulled the lever towards him. Yes! There was definitely a sound. It was like mud or thick oil squelching in a drain. He pushed the lever forward again. And back. And forward. The noise grew more pronounced and, more surprisingly, the elevator began to rise.

It rose about six inches and then stopped. The noise below became louder, accompanied now by the crunch of metal straining against metal. Danny was still holding the lamp and the machete in his left hand. He stopped pumping and placed them on the wooden floor and stood back to think this thing through. Of course! He was no shining star in the physics class but clearly this was an hydraulic elevator. It probably worked on the same principal as the mirror in the studio. An occupant literally pumped himself aloft. And it was still in working order, though at the moment something was impeding it.

Danny banged the walls and thumped his foot on the floorboards. The elevator rocked gently on its springs but the metal was still crunching. Then he slid the grille door shut so that the teeth on its handle interlocked with the teeth in the socket of the jamb. The crunching sound wound down. Danny took to the pump handle once more and the elevator rose again with ease until it was clear of the aperture of the tunnel and rising with amazing swiftness through a shaft which showed nothing but a smooth black surface beyond the grille.

When the elevator came to a door Danny stopped pumping but the machine had momentum by that time and the door flashed by in seconds. He assumed there must be another door soon and left the pump alone. But no other door appeared. And the elevator simply kept hurtling upwards.

Danny held his chin in his hand to figure it out. The elevator must be at the Top House by now, and there was just nowhere to go after that. A lone elevator shaft rising into the air above the convent would have been apparent before this.

It was the kind of thing one noticed. He closed his eyes, clenched his teeth and clutched the bars. If he prayed at all it was that there might be ramming springs, or at least a couple of old tires on the roof when the elevator crashed into the top floor ceiling.

But no crash came. A full minute passed and the elevator seemed to be gaining momentum rather than slowing down. Danny had read somewhere that the Empire State Building elevators traveled sixty floors in 60 seconds. He began to panic that he might have hurtled straight into the clutches of the demonic figure in the cloak with the fiery eyes. But if that were the case, he reasoned, wouldn't he be heading *down?*

Then the elevator suddenly stopped and the door slid open. Cautiously, very cautiously, he stepped into a small, low-ceilinged room.

# 11

## *The Anchoress*

DANNY STOOD in the center of the room for a long time. It was good to be there. It had the comfort and security of a womb. A peace rose up from the stone floor and a peace seeped out through the walls. There was a distinctive smell to the place, fresh, like apples and spring water, and the air tasted like that too.

After several minutes, during which Danny barely moved at all, a young woman entered. She wore a long gown that opened into a full skirt. Her head was covered with a sort of large, stiffly starched handkerchief, turned up at the corners. When she saw Danny she crossed her arms over her chest and made a rapid but very gracious curtsy, casting her eyes downwards and bowing her head. Then she turned to the fire, busying it with a poker and placing another log on it. When that was done she proceeded to draw back the curtains against the wall and open the shutters behind them. An arched window set with a thick iron grille looked out into a narrow stone church. In front of the grille the girl arranged two prie-dieus. As quickly as she had entered she was gone.

Candles and oil lamps flickered on the other side of the grille like glow-worms in a cave and muffled sounds could be heard as of people coming and going. Danny moved closer to peer through the bars. He made out an ornate altar, but found that the window was set at such an angle that the worshippers could not see back inside the room. Nor could Danny see them. But they could be heard and voices complained of the early hour, of the cold, of the cost of warm clothing. They spoke of a death in the parish the previous day, of how much money the deceased had left, and whom she had left it to.

The language was English, though many of the words used, the syntax, the idiom, the grammar couldn't have been in colloquial circulation in centuries, and certainly never in New Zealand. Yet Danny had no trouble in understanding it, a facility that came from some source outside himself, he realized when he thought about it later. Everything seemed quite natural and just as it should be.

As acolytes lit the tiers of candles around the altar another woman entered the room so quietly that Danny hadn't realized she was there until she touched him lightly on the elbow and indicated that he should use the prie-dieu. He did so and she knelt on the second one with her face close to the grille. Shortly a priest and a deacon, both in full vestments, came out from the sacristy and began to say Mass.

The language they used was Latin though it was celebrated in a way Danny had never seen before. The priest's manner was solemn and ritualistic and he showed great reverence. The unseen congregation joined in the responses but more, it seemed, as spectators than participants.

At the Communion the priest came first to the grille. The woman opened a small door in the center of the grille and made her communion. When she had received, the priest turned away, but the woman called him back and motioned Danny to receive the Sacrament also. When the Mass was over and the priest had returned to the sacristy the woman stayed at the grille, quite motionless, absorbed in her thanksgiving.

Many of the candles had been extinguished in the Church and the people had gone. Daylight began to filter through the high windows.

It seemed an age before the woman stood up, and bowed towards the altar with a reverential meekness that would have melted the hearts of Huns and Saracens. She smiled at Danny as if he was the most important person in the world, then nodded her head towards the fire as if to say, "Will you look after that for me while I do something else!"

Danny built up the fire while the lady and the servant girl brought in dishes and set them on the plain, well-scrubbed, wooden table. The lady pulled a chair for Danny and after he was seated she herself sat and poured a hot, colorless liquid into bowls with a handle on either side. The lady cupped her hands around her bowl, linking her thumbs with the handles and Danny did likewise. The liquid was a very sweet tea that tasted like ginger and lemon and the bowl warmed his hands. The lady gently pressed dishes on him, warm spongy bread shaped like sausages which was dipped in melted butter, little squares of dried fish, dried figs, almonds, eggs in savory jelly and combs of raw, waxy honey.

When the meal was finished she said a prayer and then spoke to him for the first time.

"You must go now, young one."

"Yes!" said Danny.

"Come again soon. There is much for you to learn."

"Yes!" said Danny.

"Pray and paint. Learn to pray here. Sketch and paint what your angel shows you. That is your mission. Develop it. And take great care of your sister. She is very precious to our sweet Master."

"Yes!" said Danny. He stepped back into the elevator cage. Then he asked, "Who are you?"

"I am called Juliana, because my hermitage here is attached to the Church of St. Julian."

Danny considered. "This isn't Lower Hutt, is it?"

"No. We are on the boundaries of the city of Norwich."

"It's not the 21st century either, eh?"

"It is the year of Our Lord 1399."

"What is this big thing I've got to do? The angel spoke like that as well."

"When the time comes, young one, when the time comes you will know. Think well on all you have learned here and come back soon."

Danny pulled the elevator door to. He was about to work the handle when he saw the Lady Juliana pointing towards his right. The knob with the ball bearing. He reached out and slid it down from the top of the panel to the bottom. She nodded and smiled. Danny started to pump.

The descent was rapid. All the way he kept a firm hold on the ivory crucifix. When the elevator stopped it was in its original place in the tunnel. Danny stepped out and took the machete and the halogen lamp and returned to the greenhouse. He walked back up to the convent like a boy hypnotized. The bell was ringing for the Sisters' afternoon Rosary so he, too, went into the chapel and sat at the back. He had so much to think about, so much to learn. His mind found it difficult to grapple with all the new concepts he was being exposed to.

All week Danny had tried to write down in an exercise book some of the things he had learned from the Lady Juliana, but when he tried to capture them and clothe them in words, they disappeared. They were things about God and people and prayer and love and the Mass and the Eucharist. He knew she hadn't said a word, but somehow her presence had been enough to communicate these things, to transmit a taste for them and kindle a rich and joyous enthusiasm.

He made sketches of her, and of her room and of the church beyond the window, but he didn't stay up late working on them. He went to bed himself as soon as he had read Angela her usual story and rose in time for the seven o'clock Mass at Holy Rosary. He still had time to get Angela to the Day Center and be punctual for school assembly.

At lunch time one day, between the Maths and the Biology papers, Sister Eileen sought him out where he sat at the outdoor tables underneath the sycamores with his sketchbook beside his tray. She suggested that he take some of his work to show Mother Madeleine. Mother Madeleine had been told that he had talent and was anxious to see samples of what he'd done. She was a bit shy of asking herself, Sister Eileen said.

Mother Madeleine shy? Even the normally deadpan Danny almost choked on that one.

Yes, yes! Everyone in the world was shy, apart from a few psychopaths. And the most extroverted people were often the shyest of all.

Danny said he would take some that afternoon. At that moment he noticed that Zelia was approaching with a tray in her hand. His own shyness took hold and, figuring that she hadn't seen him, he slipped away quietly. Zelia, preoccupied by her problems, sat down at his empty spot at the table, and began to eat.

Nearby, another teacher, Mrs. Evesham, had caught Sister Eileen's attention. Mrs. Evesham, indicating Danny's retreating form, asked, "Who is that lad? I've not noticed him before."

"Danny Mago. Year 10. A good boy, honest, no trouble. He gives the impression of being emotionless—rarely expresses himself at all. You'd hardly notice he was there except that Mr.

Grundy of Art says he's got more artistic potential than any pupil he's come across in 35 years in the classroom."

"Really!"

"He's been helping Paula and Madeleine at the convent this week. Madeleine's taken quite a shine to him. Says he makes a good walking stick. He went with her to the Cardinal on the Saturday before last—a press reception for the competition they've launched for the new Cathedral. Paula hates that sort of thing and someone has to go out with Madeleine. She won't touch money for one thing . . ."

"Won't touch money?"

"Never has done in all her years in the convent. Literally won't touch it. Impractical really, but I confess I secretly admire her stand."

"So the boy, what's his name, Mago, is that why you got him at the convent, to apprentice him to Mother Madeleine, so to speak?"

"Not really, no. We needed somebody, and his family can use the extra few dollars we pay. The father's dead and the sister's an invalid, needs constant care. His mother works at Kirkaldie & Stains in Wellington. But if he can learn from Madeleine, all the better."

The two teachers moved on. Zelia had forgotten her food because she was deep in thought. . . . So Danny worked where the nuns lived. And yes, he was good at art. Perhaps the artist in him could decipher Uncle Zeki's strange lines on the cards. But no! She mustn't confide in anyone. She had promised—unless, unless—what was it her father had said? Unless such a confidence was inevitable.

That afternoon Danny had planned to go straight to the elevator again but he didn't have the opportunity. Sister Paula had left the nun in the wheelchair on the front porch to keep a lookout for him. He was to go straight to the laundry where a blocked pipe had caused flooding. After he'd bailed the laundry dry he was summoned to Mother Madeleine's studio. He had brought a folio of work from the Art Room to show her. She didn't open it then, but put it to one side saying that she'd take a look later. In the meantime she had an urgent mission for him. He was to take the train into Wellington and collect material from the Turnbull Library, which the librarian was holding for her.

Every day passed like that and Danny didn't get back to the elevator till over a week later. He knew it was nonsense, but he couldn't help feeling that the Lady Juliana might think he was avoiding her. He came early on Saturday morning and left his bike by the bridge at the bottom of the driveway and walked through the bush around the river edge. He took the halogen lamp and the crucifix from their pegs in the greenhouse. The crucifix he hung round his neck. He ran to the tunnel.

As the elevator sped upwards he rehearsed the questions he wanted to ask the Lady Juliana. He wanted to know if her Norwich was the Norwich in England, and if it was 1399, how was it that he could go there and come back and, oh, a hundred other things like why she hadn't been surprised at finding a stranger in her house, and how she had known about Angela. He wanted to know . . . but maybe these would be enough for the moment. Communication with the Lady Juliana seemed to be through silences. There were things, though, that needed concrete answers.

# 12

===

## *A Lesson in Fresco*

EVEN BEFORE the elevator stopped, Danny could see through the metal grille that this wasn't the Lady Juliana's parlor. It was a large space, enclosed, but with much light from all sides. There were many people, going or coming or engaged in something, as in a factory. His first impression was that he'd arrived in the laundry, or perhaps the kitchen, of some large establishment, but he hadn't long stepped from the elevator when he realized that he was in an artist's studio, or rather a studio housing many artists.

Some of the men working were monks with long white gowns and scapulars. Some had their hoods over the heads so that their faces were hidden in shadows, like beings who dwelt forever in the dark vestibules of caves. The heads of those whose hoods were lowered were shaved to the skin apart from a ridge, like a halo of fine trimmed hair, encircling their crowns.

But not all the men were monks. More than half were lads about Danny's age, or not much older. Their hair was mostly dark and curly and thick. And long. The hair of these young men seemed to be their chief pride. Even those whose clothes or faces looked grubby had clean, well-brushed hair. One or two had it plaited at the back and Danny was wondering whether these men ever cut their hair at all.

58

Danny moved forward and stood behind a monk seated on a high stool behind a steeply sloping desk. On the desk a sheet of vellum was stretched on a frame. The monk was writing on it, very carefully, with a goose feather quill. On the flat surface beside the desk was a pouch of shiny black dust. Using what looked like a tiny teaspoon with a handle almost a foot long he would take a few grains of the dust and tap them into a scooped out hollow in a block of pink marble. With the same spoon he'd take a few drops of liquid from a cup and stir it around energetically with the black dust. Then he would dip the goose feather nib into this ink and, with infinite precision, write a single letter on the vellum. Each letter would take five, ten or even fifteen minutes and a fresh mix of ink would be made for every one.

Away to the left, men worked at easels in oils, and at a long bench that ran almost the length of the room, boys were busy mixing colors and washing brushes. To the right, others were chipping away at marble blocks or dying material in deep vats or turning clay.

The young men who weren't engaged with dyes and pigments wore knee-length woolen houppelandes in assorted colors, some with fur trimmings, and even patterns, but most wore voluminous blue cowl-like aprons over their own clothes, some belted around the waist, some cut away to the knee, all well splotched and dribbling with color, like a cottage garden in spring. Many of these aprons, or cowls, hung from pegs in a narrow corridor that led off nearby. Danny stepped over and took one down. He was bunching it up from the lower hem to pass it over his head when he saw that one of the young men had spotted him and was studying what he saw with curiosity.

As Danny's head emerged from the neck of the cowl the young man had not only moved up in front of him but was bending over with his fingers in the pocket of Danny's jeans, feeling the texture of the denim. "Canvas hose?" His smile was not unfriendly, but puzzled. "What pigment is this? Cobalt? Monestial? And what have you got on your feet, man? Are you Tartar or something?"

"They are just old sandshoes," said Danny. "My Mum can't afford trainers."

He knew he was speaking in a language that wasn't his own. He didn't even know which language it was. But, as with the Lady Juliana, he just thought natural and it sort of came out.

"Who took you on? Has anyone given you work yet?"

"I . . . er . . . no!"

"Well, grab that bucket of water and come with me. What's your name? How old are you?"

"Danny Mago. I'm 16." He said "almost" under his breath.

"Only a kid! I'm Benozzo Gozzoli. I'm 19 and by the time I'm 25 I'm going to be the greatest painter in Florence. And that's not boasting. That's a fact. Masaccio says so and Luca della Robbia recommended me to the Gonfalonier. I painted the ceiling in his secretary's bedroom. Fra Benedetto and his brother both believe in me. You'll see."

"What is this place?" Danny asked. They had walked along the corridor where the blue cloaks hung. Benozzo's hair was piled up on the top of his head and fixed with pins. In it were stuck many paintbrushes, which he took out and fluffed gently on the palm of his hand as he walked.

"The monastery of San Marco, surely you know that. It was a Silvestrine monastery but they found it too distracting being in the city, so they gave it to the Dominicans. The Dominicans are rebuilding it and every wall is going to be a masterpiece. Especially mine. Fra Benedetto and his brother are letting me do one of the brother's cells completely on my own. I've shown them my drawings—a Loaves and Fishes, a Palm

Sunday, A Gerasene Swine and a David and Goliath. They're all crowd scenes, you see, and I'm good on crowds. Especially faces. I put in everybody I know. I've got a mind like a mirror. Once a face has been reflected in it, it stays there until I paint it out onto something. I'll put you in if you like. You've got a fine head. Not beautiful, but there is character in the expression. Individual. Yes, a fine head, and you hold it high. I'll do you, master Daniel, you'll see if I don't."

They had moved into a large cloister, empty apart from a knot of men working on the far side. In the center was a block of marble the size of a small house. It was clearly spring because the garden was a gaiety of flowers. The air was bright and the light in the courtyard had a buttery sheen, like daffodils, but it was strangely cold, as if the door of a deep freeze had suddenly been opened. A Calvary in the center was emerging from the stone, but there were no sculptors working on it at that moment.

"I've heard of Dominican monks," said Danny, "but who are the Silvestrines?"

"Dominicans aren't monks, they're friars. The Silvestrines are monks, Benedictines, but very strict. They wear blue cowls. That's one you've put on. They left a whole wall full of them here. We use them as working smocks. Here is Fra Benedetto and Fra Giovanni. They're brothers, you know. Blood brothers as well as Dominican brothers. Fra Benedetto used to be the Superior at San Domenico in Fiesole."

Two friars and several boys were working on a section of wall between two arched doors. Two of the boys were mixing lime and sand from barrels in a v-shaped trough. Fra Benedetto, the elder of the brothers, was mixing powder colors with water while the other stood at an easel frame directly in front of the wall, making some finishing touches to a detailed drawing of a Visitation scene on a large piece of cloth.

"This is my kid brother, Danello," Benozzo announced. "He is going to be the greatest fresco painter in Florence after me."

Fra Benedetto nodded gravely in Danny's direction, otherwise Benozzo's introduction fell very flat indeed. Clearly the Dominicans were accustomed to Benozzo's flamboyance, but did nothing to abet it.

"What's a fresco?" Danny asked in a whisper as he poured the water into a vat.

"Stucco work! Where do you come from? Escotia? It's *buon fresco* we are doing here, coating the walls with a lime plaster and painting on it while it's still wet. That way the paint can't peel off. You've got to work quickly, though, before the stucco dries. If you get it wrong it stays like that unless you hack the wall down and start again."

"Fresco! Stucco!" The words held a fascination for Danny and he repeated them.

"The noblest medium of art," said Benozzo, holding his fine, handsome head up like a visionary. "And it will last into the Kingdom and pave the thoroughfares of the New Jerusalem."

"No kidding!" said Danny.

"Watch this now," said Benozzo as one of the young laymen approached the wall with a mortarboard piled with the white lime plaster. "Zanobi is layering the wall with stucco, just enough for this afternoon's work. See that straight charcoal line that comes to an angle at the base. That's going to be a column and a terrace in the scene. That is as far as he'll stucco today. A frescoist always has his day's work delineated so that the join won't show. A tree, a column, a ray of light. They're all tricks of the trade."

When the section of the wall was plastered, two of the boys held the frame with the drawing on cloth up close to the area, while the friar whom Benozzo referred to as Fra Giovanni copied the lines onto the wet surface. He worked from a low ladder, or rather three benches set in tiers one above the other. He worked quickly but with no haste or bustle. He clearly knew exactly what he was going to do from one moment to the next and allowed no distractions.

When he started painting Fra Giovanni worked with the brush in his right hand. In the left he held a thin earthenware cup which contained the pigment. When he wanted to change colors he would say loudly and clearly, *ochre, cadmium, verde* or whatever and Benozzo would take a new bowl from Fra Benedetto and be standing by with it at the ready along with a new brush.

*Crimson, burnt sienna, lemon yellow,* the words were absolute commands, but at the same time they held no urgency. The tone was exquisitely modulated and courteous. The face of the painter was hidden deep in the folds of the hood of his scapular and anyway Danny had only seen his figure from behind, but the sweetness of the voice was so compelling that Danny slowly edged around so that he was parallel with the wall which might afford him a glimpse of the face. But no matter how diligently he craned, he caught no sight of the features of the speaker, who didn't move his head from the work in front of him. Even when Benozzo was handing him new pigments, he simply stretched his arms to the side but never moved his head so much as a millimeter.

Benozzo whispered what Danny had already worked out for himself, that the painting was a Visitation—or would be when it was finished. That afternoon's work only revealed some distant hills with a tree-lined road and a cluster of angels along with the beginnings of a column and a patio. Yet even as these emerged they seemed all of a piece with the golden voice of the painter and, at the same time, familiar, like a tune associated with a favorite person or place; like the handwriting of a friend.

As Fra Giovanni was applying the final brush strokes to the hardening stucco, a cry went up and all eyes turned to the courtyard. There was a general gasp of wonderment, and then the whole monastery seemed to pour into the cloister garden, the friars endeavoring to restrain their gait, but the boys howling and cartwheeling, for it was snowing. It was clear that many of the people had never seen snow, and no one, ever, in the middle of spring, as they all said over and over. It was a miracle! Though to what purpose no one knew.

The snow fell down rather than flurried, cascaded down as if a fat feather pillow in the sky had been split asunder and the duck down left to enjoy the free fall.

The boys rolled in it, balled it up and threw it at each other. They pushed it in each other's faces and down the backs of their cowls and houppelandes, and still it came in great drifts, burying the shrubs and flowers and sitting like a mantle on the unfinished marble crucifixion. Then they built snowmen. Five, six, seven groups of them built snowmen in various parts of the cloister garden and even the friars joined in. They called their snowmen St. Dominic, St. Augustine, St. Bernard, and John the Baptist, etc., but didn't think it undignified to give their saints metal noses and horsehair beards and bottle-bottom eyes.

Benozzo pulled Danny into the fun and he went willingly, forgetting his desire to see the face of Fra Giovanni, but in the midst of the activity he looked up and for an instant caught the eye of the friar who was standing with his brother in the cloister and smiling at the antics of the boys. Yes, it was a face of poignant tranquility, but a face of fire too. It made Danny inordinately happy just to have glanced at him.

The snowmen were barely completed when each faction rose noisily to defeat the others. It was a half a dozen ebullient Civil Wars, all compounded into one. Never, thought

Danny, who usually curled up like a hedgehog at a glimpse of violence, was fighting such a lark. He had knocked at least three fellows into the snow and single-handedly demolished Thomas Aquinas when Benozzo, in an effort to protect him from an ambush by the champions of John the Baptist, accidentally grasped the crucifix that hung around his neck and severed it from its cord. Then, amid all the chaos, Danny heard a voice behind him say with ominous solemnity and in his own language, "You will never find it. I swear by fire and by despair, THE FACE WILL NEVER BE SEEN!"

He knew the voice. It turned his blood into needles and his nerve ends into razor blades. He turned very slowly and the snowman he faced hadn't been put together by the high spirits of some medieval apprentices. It smirked the ghastly smirk that had terrorized Danny before, then grew, rose, swelled into a horrible darkening specter whose substance ran into folds and dripped like venomous treacle. And its shrieking seemed to echo back off the walls of hell.

Suddenly the elevator was there and he was inside it, slamming the door to. But the heinous presence was with him in the elevator all the way down to the tunnel, and the noise it made rang through every channel in his body until he had left the elevator and was racing along the fern path towards the conservatory.

# 13

## Cowls & Cloaks

DANNY RAN around the river path, leapt onto his bike and pedaled rapidly to the main upper house of the convent. He needed time, and a place to calm down. He went round the back way past the laundry and entered the chapel through the side door. He sat in his usual seat at the back and took deep controlled breaths. After five minutes he'd calmed down enough to think rationally. Strange things were happening to him. He couldn't explain any of them, but he couldn't deny them either. The demon was the only aspect of the phenomena that actually frightened him—frightened was too tepid a word. Whatever it was it filled him with dread, real gut-curdling dread. Before the demon, he thought he'd feared death. Now he thought death would be a piece of cake compared with the presence of the demon. And what was all that about a face that would never be seen? What face? Why? It was all very harrowing.

Sister Clare, an older nun whom Sister Paula had laughingly described as the convent intellectual, entered the chapel and was about to move into her stall when she saw Danny. She jerked her head back slightly, then smiled apologetically. She knelt in her stall but was obviously ill at ease. Presently she turned around and said to Danny in a chapel whisper, "What ever is it you are wearing?"

Danny looked down. He was still dressed in the blue cowl he had taken from the peg in the corridor off the studio in the Monastery of San Marco, Florence, Italy, five hundred and sixty something years before. It had looked quite normal there. Here, in 21st century Lower Hutt it looked quite bizarre. Sister Clare stepped over and inspected it closely. "Wherever did you get it?" she asked.

"It's just an old thing to paint in," Danny mumbled.

"But where did you get it?" She was studying it closely now and feeling the texture of the material with much the same curiosity as Benozzo had felt his jeans. "Was it a stage costume?"

Danny had the happy facility of never jumping to concocted excuses when he couldn't explain something. He simply remained silent.

Sister Clare muttered as if digging up a fact from archives hidden deep in the cellars of her brain. "It's a Benedictine cowl. A rather obscure branch of the Benedictines called Silvestrines wore these blue cowls."

"That's right, Sister!" said Danny. "That's what I was told."

"Amazing!" She shook her head as she returned to her stall. "Amazing!"

Danny left the chapel. There was nobody around the side entrance, so he wriggled out of the cowl and folded it into a bundle. He was figuring out where to hide it when Sister Paula saw him on her way to the laundry. "You're nice and early," she said. Then she told him to go directly to Mother Madeleine's studio as she'd been asking for him. Nice and early? Nice and early? Something seemed odd. He consulted his watch. It was half past nine. He looked up at the sky. It was clear, and sure enough the sun was at about half past nine in the east. So all the time in Florence didn't count as time in Lower Hutt. That was interesting, but, he told himself, it didn't mean much to him now because he would certainly never go back in that elevator. Nothing could induce him to risk meeting with that demon again. He'd rather be thrown into a pit full of crazed katipo spiders.

Danny walked in the direction of the studio. Mother Madeleine was sitting on the veranda that would have commanded a view of the stream and the land beyond it, which had been the convent farm, if the tangle of native bush hadn't obscured it.

She looked up from her book as Danny approached. "Big Boy!" she said. "I've been browsing through your portfolio and, hey, yes, I like what I see. I don't know if it's any good or not, but I like it. That's the only judgment I can ever make of pictures, whether I like them or not. Don't quote me but I can never tell what all the professors are talking about when they start up about pictures. Especially my own pictures. I get letters from authors of heavy books, I mean big, fat, heavy books, hey, asking what was the symbolism of the carrot on the footpath in a painting I did fifty years ago called Tinakori Hill. They smile as if to say my secret is safe with them when I say that there was a carrot on the footpath when I set up my easel there that morning. I couldn't account for it either, but that was no reason to exclude it—whatchasay, Big Boy?"

Danny was pleased but confused. "I don't know what to say. I want to be a painter more than anything. It's all I've ever wanted since I was little."

"Hey, you're hardly a giant now. I only call you Big Boy because you're not to give up hope that you might be one day. Ha ha ha ha!"

"I'm sixteen," he said. And added "almost" at a slightly lower pitch. "I know when I do something good. Not right away, but later, a few days later, maybe, I know if something of mine is good, even if it is only good by accident. But even when it is good I always know it can be much, much better. I want to be able to paint . . ." Danny groped about in the air for the words he wanted. "I want to be able to paint a soul," he said.

"Well," said Mother Madeleine, as she heaved her large body out of the garden chair. "You'll need some mighty subtle colors for that one, hey! Mighty subtle colors. Come on with me now." She clutched her skirts with her fists and shook them till her rosary rattled and shook her head so that her veil smoothed itself out. Mother Madeleine had not changed from the full billowing black skirts with belts and rosaries, the starched linen headdress and flowing black veil of the religious congregation she had entered before rules were relaxed in the '60s. "It's the reason I joined," she used to joke. "They won't take that from me unless they bring the obedience clause into play."

She led the way into her studio, the one-time billiard hall. The blackboard read *November 17th, St. Elizabeth of Hungary.* She crossed the room behind the large canvas she was currently working on. Mother Madeleine opened one of several doors, which led into the annex on the far side of the studio where Danny had set up the computer. The great hydraulically-worked mirror-door was still open.

"I reckon now that you've got the computer set up in here," she said, "you could take charge of it and use this room as your private studio. It has its own back entrance over there, which leads straight into the bush, but there's a path running round to the rear parlors so we can avoid bumping into each other. And through that little door you have your own little bathroom. It has running water and, hey . . ." The old nun shuffled across the room and peered into the room beyond the mirror, which smelled of mothballs and housed the old dressmaker's dummy, and the splendid, knee-length Weka-Feather Cloak. "You've seen this, hey? You carried it to the chapel the first day you were here. I'm real proud of this. It came with the house, you know, but it belonged to the last Chief of the Te Ati Awa—that's my people. When I was Superior here I wanted to give it to the Wellington Museum, but the sisters wouldn't hear of it. Twice a year, for Martin de Porres and again on Fatima day, May 13th, out it comes and goes round the shoulders of the statues in the chapel. I reckon it must be almost as heavy as the cross. Feel it. Thick, hey! Beautiful, hey! Whatcha think, Big Boy?"

# 14.

## *Raphael the Castaway*

AT MOTHER Madeleine's insistence Danny spent the rest of the morning making the studio his own. She gave him an easel, and canvases and boxes and boxes of paints and brushes. He stapled some of the oils he had brought to show her to frames and then placed them on the easel, one after another, moving it six inches here, a foot there, to capture the most favorable light from the skylight in the roof. Unfortunately a branch had fallen over the frosted glass. Danny stood on a chair and tried to open the skylight to clear the branch, but he wasn't tall enough. He reckoned he'd have to find some way of getting onto the roof itself to do it.

After lunch Danny had cycled home to fetch things of his own he'd need for his new studio. As he came round the corner from the main drive, he saw someone sitting cross-legged on the gravel at the top of the steps that led down to the Lower House. He was a fellow in his early twenties and, Danny thought, probably one of the New Age hippies he'd read about in the papers. He had bare feet, frayed jeans and an open-neck white shirt. He had a fine, handsome, pleasing face and a shock of very blond, curly hair. The fellow called, "Hi!" and Danny called "Hi!" back. He hadn't taken more than two steps towards the young man before he recognized the fellow from the plane

crash, the one who had stepped bedraggled out of the helicopter and walked like a prince.

"You look an intelligent sort," the fellow said with a most
engaging grin. "What do you do?"

"I'm a schoolboy."

"Why aren't you at school?"

"It's Saturday. Anyway, the exams are over and it's almost
the summer holidays."

"Do you live here?"

"Of course not! This is a convent."

"It is? Great! I was hoping this was the place. I want to see
Mother Madeleine Atuahera. She's the greatest painter in the
world, you know. I've come to pay her homage. Do you think
she'll let me shake her hand? I'm in no hurry. I can wait.
Here—my card!"

He produced an expensive-looking gold and crimson paste-
board from his breast pocket. Danny took it and read:

*Raphael da Vinci*
*Artist*
*Commissions Accepted*

"No address?" said Danny, sitting down on the gravel beside
his fellow artist. "No phone number? How can you accept
commissions if people can't contact you?"

"Ah ha!" said Raphael, nodding sagely. "All art is a paradox,
a conundrum. My teacher, *Monsieur Peinture,* taught me that.
He also taught me that a true artist shuns self-advertisement.
Do you know Mother Madeleine Atuahera? What time will
she emerge from the convent? I rang the bell and asked to see
her, but the Sister who answered thought I was a burglar, I
think. She squealed and shut the door in my face. So I reckoned I'd just wait around."

At that point one of the sash windows of the old billiard

room slid up and Mother Madeleine leaned her aging bulk out of the open frame.

"Who is that?" Raphael whispered. "It looks like the Press Secretary for the Last Judgment."

"That's Mother Madeleine."

"No! Really?" Raphael was suddenly awed. He tried to stand up and then fell on his knees. Then in a loud, clear, but not very melodious voice he began to sing *Rock of Ages*. Danny was sorely embarrassed. "Please be quiet," he said urgently. "What are you doing that for?"

"It's the only hymn I know."

"You don't sing hymns to nuns. No wonder they shut the door in your face."

"Hey! Big Boy! Who's that canary you've got there? What's he playing at?"

"He's a . . . just a passer-by, Mother."

"Another beggar! What's he doing kneeling on the stones? Tell him to be off."

Raphael pleaded. "Tell her I love her. Tell her I think she's the greatest."

"I can't tell her that."

Mother Madeleine had another thought. "As he's into expending energy, you can get him to help you this afternoon. Sister Paula might even give him a buck or two if he shows willing."

Inside the studio Raphael displayed a sort of gallant charm which amused Mother Madeleine, though it didn't prevent her from telling him to get some decent clothes on his back. "How come you're begging when your voice shows you've been to good schools, hey? Drugs, is it? Alcohol?"

"Art," said Raphael. "I'm a slave to art."

Raphael followed Danny into his studio. His eyes lit up as he inspected Danny's drawings and canvases. He didn't praise them, but he didn't criticize them either as he fingered all the paint tubes and brushes and books.

Danny pointed out the branch wedged in the skylight to Raphael, who grabbed a chair and easily cleared it. While he was standing there, stretching up with the rays of light spilling down over him, a concept that Danny had been toying with for some time all came together.

He was so excited, it was as if he was possessed by a benign force, the spirit of the Old Masters, or the Maori chiefs in Hawaiiki. Danny told him to hold it and grabbed his pad. He made some quick pencil sketches and they came together without any effort at all. Phenomenal! It could be a Christ! A Kiwi Christ! He was concentrating on the figure, of course, but even the background drew itself, more or less. This Christ was standing in the Tasman Sea facing the rest of the world. His arms were stretched the length of both islands and he was protecting them, but at the same time the islands are the cross-beams of the cross and his hands are nailed to them.

He did about 15 rapid sketches but there was something jar-ring. It was Raphael's clothes. Danny thought of fetching the cowl from the conservatory. But no! A Christ in modern clothes was a great idea, but not these clothes. The jeans looked vulgar and the shirt was too beachy.

They took a break and Raphael looked at the sketches. He was very pleased with himself. Danny told him the clothes were all wrong, and he agreed, but asked why Danny didn't just leave the pattern off the shirt and draw other trousers. Danny said it wasn't just the pattern. It was the cut and style of the thing. It had no dignity. And then inspiration struck. The Kiwi Christ! What was the obvious garment? Right there on the premises? The Weka-Feather Cloak! Danny brought it out from its dark, walk-in wardrobe and secured it around Raphael's shoulders.

It worked. The weka-feather, the concept—the whole thing. It worked!

Mother Madeleine had given him a canvas, which was already primed, so Danny set it on the easel and started to realize his concept then and there. He painted right through the afternoon—as if in a fever, as he told Angela later that night.

*And it grew, Ange, fantastic! It was like those plants you see on television whose growth is speeded up. The background can wait. I'm only doing the Christ while I've got the model.*

*You'd have liked him, Ange. He had a pleasing way about him, a cool smile, which was gentle and dreamy without being weak . . . He didn't mind posing for hours on end. Said he was used to taking his time. We got talking . . . he has been wandering around New Zealand the last couple weeks, sketching. How old? About 19, 20, I suppose. He had long hair, curly, burnt sienna with highlights of very washy yellow and brown eyes that weren't afraid to look at you. Skin like real old ivory, polished till there's a bronze behind the white. What? No, not Kiwi. Almost certainly not Kiwi. But he could have been. To look at him you'd think he was the perfect Kiwi. A Kiwi prince. Actually, I think he was one of the survivors from that plane crash by Somes Island a few weeks ago, though he doesn't admit it.*

*Anyway, he's promised to stick around and model for my Kiwi Christ until I've finished it. Just wait till you see it, Ange, just wait till you see it!*

<hr>

The day before, on November 16, the feast of St. Margaret of Scotland, the Generalissimo Odo von Blumenkohl met with Abu Kyed at the Syrian's own home in Camden Hill in London; not that either of these rogues, the fat, gruff, cigar-smoking, ignorant-in-all-things-except-money-and-power Odo, nor the refined, well-spoken, cosmopolitan, the final word in art critique, diabolically cunning, Sir William, knew of St. Margaret of Scotland. She had no commercial value and was quoted on no stock exchange.

Abu Kyed, like Odo, had had a change of name. He had taken British citizenship and received the Royal Honors. He was now Sir William Kydd. He rarely lectured these days; his function was to advise governments on art. "Art is the true peacekeeper," he would announce at diplomatic receptions. "Art and music need no passports, they recognize no frontiers. I can be working on behalf of warring nations and be the only pure, unprejudiced contact between them."

His home, at only four stories, was not exactly palatial, but taste and refinement manifested itself in every room.

Syrian domestics who lived below stairs served dinner. The Generalissimo was never prodigal with small talk. He came straight to the subject of Claude, Paris and the New Zealand *Lampadephoria*. Sir William had concentrated eyes and a furrow of determination that ran from his hairline straight down to the meeting of his black brows. "Has the boy any talent?" the Anglicized Syrian asked in his finely fruity, debonair, rather emotionless voice.

The notion was alien to the Generalissimo. "Does it matter?" he asked, his bull-like face veiled behind cigar smoke.

"Not necessarily," was the suave answer. "But it helps."

"If I were to raise the prize money to five million? And if young Claude could win this competition . . . ? On his own merits, so to speak. . . ." Merit was a word the Generalissimo had never used in his life and now that he was doing so his self-consciousness was scratched slightly, as the skin of a pachyderm is scratched by a thistle. "No help from dad. Independence is important to the boy. I can see that. Can it be arranged? This is where you come in."

Sir William did not answer immediately. The talk had

opened his mind to other avenues, avenues of more personal concern. New Zealand! There was that matter of Agent Mamoulian's long silence.

Perhaps, just perhaps, in helping the Generalissimo he could acquire the object that had eluded his family for two thousand years. After all, to locate it had brought him into the art world in the first place. . . . And with the Generalissimo's money and influence . . .

Sir William twirled the stem of the crystal wineglass between his fingers. When he spoke it was very slowly and very deliberately. "I can't see that there is very much I could do," he said. "I know very little of this competition and nothing of the people involved. And it only has a few weeks to run. To be frank, I consider it somewhat vulgar."

The Generalissimo blinked. "How can five million smackers be vulgar?" The question answered itself.

"That requires no effort, I fear."

"I'll top it up to ten million. No one must know it's my doing. No one. Got that? We can't have the kid suspecting. My brewery out there can take the credit, they started the whole thing as a gimmick anyway, I hear."

"I'm not entirely convinced . . ." Sir William spoke with studied circumspection.

"You'll be my ambassador, my agent, my front man. Just go out there and take the whole thing over. You've got that sort of clout."

Sir William eventually agreed to go to Wellington and survey the scene. But he guaranteed nothing. If there was the merest possibility of his prestige being undermined, or of the committee in Wellington smelling a rat (he winced as he repeated one of the Generalissimo's clichés) he would shut the door on the whole business and lock it.

"The big job now is to find the boy. He's somewhere in

Paris, I reckon. I've got 50 private detectives on the job. Kids can be so willful."

"Quite!" said Sir William.

An honorarium, equal to 25% of the prize money, was agreed on.

The Syrian could scarcely believe that he had been dealt every trump card on his first hand. When it suited the devil, he was lavish with his own.

# 15

===

# *Sister Eileen*
# *Reconnoiters*

SISTER EILEEN was concerned for the foreign girl who had been enrolled by the Mamoulians, not a family of great repute in the community, and who didn't seem to be settling in along the normal lines. Zelia was no trouble, her attendance was regular and not a single teacher offered a word of complaint about her. She had an excellent command of English, both spoken and written, and clearly enjoyed an uncommonly high I.Q. But during the weeks she had been at Holy Trinity she didn't appear to have made a single friend among the other students and now, Sister Eileen noticed, the Mamoulians had advised central office that Zelia no longer lived with them and had furnished the secretary with an address in Knight's Road.

The girl was clearly mature beyond her years and appeared to be sensible and self-sufficient, but she was still only sixteen. Sr. Eileen was reluctant to question the girl directly because on the several times she had made friendly overtures, Zelia had brought down her safety curtain with a bang.

These things were on the Deputy Head's mind one afternoon when she had returned to the convent. It was her duty to find out under what conditions Zelia was living. At the same time she must not be thought to be prying, or there would be no foundation for confidence. And then, when the community assembled for the rosary, she saw Danny accompany Mother Madeleine to her stall and quietly kneel at the back. Of course, why hadn't she thought of Danny? He would be discreet, almost to a fault.

A day or two later Sister Eileen went round to Danny's own little studio by way of the back path. It was not a cold evening and the door was open. Danny was working on a canvas and didn't see Sister Eileen until she spoke.

"Well, Danny Mago, you have settled in here nicely," she said, laying emphasis on the *have*. "Am I allowed to look at what you're working on, or are you a sensitive little flower in that regard, like Mother Madeleine?"

"You can look, Sister," said Danny. "It's almost finished, actually, but it's not like I want it."

Sister Eileen walked around the easel to face the painting. "Why Danny, it's extraordinary," she exclaimed, too spontaneously to allow of any manufactured enthusiasm. "Charming and so full of atmosphere. What is this room? Who is this woman? This is not a New Zealand picture. Did you get it from a book? But it's so life-like."

"Her name is Juliana," said Danny, rather matter-of-factly. "Her house is next to a church called St. Julian. This window here looks onto the sanctuary, but I haven't painted that yet. It's behind a sort of grille. I've done the drawings." He pointed vaguely to the heaps of paper on the table.

"Julian of Norwich," said Sister Eileen, more to herself than to Danny.

"That's right! Norwich! How did you know?"

"She was a 14th century anchoress. Where did you get the idea? And the detail?"

Danny was about to say that he'd dreamed it, sort of, but then thought he'd better not. He retreated into himself, which created one of the silences which other people often found so disconcerting.

Sister Eileen decided to change the subject. "Danny, I believe you share several classes with the new Syrian girl (or is she Turkish?), Zelia. How do you get on with her?"

Danny blushed a cadmium red and stammered something unintelligible. Sister Eileen had remembered being young well enough to be able to read the signs. She turned her attention to the books and picked one from the shelves. She opened it and began to turn the pages. Then she said, as if the subject of Zelia was merely secondary, "I'm a little concerned about her. She seems to be too shy to make friends. I wonder if you'd try to get to know her . . ."

"I couldn't," said Danny. "No, I just couldn't, Sister."

"Don't you like her?"

"Like her! She's the most beautiful girl I've ever seen in my life. But she wouldn't look at me. Ask Colin Myers, or Duffy, or Pascal. They're the sort of blokes who'd love to look after her."

"That's precisely why I'm asking you and not them." Sister Eileen let the subject drop, but she stayed longer and talked some more. She was clearly very pleased with Danny's work, made some points about the unfinished Kiwi Christ, and called him her "budding Michelangelo." They discussed the uses the computer might be put to in the interests of the convent. Then, just before she left, Sister Eileen said, "I have an idea to get you and the girl Zelia better acquainted. I believe something is coming up next week. Leave it to me," and with that she was gone.

Danny was slightly irked. He would, of course, dearly love to know Zelia, but Sister Eileen was saying it as if he'd asked her to help him, and as if she was putting herself out to help him. In his distraction he ruined an hour's work on his Kiwi

Christ picture. Where was the mercurial Raphael when he was needed? He'd promised to pose till Doomsday, if necessary, because "no sacrifice is too great in the cause of art." Be that as it may he'd vanished, and the only clue to his whereabouts was a hastily scribbled note left with Sister Paula, which told that he'd gone in search of the quintessential New Zealand.

"He won't have to go far," Mother Madeleine had chuckled. "He'll find that commodity at the end of the nearest rainbow."

*I've got a surprise for you, Ange. Look here! Those chocolates you like, Queen Anne, with the soft white middles. A whole box. No hurry. Plenty of time. This one here. Come on now, in the mouth. That was agile, Angie, you got it first try. Have another. This one, it's got a sort of nutmeg flavor. The bees' knees, eh!*

*Remember how I was telling you that I was never going to go back into that tunnel again, or into that elevator, because I'm scared to death of that demon? Well, I had a dream last night, and the Lady Juliana was in the dream and she smiled at me and said, "You haven't been to see me again, Danny. When are you coming to visit me again?" I tried to tell her about the demon, but I couldn't open my mouth. I kept straining and straining, but it was like trying to talk underwater, Ange, and in the finish I just gave up.*

*Then today it occurred to me that when I had the crucifix there was no sign of the demon. It was only when Benozzo accidentally tore it off my neck when we were fighting during the snowstorm that the demon reappeared. Remember me telling you about that? So perhaps if I get another crucifix as protection, I'll be able to go back to see Lady Juliana and Benozzo. What do you say? A bit Dracularish? Well, I suppose the principle is the same.*

*Did you like that one, Ange? Here's a good one. The card says Peppermint. You've had enough? Right, I'll leave the box here beside your bed. The Sisters pay me good money for helping at the convent, Ange. They pay me even when I'm painting. I told them that I really didn't expect that, but Mother Madeleine said that I was on call if she needed me. She said that's the whole point of my being there. That was another hundred-dollar check Sister Paula gave me today. I bought the chocolates and some good paints and gave the rest to Mum for the mortgage. She cried. I wish she wouldn't cry. If I went out and got drunk or something with the money, then I wouldn't mind her having a good cry.*

*There's so many things, Ange, and no one else I can talk to except you. Remember me telling you about the competition that Mother Madeleine and the Cardinal launched for a design to go behind the altar of the new Cathedral? Well, she gets dozens of letters every day from artists asking if this and that idea is O.K. Some even send detailed plans with every square centimeter of space accounted for and costed. Sister Clare put a standard letter into the computer saying that, as Mother Madeleine is one of the judges, she is unable to correspond with entrants. Very icy the letter is. Nobody at the convent says 'no' anymore. If you want to answer in the negative you say, "I regret to inform you that no correspondence on this matter can be entered into." How do you like that? Of course the proper place to send stuff is the office they have set up in Hill Street in Wellington. It says that clearly on the Internet site.*

*But the point is, Angie—what do you want, a drink of water? No?—that none of the work is much good. I mean, it's professional and all, and the sketches and layouts that are sent are slick and colorful and arresting, but none of them have blood or spirit or nerve. Modern artists seem to think that for a work to be religious, it's got to be all pastels and platitudes.*

*I wonder what Benozzo and Fra Giovanni would have entered for the Lampadephoria? Frescos, to be sure. They'd probably make the new Cathedral look like the Sistine Chapel. Well, Benozzo would. Fra Giovanni would make it like a window into heaven with exquisite*

*angels everywhere. But you know, Ange, in all the inquiries and let-
ters and suggestions we've had from just about every country in the
world—one from Chad yesterday, I've kept the stamp—nobody, not
even the Italians, have proposed to do a fresco. People want to paint
it in oils and acrylics and pastels and water colours, they want to mold
plaster of Paris and papier maché into it, they want to work in glass
and bells and leather, in gold and mercury and florescent lighting and
lapis lazuli and laser beams and every medium but the one the wall
calls out for. Fresco. Admittedly I'd never heard of it till Benozzo
explained it to me, but now that I have heard of it, I reckon nothing
else will do.*

*I wish I was older and more experienced, Ange. I'd love to enter
that competition—not necessarily to win, there are too many experts,
but to show the sort of thing that could and should be done. I'd design
a fresco and make it specifically New Zealand. Not exclusively, and
not all Maori either, but New Zealand, Maori and Pakeha equal
among each other in the New Jerusalem. I don't know what the actual
picture would be, I'd have to give that some deep thought. There are
all sorts of possibilities. What do you think of a. . . .*

*I'm getting carried away, aren't I, Ange? And you want to get some
sleep. There's my goodnight kiss. I don't know where I'd be without
you, Ange. Nobody's got a sister as valuable as you. And I know you
understand me, in spite of everything. One day the world is going to
know what a treasure you are.*

*Good night now. There you are, I'll tuck you in so's you don't fall
out like you did at Easter.*

*Oh, and one last thing. Sister Paula has given me new rosary beads
with a large crucifix, so I'm taking it to Mass in the morning and
getting Father Doyle to bless it, and after school I'm going to try the
elevator one more time, so say a prayer that the demon doesn't appear
again.*

# 16

---

## *The All New Zealand College Challenge*

 DANNY WOKE up the next morning full of resolve. After school he would cycle directly to the conservatory and face the elevator. He had hidden the blue cowl under a bench there and he decided he would slip that over his head too, so that he wouldn't look out of place if he went back to Benozzo's monastery.

He attended early Mass—Tuesday, November 27, Our Lady of the Miraculous Medal. On returning home he had breakfast, then wheeled Angela to the day center before joining the school assembly.

After the prayer and the Head's address, Sister Eileen stood up on the podium. "An item of good news," she announced. "Well, let's hope it's good news and that we don't disgrace ourselves in front of the nation. Holy Trinity has been chosen to represent the Hutt Valley area in the inter-college television quiz *A to Z All New Zealand College Challenge,* which I have always considered a strange name, but there we are. This season it is 10th Grade Students and the two that have been chosen to represent us in the studio in Wellington this afternoon are Danny Mago and Zelia Mazloum."

A low but distinct moan issued from the ranks of the tenth graders. "Do I hear some dissension?" Sister Eileen asked.

Pascal, who was used to relying on his good looks to get him chosen for any public showing, said, "Mago's as dumb as a pukeko, Sister. He sniveled his way onto television a few weeks ago and just sat there looking dumb the whole time."

"Would you rather go yourself, Pascal? Let's see, just off the top of my head, what is the capital of Canada?"

"Toronto," Pascal grinned with confidence.

"Not according to the Canadian Yearbook, it isn't. Ottawa's the capital. Would you like to ask Danny Mago a similar question?"

Pascal closed his eyes and screwed his face in a show of intense thought. When it seemed he couldn't come up with anything, Colin Myers said, "The capital of Chad?"

The eyes of the whole school turned on Danny. He flushed nervously and mumbled something.

"Speak up, speak up!" Sister Eileen spoke with uncharacteristic harshness. "What's the capital of Chad. Answer the fellow."

"N'Djamena," said Danny.

Sister Eileen didn't drive home the victory. She didn't need to. But she paused long enough for it to sink in, then she said, "They'll be sending a car to collect you both at one o'clock. Come to my office a little before that. School uniforms, please."

When the car arrived at the television studio, Danny and Zelia had barely exchanged a word. Danny felt awkward and embarrassed and inadequate alongside the mysterious girl who was as aloof as a leopardess and probably hadn't even noticed him any more than she would notice the taxi driver or the attendant who filled up the tank at the petrol station. It probably wouldn't matter so much if she weren't so incredibly beautiful, if she didn't have color-changing eyes. No human being had a right to be as beautiful as that, to have eyes like that. It was almost painful to look at her.

At the studio nineteen other pairs of college pupils from the Wellington province were assembled. They were all taken into a makeshift, horseshoe-shaped room. Tiers of desks with the names of the colleges ranged around the horseshoe. A card with each student's individual name stood on the desk in front of each place. The quizmaster's table was centered in front of the horseshoe. Beyond that stood three cameras on wheels and technicians stood in groups, talking.

When the contestants had found their places the quizmaster began a rehearsal. Danny was nervous. The nervousness took the form of a dread, not unlike the dread he experienced in the presence of the demon. His stomach had developed a horrible form of weightlessness. He felt that any moment he might scream and go rushing from the room. And it was getting worse.

He was considering whether to announce that he felt ill and see if they mightn't take him off to a first aid center or something when he noticed that Zelia beside him was shaking. Her eyes had turned a sort of pale opal color. They were staring directly ahead, but they looked like dead stones and not organs of sight. "She is more terrified than me," thought Danny. With the same sort of impulsiveness with which one might pick up a wounded starling that was disorientated and flightless, Danny reached over his hand and clutched hers.

She clung to it. Her nails dug into his skin, but the pain and the pressure injected him with strength and confidence. His own nervousness fell away like dawn mists under a strong sun. This new confidence continued throughout the program as Danny held Zelia's hand in his own beneath the desk. They didn't win the quiz, but they didn't disgrace the school either. Indeed, Zelia gained a greater number of points than any individual contestant by answering a question that no one else could even guess at. The question was *What is the name of the*

*New Zealand author of the autobiographical novel "Children of the Poor"?* When Zelia answered, "John A. Lee," there was a stunned silence before spontaneous applause.

Danny whispered under his breath, "How did you know that?"

"His picture is one of the *Great New Zealand Writers* on the cover of the Wellington and Hutt Valley Telephone Book," she said.

After the show had been taped, all the contestants were invited back to Wellington College for tea and cakes. There was a bus laid on outside the studio but Zelia wasn't on it and Danny couldn't find her anywhere. Eventually he made his own way to the railway station and took a train to Woburn and ran home to collect his bike. Sister Madeleine was expecting him, and he was determined to enter the elevator once more with the crucifix of his new rosary.

He had never felt more ready to combat the demon.

# 17

## The Temple

 AS THE elevator ascended Danny had time to say two decades of the rosary; it seemed a sort of double protection against the demon. Even before the elevator stopped, he knew that yet again he wasn't at the Lady Juliana's parlor. A pervasive sense of doom grew thicker and thicker. And there was a heavy smell, the sort of smell that pervades a freezing works, the smell of blood and guts and death. There was smoke too, and burning flesh.

The ghastly dread attacked him and he clutched the crucifix. He wished he hadn't come. He turned back towards the elevator and felt for the gate in the darkness but it wasn't there. Presently a gentle, calming arm enfolded his shoulder and led him forward. There was great strength in the arm and he trusted it completely. Amid all the shouting and frantic movement and the wailing of animals he felt secure as if in a protective capsule. The arm did not indicate a material presence. Even in the darkness he knew that it was his angel that hovered beside him.

They climbed steps. Slowly the darkness was lifting and Danny could see more of what the noise was all about. He saw numerous people on their knees; others were prostrate on the ground. The crowds, wearing robes and headdress like turbans or folded towels, moved erratically, and every individual seemed to be shouting. Sheep and goats on leads were running back and forth entangling people and each other. In the distance, ranged over a great area, men dressed in identical ceremonial robes were cutting the throats of the animals at elevated tables and bleeding them. The blood was carried off in bowls and sprinkled in various places. The carcasses were handed back to those who had brought them, though some were fleeced and gutted and thrown onto flaming barbecues around the altar.

The more light that came into the area the more the general consternation was revealed. Danny and his protector moved through several courts and vestibules and up more steps. He felt that he was gliding rather than walking, but wasn't sure.

He was in a vast hall with a long, marble table in the center. A ramp led up to this table, and around it men in solemn robes with almost conical hats, high and veiled, threw incense into dishes of hot coals.

Danny's attention was drawn to one of the central sacrificial tables. A lamb, sprightly and most fetching in its innocence, broke away from its lead and gamboled up around the legs of the knife-wielding priests. They picked it up, threw it on the table. It began to bleat in a way that would soften the heart of the hardest of executioners. Routinely, they slit its throat.

At that moment the earth began to rumble. The rumbling grew louder. Eventually it sounded as if a herd of buffaloes was stampeding through the Halls. The people, so recently soothed, screamed again and lost all control in sheer panic. The outer walls swayed, then shook, then danced till many of the upper ramparts tumbled to the ground.

With the slain lamb still a vivid image in his mind, Danny was taken up another flight of steps behind the central table and through a set of doors ten meters high. He was in a large room, which was empty apart from a table and a seven-branched candlestick. Some ways down there were more steps leading to a house built within the room. At the entrance to this house stood two great columns of black and green marble, and between them hung a curtain which was striped red and blue and white and yellow, and there were spheres and serpents described upon it.

The noise of the earthquake had grown to an intolerable pitch. Then the ground split open in various places, the crack zigzagging as if traced by forked lightning. At the same moment the two great porphyry columns folded in their centers and fell away from each other, ripping the magnificent curtain from top to bottom with a noise like the hissing of a snake.

An ornate altar which contained the originals of the Sacred Books, itself an imitation of the old Ark of the Covenant which had been destroyed 500 years before, was exposed within the house. This had slumped onto its base like a carriage whose axle has snapped, and its top and sides were caving in. Stone angels had guarded it, but the angels were losing their heads and their wings and their gilded bodies.

For an instant Danny saw beyond the halls and the courts and the walls to where, about a kilometer away, the earthquake had cracked a huge rock that formed the summit of a hill from one end to the other. Already men, scientists, geologists or whatever, were letting down lead lines to determine the depth of the gash.

Quite a crowd had been standing on the hill even before the earthquake and the darkness. Somewhere there in the middle of the crowd three cross-trees had been buried in the rock and three criminals had been fixed to the wood with ropes and nails and left to die, because that had been the sentence passed on the poor wretches by the courts of the city.

The depth of the fissure measured by the scientists or geologists was never recorded. Perhaps it was fathomless. Perhaps they fell in.

But this glimpse of Golgotha was all too brief. Danny had scarcely time to think about it before he was back in the elevator and hurtling down to where he had started from.

# 18

## All the Makings

A COUPLE of days later, two days before the *A to Z All New Zealand College Challenge Program* was to be transmitted on television, Mother Madeleine knocked on the door of Danny's small studio at the back of hers and asked if she might come in. Danny was touched by her courtesy. She lets me use her room, provides me with all the brushes, paints and canvas and then asks permission to enter, he said to himself. I wish I were that gracious. I wish everyone were. The world would be a more amenable place to live in if we managed to defer to others like that. But just to will it wasn't enough. There was something vast and stubborn in human nature that got in the way.

Mother Madeleine hobbled into the room with that great smile of beatific mischief lighting up her face that Danny found he could only respond to by smiling back.

"What are you working on, Big Boy?" she asked. "Are we allowed to look, or are you a mean dauber like me who won't let anyone look at anything until after the final brush stroke?"

Danny said, "I don't mind," and stood back from his easel to make room for the nun's inspection. "It's only a study, really. A study for a mural. If I ever get it right, I'd like to do it in stucco."

Mother Madeleine wasn't the type to sink into long contemplation of pictures. She had the knack and the experience and the intelligence to be able to assess a work at a glance.

Enjoyment could come later. "Aue!" she exclaimed. She cherished her Maori exclamations, but used them sparingly. To her they were the expression of deeper delights, independent of the pakeha. "What's all this, Boy, what's all this? Where did you copy it from?"

"It was just an idea," Danny stammered.

"'Course it's an idea. But where did it come from, hey?"

Danny wasn't prepared to tell anyone, not even Mother Madeleine, about the elevator. "From my head," he said. "A combination of things. It was an idea for the Cathedral wall. Just an idea, mind. It wouldn't be good enough to enter or anything, it's just an idea."

"If half a dozen ideas are as apposite as this, the venture will have been worthwhile," Mother Madeleine said reflectively.

Danny looked blank. "What does *apposite* mean?" he asked.

"Appropriate. Seemly. I mean, for an altar backdrop this is perfect. I mean...it *is* the Mass. Tell me the truth, Boy. Where did you get the idea for this? I don't believe it just came to you out of the sky!"

Danny tried never to lie. If you need to dissemble, he often told himself, the truth does it for you. "In an elevator," he said.

"I suppose I'm one of the judges, so I mustn't say too much, but I'm telling you to keep working on it. On the strength of this I see no reason why it couldn't be entered for the competition. Hey, as long as you don't let it go to your head, I think it would be rather fun to set your work up alongside the offerings of the successful and the celebrated. The identity of entrants is only known to the computers."

"Do you know anything about fresco?" Danny asked.

"Nothing," Mother Madeleine said flatly. "I don't think anyone does it in New Zealand."

"I'd love to learn about it," Danny said. "Maybe Mr. Grundy knows about it."

As she was leaving Mother Madeleine caught sight of the beginnings of Danny's Kiwi Christ leaning against the wall at ground level. She asked what it was. Danny told her. "Where's he gone, that beggar boy?," she said. "You get him back here and finish this. You've got all the makings, Danny, all the makings. Time, prayer and a whole heap of work and who's to know what you might do, hey."

That evening in their communal dining room Mother Madeleine was telling the Sisters about Danny's painting. "There's a lot to be done and his inexperience shows, but the composition holds an element of genius. I can't for the life of me believe that the boy conceived the whole thing in his head—bespoke, as it were."

The Sisters wanted to know what the subject was, exactly what Danny was depicting. For all her praise, Mother Madeleine hadn't mentioned that.

"Well, it's the temple in Jerusalem. There is no mistaking that. It is vast and lofty and awesome. In the foreground there is a crush of people and animals for sacrifice, all in a frenzy of fear. It does no good to look closely because all you see is a blur of paint. He has given no definitive features to the people. Yet if you stand back you can see all sorts of wonderful, frightened faces. Collectively he presents individuals, but if you try to single one out, all you can find is a blob.

"At an elevated central altar are a row of gruesome, eerie-looking priests all splattered with blood. One of them is holding down a lamb, which is struggling to stand on new legs. Another is slitting its throat with an enormous knife. People are taking their slaughtered animals away, but around the altar are troughs of fire where men, their faces twisted against the stench, are preparing the slaughtered animals to be roasted."

The Australian sister was unimpressed. "It sounds like an illustration for *My First Bible Picture Book,*" she said curtly.

Mother Madeleine probably didn't hear her. She held her hands out in front of her and was moving them as if she was creating the scene in the air. "Behind all this is an enormous curtain, very colorful, very splendid. But imagine that a maniac with a knife, hey!—that priest, perhaps, who is slaughtering the lamb—imagine him stepping out of the picture and stabbing it, zigzagging his knife from top to bottom. That is the earthquake. It has started to topple some of the walls of the temple. It has split the great curtain to reveal Golgotha, but from behind the crosses. They look like three trees in the starkest, darkest day of winter, brought into relief by a flash of distant lightning. You can't see much of the bodies on the cross but you can almost hear the wind blowing into the open wounds. The earthquake has split the rock behind the crosses and some men with scientific instruments are engaged in measuring the depth of the fissure. In the temple itself people and animals are falling into the crack in the floor. If you look over the edge, so to speak, you can see flames licking the sides within."

"I told you we have a budding Michelangelo in our midst," said Sister Eileen. "He was painting Juliana of Norwich last time I was in his studio. A fifteen-year-old. Most fifteen-year-olds haven't heard of Norwich, much less Juliana." Then Sister Eileen looked concerned. "We must be sparing in praise in front of Danny," she reflected. "He's a modest boy and I'd hate to see his head turned by too much attention."

Sister Clare, ever practical, slapped her hand on the table. "Why all the talk? If this is a masterpiece let's see it for ourselves. It's only a few meters away, after all. Let's go and take a peek."

A debate as to the ethics of taking peeks ensued. Mother Madeleine thought it a violation of artistic privacy, while the younger nuns were swayed by Sister Clare's assertion that the Children of Israel might have been spared a heap of anguish had they paid more attention to Moses' blocks of stone the first time round. So, as soon as the Grace after Meals had been said, they all walked to the small door at the back of the billiard room and took a peek at Danny's large, ambitious, half-finished canvas.

*Angela, I've picked you up early because we've been invited out. Both of us. Together. Really. And guess who by! The Splendor of the East, the Muse of Poets, the only really beautiful girl in the whole school. By Zelia Mazloum, that's who! They're showing the Quiz program they taped on TV tonight. This morning she asked me if I'd be watching, and I said I wasn't sure because we don't have a television at home, and straightaway she said to come to her place to watch it. When she said it was at eight o'clock, I said I had to pick you up at eight o'clock so she said to bring you too. She even said to bring Mum. I phoned Mum at work, but she's staying in town to watch with friends after work.*

*Zelia's cooking for us, Ange. Armenian food, she says. I hope I'm not nervous. I don't feel nervous right now. In fact I feel great. I hope I don't talk too much, though. Or not enough. I wonder what we'll talk about. I don't even know what her interests are. And all she knows about me is that Myers and Pascal and those smart-alecs take the mickey out of me during Mr. Grundy's class. You want to hear them put on their English accents. They sound like high-steppin' poofters. I bet no Englishman ever really talked like that. They carry on like those baboons in the zoo when you give them a mirror. Why do they do that, do you think? Probably because Mr. Grundy's English, and they watch too much English stuff on TV. It can't be us, Ange. We haven't got any English blood in us. Mum and Dad both go back to early New Zealand days. Mum's family was Irish and Welsh and her mother's mother was Ngati Tawa. That's where our Maori comes from, though it seems to have washed out in you and me. Dad's was Scottish Catholic. Dad's mother's father's father's mother's elder brother was the first pakeha to be born in the Wellington province. No, wait a minute. I've got it wrong somewhere. Dad's mother's mother's father . . . well, it doesn't matter. But they were Scottish. They'd immigrated to Australia, but were always being mistaken for convicts, so they moved on over here. There's a book about them, Mum says.*

*That must be the house over there, Ange. The one on the corner of Knight's Road with the magnolia tree and the ponga. That's where that Member of Parliament used to live, the one who lost his seat and went to the Chatham Islands. Now, don't go getting excited, Angela. Everything's going to be O.K. Zelia knows you're not well. She's looking forward to meeting you. Remember, if you want to go to the bathroom, hit me twice on the arm as usual. No problem. And try not to make that howling noise, Ange. Not here. It doesn't matter at home, but sometimes people who don't know you don't understand.*

# 19

## *Whisked Off by the Angel, Again*

 DANNY DIDN'T see much of the television program. At first he sat in Zelia's living room, gazing at her with hung-jaw admiration at the way she took over Angela. It was a ballet of tact and ebullient affection, not so much as a hint of recoiling at physical deformity or condescending to the less happily endowed. Indeed, the two girls might have been sisters from the same cradle.

Then, just as Danny caught a glimpse of himself on the screen, he was plucked up into the ether. The angel was holding him and they went almost as high as the moon. Even though he knew the angel might not talk to him, he couldn't keep quiet.

"There are a hundred questions I want to ask," he said. "Like—are you my guardian angel?"

"I am the custodian of the Mandylion."

"The what!"

"Patience, silence, trust. Pray for these and all things will be shown in their season."

"I don't suppose I'm allowed to stay here with you, am I? The trouble is when I leave you, when I leave the elevator and everything is back to normal, again I don't even know if I believe I've been away. One minute chatting with angels or taking a stroll through the Middle Ages, looking down on the earth like it's a bubble in a fizzy drink or getting my head kicked in by the ugliest brutes in creation—and the next, well, mowing the lawn in Lower Hutt. A bloke can go mad like that. What's it all about?"

The angel didn't answer at all this time. They began to descend, swifter than a lightning bolt, and joined the fingers of the sun as they raced along the ocean top, tripping over waves, surfing the dawn.

The great city looked as if some sharp-toothed monsters from the deep had fed on the land from both sides until only a narrow, twisted isthmus remained to house the mass of people. Here a number of the lights shone, throwing up a beam which went beyond Danny and his angel into the deepest heaven. It was while they flew over a quilt of farms, and saw the stately silver of the mighty river beyond, that Danny became aware that the light was from the tabernacles of churches housing the Eucharist and that what had looked to him as the petals of the flowers were tier upon tier of angels, massed in amazement and adoration.

Danny felt enormous pleasure in the simple things, a farmer bringing in his cows for milking, children reluctant to leave their beds for school. In the next city a woman watering her cottage garden told her dog of an impending family visit. Eastward, among the hills of a rolling range, young hikers were taking an early dip in a thermal pool deep in the native bush.

From the Tattooed Rocks to the since-destroyed Pink and White Terraces, time's curtains melted away and Maori tribes made of the land their markets, their arenas, their sanctuaries and their burial grounds. Danny clearly saw a gathering in a great *pa,* which he estimated as taking place at least a thousand years before. A chief had died young and childless and there was a dispute about a successor. While the warriors danced in stylized argument, their women sat in circles piercing small eggs with sharpened hollow reeds and sucking out the liquid. Although he couldn't interpret the ritual, Danny was moved by the innocence of it. The dance symbolized ferocity, but the people were gentle and protective of each other.

As vista after vista unfolded beneath them, Danny was all but overwhelmed with the beauty of it. It was so beautiful it was painful to have to pass by and have no part of it.

They veered eastward and flew over an island, a floating cauldron, constantly on the boil. Amid the smoke and fumes and gases that belched from the groaning crater, Danny was put in mind of Myers' motorbike and compared the island to the exhaust pipe of that unruly machine.

In a great sweep back across the mainland, the angel passed above the thermal triangle, the explosive pools of subterranean energy, of lakes of boiling mud, of spurting fumaroles, nature's kitchen, and rose to cover the silver and cobalt lake in the center of the land which, his guide confided, was known as the Moon's Mirror in the realm where they now moved.

At the farthermost shore they rose yet higher to brush the summits of the three snow-capped volcanoes, the first of which was breathing fire and smoke from her sulphurous nostrils. The land around was parched and lifeless, but soon color returned and the land appeared as a crumpled green carpet flecked with yellow and red and here and there a pattern of towns. Rolling sheep country gave way to river valleys and flat land, farmed and forested. Never far were the ubiquitous motor vehicles on their ribbons of roads, which crossed and crisscrossed paths along which native warriors and hunters strode behind gauzy veils spun by time.

They followed the course of trenchant rivers through gorges and plunging ravines, around sedate hills of fern and pine and rimu and past trim banks manicured by municipal councils before running wild in rapids, drifting into deep, bottle-green pools or tumbling over cliffs in cascades of spray and foam.

"You must absorb all this," the angel said. "Reduce it to a single entity, then represent it."

Danny sat bolt upright as if an electrical charge had been administered to his body. His own head and shoulders, alternating with Zelia's and pictures of penguins, took up the entire television screen. They were making a hash of identifying the different species. Angela reveled in making noises like a jungle cockatoo. Zelia's head was turned in his direction. "Oh, there you are," she said. "I thought you had gone outside for a moment. My head must be addled by the embarrassment of watching this program. I'm so glad it's not being transmitted to Urfa. I don't think I could face the family again if it was."

# 20

## *Sir William Arrives*

IMMEDIATELY after his talk with Odo, Sir William had sent his agent, Ferhat Ferhat, ahead to Wellington to prepare for his arrival. Ferhat Ferhat had often been forerunner to Sir William's redemptive missions, clearing his ways and making straight his paths. Ferhat Ferhat was an accomplished diplomat, actor, front man, trouble-shooter, jailbird, swindler, toothpaste commercial and psychopath. He had one love, one goal, one motivation, one single principle, immutable and absolute, the deification of the ego of Ferhat Ferhat. And he could be very modest about it, too, if modesty was what it took. Or ruthless, depending. In Sir William he had found an ally and a champion. Their egos were identical twins. Eventually, of course, one would have to be sacrificed as part of the deification process of the other, but for the present they circled in mutually indispensable orbits.

Ferhat Ferhat was a Greek from Izmir in Turkey, not that there was any way of knowing that unless he told you. He held fifteen passports, valid to all appearances, and could convince as a Californian beach boy or Cambodian kick-boxer at will. Or any permutation in between. Such was the power of the ego.

Within a week of his arrival in Wellington, Ferhat Ferhat (using his Russian identity Boris Abladavich, Research Fellow of the Hermitage, St. Petersburg, seconded to the British Museum) had taken Tera Whare, a house overlooking Oriental Bay. Built of kauri and rimu in the last decade of the 19th century and traditionally rented to high-paying foreign interests on a temporary basis, Tera Whare possessed a happy blend of simplicity and opulence, of domestic woodwork and foreign prestige, of urban centrality and mountain remoteness, plus a medley of further paradoxes all in merry harmony with the persona of Sir William Kydd. Like, for instance, its north-face haunted turret, an architectural folly if ever there was one, but popular—proof positive that a ghost or two can absolve even the most crimson abuses of taste and discretion.

Using nothing but charm, cunning, animal allure and the name of Sir William, Ferhat Ferhat prepared the forces of the media, the galleries and the museums of the capital for the coming of the renowned maestro of ART until his name felt as familiar as a coin in the palm. Citizens from university professors to pink-haired punks jabbing their arms with deadly liquids in the shadows of upper Cuba Street were programmed overnight to hail the imminent arrival of Sir William Kydd as civilization's stamp of approval on New Zealand culture.

But Sir William was too cynical an egotist to believe in his own hype. Superstitiously discouraged by the recent plane crash, he entered New Zealand by private yacht from Australia a week or so later, tiptoed in through the back yard, one might say, and had seen everything he wanted to see before the press had any inkling of his arrival.

He visited the Cathedral and assessed the potential of the surface proposed for the *Lampadephoria* in terms of area, light, visibility, visual impact, circumambience, durability and maintenance. The volume of light was too intrusive for a conventional oil, he thought. In a few short years an oil would scorch like newsprint. The space required a solid medium, tiles, mosaic perhaps, tableaux of stained glass angled to digest the light. Plaster figures, gilded wood. The space would make a perfect vertical garden, Sir William mused. Lush tropical foliage with a ribbon waterfall in the center. Ferns. Moss and lichen. Orchids. Windowed in it could be said to represent Eden, which was a perfectly respectable religious theme. But, of course the Church Authorities would never buy that. An ornamental greenhouse, they would say. A pretty conservatory. A fernery. That sort of thing was all very well for the foyer of a prosperous banking house, but it would detract from the dignity of their Mass. They wouldn't object to naked cherubs or the gore and barbarity associated with martyrdom, but aesthetic horticulture, never.

Yet Sir William would not publicly betray his contempt. He considered religion to be the acceptable face of hypocrisy, and as such showed it the same deference as he showed to politics, war and sartorial fashion. He valued these things as enemies of anarchy; essential niceties to keep society's clock ticking. He was a man of deep urbanity, one who hadn't so much sold his soul as locked it out of his life so that it had become dried and wizened from lack of nourishment, a hot house for devils. The visible and the tangible absorbed all his efforts towards perfection.

Before going public in Wellington Sir William arranged a meeting that was, to him, the true purpose of his visit to what he thought of as "the last outpost of the known world."

Long after midnight he sent Ferhat Ferhat to fetch Qetik Mamoulian, the head of the family who was supposed to have looked after Zelia for her parents back in Urfa, but from whom she had fled. Ferhat Ferhat was to take the Armenian to a suite in a motel in Petone, which he'd booked by phone that afternoon. Qetik Mamoulian, unshod and wearing only a singlet and jeans, was still carrying a gutful of beer. He arrived with little idea of where he was or why he was there.

There was a cane chair in front of a dressing table and he slumped into it. Straightaway Ferhat Ferhat jerked him out of it. As he staggered on all fours Ferhat Ferhat tied a blindfold around his eyes.

Sir William entered from an adjacent room. He set the ferule of his walking stick on the floor before him and placed his hands, one on top of the other, over the silver ram's head. He studied the pathetic form of Qetik Mamoulian as a fastidious housewife might study a brisket of beef which she suspects of being unworthy of her pot.

"What the heeeeck's going on here?" Mamoulian spluttered in dazed defiance. He spoke the language almost without trace of an accent. "Dragging a bloke out of his bunk . . . some sort of Gestapo . . . is there a war on that no one has told me about . . . ?"

Sir William continued to inspect the overweight, unshaven Mamoulian with distaste. When he eventually spoke, the disdain transferred itself to his voice. "Five years ago you were recruited to come out here and instigate a search for the Mandylion which, we suspect, was secreted somewhere on these shores in the last century. You offered yourself, Mamoulian. We didn't solicit your services. As a renegade, or convert, as you wish, from the Mazloum family who has managed to retain the Mandylion in their possession for most of two millenniums, we assumed you would be an asset to our cause. We financed your move here, housed you, and pay you a monthly emolument. We have been exceedingly patient, Mamoulian, exceedingly patient, but to date your part of the bargain has not been in line with expectations. Until I chanced to watch television last night—some adolescent quiz program, a gratifying departure from rugby football and free-range politicians—I didn't even know that the Mazlooms had sent their girl here."

"I didn't know myself . . . didn't know . . ."

"Highly peculiar, Mamoulian, considering she was living in your house until your drunken debauches drove her to arrange independent accommodation. My informants have no doubts on the matter. Not a happy eventuality, Mamoulian, because until then the Mazlooms weren't aware of your defection. Now, we assume, they have lost faith in you and that means, oh dear! That means that you are no longer of any use to our organization."

"You've got it all twisted about . . . I can explain . . ."

"Indeed you are a liability." Sir William's bland face betrayed nothing of a line of action that had suddenly occurred to him. The television program . . . the Mazloum girl . . . no threat, of course, just a baby, but she could be an asset. What was the School? Holy Trinity in Lower Hutt. She would be in need of a protector and who more suitable than he would . . . ?

"Listen, mate, if you'll take this bandage off my eyes . . ."

"You are superfluous to our needs, Mamoulian. Superfluous."

Sir William nodded briefly to Ferhat Ferhat and left the room. Sir William was not at all averse to the idea of violence, but he preferred to involve himself on the management board rather than on the floor of the abattoir.

Zelia wrote her long weekly letter to her parents in Urfa. She told of her failure to come up with any lead at all concerning the Mandylion. She told how she had spent many hours in the Public Library in Wellington, sifting through the newspapers and the archives of Uncle Zeki's time, looking for some clue that might open a window, however tiny, on the mystery of the colored cards and the apparently simple message written on them. But there was nothing. Nothing at all. She might as well be trawling outer space with a magnifying glass, she wrote.

She apologized once again for any concern she had caused them for leaving the Mamoulians, but they were not to be trusted. She acknowledged that she had been lonely at first, but that she had made friends with a student in her class. She proceeded to tell them everything she knew about Danny and suggested that she might share the secret of the Mandylion with him, but only if they consented. A burden shared is a burden halved, she wrote in English, quoting from a cracker she'd found in a packet of breakfast cereal, and then translated into Aramaic. Above all, they were not to worry. She was quite aware that she was young and vulnerable and that normally it would be folly for a girl of her age to be living alone in a strange country on the other side of the world, but, she insisted, the circumstances were exceptional, and she believed that the Blessed Virgin was giving her special and personal protection. Sometimes, it was as if she, Zelia, felt Mary's hand on her shoulder, caressing her, guiding her, and that her quest was not only approved of, but that Mary herself was the instigator of it, the patroness, the manager and the one who would bring it to fruition.

Zelia tapped her teeth with the hilt of her pen. It occurred to her to wonder why, if heaven knew the answers, it didn't simply reveal them? There was no future in speculating on the "what ifs." The Promised Land was not a matter of luck, or chance, or serendipity. It was necessary for her to fumble in darkness for a while. Asking "why" impeded progress. A light would emerge slowly, or maybe even suddenly, who knew? But in the end it would reveal the essence of all. . . .

Zelia's mind was wandering. It often did that. It was like

prayer. Perhaps it was a form of prayer, a sort of knocking on the door, a waiting in the atrium, preparing those things that needed to be said.

But at the moment she was writing a letter to her parents. She jerked her head back as if to shake off thoughts alien to her present purpose. Once more she applied her pen to the paper.

On the morning of December 6—St. Nicholas—the Cardinal's secretary phoned Mother Madeleine. The secretary's voice was breathless with shock. All Mother Madeleine said was, "Ridiculous!" though she did add, "And on the feast of St. Nicholas, too!" as she put the receiver down.

By lunch time word had leaked out in the government offices and in the university.

Before the lunch dishes had been cleared away, all overseas telephone lines were jammed and the Electronic Mail Delivery system became overloaded and the words FATAL ERROR flashed on and off on computer screens all over the country.

A press conference was announced for 2:00 pm. It took place at the Basin Reserve Sports ground. Sir William Kydd himself spoke. It was true, he confirmed. An anonymous benefactor had upped the prize money for the *Reredos Lampadephoria*. The winning entry would now receive the magnificent sum of . . . Sir William, black soul that he was, knew how to work a crowd and did it with aplomb. He waited for silence. Then, when he had such a silence even an egg being laid could disturb it, he held one finger aloft. Then another.

"Million?" people gasped. Sir William nodded.

Four fingers . . . six . . . eight. The Basin Reserve had never known such tension, no, not even in a final innings with an equal score. It was like blowing up a balloon. Any second it must burst in your face.

Ten fingers! "Ten million dollars!" Sir William announced.

"Is that American or New Zealand dollars?" a practical pressman shouted above the hush.

Sir William had no idea, so he treated the query as an impertinence, and ignored it.

On the Second Sunday of Advent, Danny cycled to the convent with a view to working undisturbed on his paintings. His mother had taken Angela somewhere in the old Ford and Zelia, although he had courageously knocked on her door, hadn't been at home. He took the back path to his studio.

In his studio Raphael da Vinci was stretched out on a chair with his feet on an upturned bucket. He was wearing the same clothes he had been wearing when he had first arrived at the convent, but they were not dirty. Indeed they appeared to have been freshly laundered. His skin was burnished with exposure to the sun, which gave his engaging smile an extra depth and charm. "Hi!" he said, shaking himself out of a doze and smiling as if Danny was his best friend in the world.

"Hi!" said Danny. "Where have you been for the past three weeks?"

"Walkabout. No roads. Strictly bush. I've been as far as Hawkes Bay—wrestling, young Daniel, wrestling with the dispensers of inspiration. I had to come back to show you the results." Raphael jumped up and spread out a rather untidy role of small, thick paper sheets on the table. "What do you think?" Raphael asked.

Danny studied each drawing. When the first arrived back at the top of the pile he removed his hands and they rolled up of their own accord, as if embarrassed for their creator.

"Well, what do you think," Raphael glowed.

Danny took his *Kiwi Christ* canvas from where it leaned against the wall and lifted it onto the easel. He placed the chair beneath the skylight.

"Do you like them?" Raphael was eager for credit. Danny fetched the Weka-Feather Cloak from the back of its sailcloth dummy in the mirror room and placed it around Raphael's shoulders. When he spoke he was careful with his words. "Monet and Gauguin couldn't have done them," he said, helping his model onto a chair and directing his pose.

"Do you think so? Really?" Raphael was as proud as a cat with kittens.

Danny painted till it was almost dusk. Raphael posed patiently, though he talked a lot. His main theme was the *Reredos Lampadephoria.* He thought that two months was "far, far too short a time for serious artists to get their stuff together."

Danny pointed out that it had only started out as a small affair, and that the committee couldn't change the rules just because someone had augmented the prize money. Anyway, they were only looking for ideas from those with the skills to implement them. They weren't looking for a finished work, not at this stage. After all, the final work would have to cover an area the size of a tennis court.

Before he departed, Raphael looked long and hard at the images that were emerging on Danny's *Kiwi Christ* canvas. He didn't comment on the work, but he did ask for the train fare into Wellington. Danny didn't have any money with him, and said so. "Oh, don't worry then," Raphael said cheerily. "I'll take a taxi. And I'll leave my paintings here until next time. You can choose which one I should enter for the Reredos thing."

He sauntered off smiling while Danny stood in the center of his studio, biting his lower lip in bafflement. No money for

a train so he takes a taxi. A batch of thoroughly dreadful paintings and he wants to enter one for the Reredos. And—it was
always nagging him—why was Raphael's face and bearing so
familiar? On television after the Somes Island plane crash, yeah,
but apart from that, before that, more general than that. He
was as familiar as a movie star.

# 21

## Première and Afterwards

ON THE last day of school before the long summer holidays, Myers and Pascal and those others were being more caustic than usual. Danny's television stint in the quiz show had jabbed at their pride and bruised their self-esteem. In class and in the corridors, in the yard and in the gardens by the river they had been firing off at him, volley after volley of invective. And it always seemed to be at its worst when Zelia was within earshot.

"I wouldn't look to a career in television if I were you, Maggot. Our set broke down in protest."

"Ours too. We've sent your mum the bill."

"Try navvying . . . or plumbing! Yeah! Take up plumbing. You talk it all the time so you might as well make it your bread and butter."

"Oh Danny boy, the pipes, the pipes are calling . . ."

Myers revved up his motor bike whenever Danny passed, as if it was a mastiff growling its displeasure at an undesirable presence.

All the newspapers, journals, television, and radio stations that week were coupling the news of the $10,000,000 prize money with news of the grand première of an American-financed New Zealand film called *Albatross*. Pundits were already claiming it as Oscar material and a global money-spinner. The American star and a number of Hollywood names were flying out for the event.

"Mr. Grundy," Pascal said in the art class. "Mago's head has swollen out of all proportion since he made a goat of himself on the TV. Permission to lop it off, Sir?"

"All of it?" gasped Duffy, feigning incredulity. "The entire mass?"

"He's become insufferable, Sir."

"Intolerable, Sir."

"He thinks he's a cut above us, Sir. He'll be telling us he's been invited to the *Albatross* Première next."

Upon this remark Zelia, who had never uttered an unnecessary word in class from the day she enrolled, rose from her desk, middle row, third from the back, and spoke. Her voice was clear and controlled and very attractive with its accented lilt. "He has!" she said. She reached into her satchel and withdrew an envelope and waved it happily in the air. "I have the tickets here. We're going together."

Danny was as surprised as anyone was, but he didn't show it. Danny rarely showed any emotion in public. It required no effort on his part. It was his way. He always looked like he was alone in a field of flowers, inhaling the summer juices and musing on the largess of nature. It was probably this more than anything that infuriated many of his peers.

After school Danny cycled into the High Street and bought himself a new outfit; warm, beery brown trousers, a blue suede jacket, a light peppermint shirt and the latest in trainers. It wasn't impulse buying. He had been eyeing these garments for weeks and diligently saving for them. (He actually gave his mother all the money he earned in the convent, but she insisted that he keep a portion for himself.) He was pleased with the color combination, and with the sense of confidence that the newness of the clothes and the quality of their cloth imparted. It was like he'd been given a fresh persona. True, his flesh didn't quite fill out the trousers, but he would thicken. Most kids did in the eleventh year. Or in the twelfth at the latest.

He spent an hour at Aniwaniwa catching up with Mother Madeleine's mailbag, which swelled daily. It was as if it contained a yeast of its own. The mailman no longer delivered, the Post Office sent a van with the latest arrivals each midday. "Mother's mail has an exponential life of its own," Sister Paula said.

"What does exponential mean?" Danny had asked, but Sister Paula had turned to other things. The word stayed in his mind and he mentioned it to Angela when he collected her from the day center, but only because he mentioned everything to Angela, he scarcely expected a definition; and then again to Zelia during their twenty minutes' train journey to the cinema in Wellington.

Actually, it was a pretty dumb thing to come up with out of the blue. "Have you any idea what exponential means?" but every other conversation opener seemed as empty as a flat tire. The truth was that he felt sorely self-conscious in the presence of Zelia, even though he would rather be with her than in any other place in the world. Or, indeed, any other time in the world. He wondered if he should tell her about the elevator. That was a secret that would surely fuse their friendship. Of course he could tell her. He had nothing to lose. She wasn't the type to go round blabbering to everyone else. The problem was how. And would she believe him? And was it true anyway? Perhaps he was just imagining the whole thing. Perhaps he'd gone barmy.

"Getting bigger as it goes along," said Zelia. "Like a snowball. It was in *Time* magazine last week and I looked it up."

"Oh yeah!" Danny looked at the train tickets. He looked out of the carriage window. He looked intently at the objects on the floor, two lolly wrappers and a crushed Coke can. He hadn't a notion what she was talking about, but it didn't matter because every word that spilled from her lips was a jewel from a secret casket to be caught and held and cherished for eternity. *Time* magazine. Danny parroted the words. Snowball. Was there no limit to her loveliness?

"Sister Eileen has offered me a job helping you with the mail in the convent," Zelia said.

Danny simply gaped. Then he managed to say, "Oh. Oh, good! She never mentioned it to me."

"She was busy. She told me to."

Pigeon Square was crammed full of people, and traffic was diverted around the north side. Zelia gave Danny the tickets and looped her arm through his. With all those people watching, Zelia looped her arm through his. Danny presented the tickets at the barricade. No one presented tickets with quite the same degree of confidence or strolled off along the cordoned passage in the middle of all the people as Danny did with Zelia's arm looped through his. Cars were pulling up and overdressed people were stepping out. Flashbulbs blinked in the dusk. The crowds were cheering, and even at times jeering at some of the pretensions of the event, because this was a Kiwi crowd and Kiwis weren't to be impressed with a Hollywood imitation. The crowd had gathered to see the crowd. If the movie people who took themselves seriously didn't like the attention diverted from their famous selves, the crowd sensed it and laughed at them. It wasn't rudeness, it was the mirth that wasn't at home with flattery. But Danny wasn't conscious of any of this. He walked on through the crowd and into the cinema foyer with Zelia's arm looped through his.

They were shown to seats in the center stalls. The lights went down and the film was screened without a break. Later the lights went up and so did the screen, right up into the trees to reveal a buffet laid out there on the stage, and after some speeches and a lot of clapping, a cocktail party started. On the stage itself, in the aisles and in the foyer, girls in short black skirts with aprons like doilies and paper caps appeared with trays of drinks.

Zelia took a glass of white wine and Danny followed her lead. From the table on the stage they took plates of meats and salads and things impaled on toothpicks and stood against the wall at the top of the proscenium steps. A strong light from above the stage was surfing Zelia's thick black hair, so black that where it swelled to a wave it was almost blue.

"What did you think of the film?" Zelia asked.

Danny was suddenly aware that he was enormously happy, that avenues of happiness never before imagined were opening up to his vision. I feel like a mole, he thought, a foraging mole that breaks the surface of the earth and gazes for the first time on a moonlit universe. Straightaway, remembering that a mole was blind, he substituted a badger and chuckled into his drink.

"You thought it was funny?" Zelia was puzzled and amused. "I thought it was anything but funny. All that fighting. All that bad language."

"No I . . . It wasn't . . ." Danny couldn't have told her what the film was about if survival depended on it. Movies, for him, were always instantly forgotten, like dreams, like reflections in water. Films had no substance. Not like paintings. If only he could paint Zelia as she stood then. To take that loveliness and set it on canvas as a hostage to time. He would mix his own exquisite happiness with the colors and they would be preserved together as a single entity; like lovers buried together for eternity, hand in hand.

"It said more about original sin than Genesis," Zelia said.

The girl was fantastic. Even in her plain cream dress, blue

cardigan and a yellow scarf, she out-dazzled all the rich and the famous and the well-scrubbed. I'll bet there wouldn't be a single person here clever enough to say that about original sin and Genesis, Danny mused. She was superb. And she liked him. Danny could tell. There was something about the way she stood, the angle of her elbows, that declared she was with him, that she depended on him, Danny Mago, not on the Prime Minister, not on the Mayor, not on the Hollywood people or the muscle boys in suits. Danny Mago was her companion and protector and she was proud of him.

Danny took a sip from his glass and pulled a wry face. "I don't like this wine," he said. "Tastes like it's been brewed in a soap factory."

Zelia smiled gloriously at this image and Danny felt he had given felicitous expression to an ineluctable truth until Zelia commented, "Do you brew wine in New Zealand? I thought brewing was for beer."

"Distill. Ferment. I don't know much about alcoholic drinks." She was possibly the most perfect being currently on earth. And he no longer felt in the least self-conscious with her. Or awkward, or tongue-tied, or shy, or anything. Just glued.

She said, "Do you like it in here?"

Danny shrugged.

She said, "Me neither. I'm hungry, but for something more substantial than piked pickles. Let's go."

Was there no end to her talent?

They put their glasses on the floor in a corner and twisted their way between clusters of sippers and chatterers, excusing themselves.

"How did you get those tickets in the first place. (Excuse me!) I forgot to ask."

"They were delivered to me at school. (May I? Thank you!) This morning. Before school."

"Who by? (Sorry. A tight squeeze!)"

"I don't know. There was a note. It was in Turkish. It simply said, *From a friend.*"

"Turkish! (Not to worry. It's suede. It'll wash out.) In Lower Hutt!"

There was more space to move in the foyer. They had almost made the door when a fellow with a faceful of teeth spoke to Zelia, and she stopped short. Danny stood still too and would have stayed like that, in a state of suspended ecstasy, for eternity, but she was speaking to the man rapidly in a language, which seemed to have more than a fair share of Z's in it. After a while Ferhat Ferhat said, in English, "I assure you, the communication I have been entrusted to deliver to your uncle confirms the whereabouts of the Mandylion. Please, do come immediately. We have no time to lose." In a very short time Zelia had taken Danny's arm again, and they were following Ferhat Ferhat out of the theatre and into a car.

"What's all this about?" Danny whispered, but Zelia frowned him into silence. Danny exalted in the intimacy of the frown. He experienced such joy in her company that he found no difficulty in staying by her even if he felt a strong distrust of the bloke with the teeth.

In the car Ferhat Ferhat kept up a steady flow of talk. Zelia maintained a grim silence, but the pressure of her arm in Danny's betrayed her tension.

Danny didn't much like the look of Ferhat Ferhat. He didn't trust him. True, Ferhat Ferhat smiled a lot, those teeth were flashing on and off like a police car on a chase, but the smile was a gloss, a commercial, a sham. Anyway, the bloke was downright rude. Ferhat Ferhat hadn't so much as glanced at Danny. Indeed, to Ferhat Ferhat, Danny might as well not have existed.

Ferhat Ferhat drove them to the Hutt Valley. Suddenly he

said he would drop Danny at his place and then take Zelia to her uncle Mamoulian's place. Danny caught the glint of fear in Zelia's eye and did some quick thinking. "O.K." he said. "Then you want to drive us to Aniwaniwa. Drive right of the railway line and turn right again at the end." When they came to the end of the boxwood hedge Danny told the Turk to stop. He jumped out of the car and pulled Zelia after him. Ferhat Ferhat grabbed out at her over the seat but only managed to get a grip of her yellow scarf.

"Zelia planned to stop with us for a bit before going home," Danny called before slamming the door, leaving the scarf still wedged in it. They moved off rapidly across the car-bridge that spanned the stream.

Danny didn't take the back drive that led to the convent. For one thing it was late and the Sisters would probably all be in bed. Furthermore, if Ferhat Ferhat did follow, he would automatically take that way whether in the car or on foot. Instead he took Zelia's arm and then ran her along the riverside path that led to the conservatory.

In the conservatory Zelia was still nervous. "I am sure he is following us," she said.

"I don't reckon so," said Danny. "But better safe than sorry." He took the halogen lamp and the rosary from behind the pagan statue. "Grab these; I know somewhere he wouldn't find us in a thousand years." He folded the blue cowl up under his arm.

They crept out into the dark.

Danny didn't switch on the lamp until they had walked up the ten steps and were in the mouth of the tunnel. When he did, the sudden brightness was so overwhelming that Zelia gave a sharp cry and stepped back into Danny's arms. "This place is spooky," she whispered when the bats had shrieked and flapped their way to remote perches. "I feel like Jonah must have felt in the belly of his fish."

When she spoke like that Danny marveled that any being could be so rare. Poetry. Utter poetry. That was how he wanted to paint. "It's O.K.," he said. "Nothing can harm us as long as we have this," he said, touching the cross of the rosary. "Come forward a bit. You see that grille door. It's an elevator." Then he told of the places and the times in history that it had taken him to. He told of the painter monks in Florence, of the Lady Juliana and how the whole world and everything in it took on a new perspective when he was with her even though she barely spoke. He told of the monster, too, but was inclined to make light of it. He said that it never appeared when he held the crucifix, and that even when it did appear, it only had the power to frighten, it couldn't do any actual harm.

He told her all this in about ten sentences, then he opened the gate. Zelia was willing enough to enter but her movements betrayed her apprehension.

He slammed the gates shut and clutched the lever. There was a sound from beyond the tunnel. It could have been a possum, or it could have been a big-toothed Ferhat. The elevator started to move, slowly at first and then very rapidly. To deflect from the tension Danny asked, "What was he talking about, that oily fellow? What did he say to you to induce you to get into the car with him?"

Zelia was embarrassed. "I can't . . . it's a secret," she said.

"So is this, " said Danny. "My time-defying elevator."

"This is something sacred that my family has guarded for centuries—for millenniums."

"You sound like my angel . . ."

# 22

## *Phoenicia 32 AD*

 THEY FOUND themselves on a hillside looking down on a town of great visual charm. It was built on the confluence of two rivers and, criss-crossed as it was with canals and pools, it gave the illusion of floating on water. Fruit trees, palms and weeping willows grew on the banks of the rivers and the courtyards, and even the flat roofs of houses were dancing with color in the heat. The position of the sun in the sky and the pace of the few people and animals in the streets and on the solid stone bridge of the town told that it was early morning.

Zelia was stunned with amazement. "This is incredible," she said in her own language; then, in English, "Where are we? What is this?"

Danny winked. "Swap you," he challenged, like a card player who holds a golden hand. "Your secret for mine."

The dress of the people suggested that he was somewhere in the Old World of Europe, probably what they called the Near East. The dusty, stone-paved roads out of the town and the number of animals indicated that it was before motorized vehicles. Furthermore there were no TV aerials, telephone or electricity lines. No church steeple, or even a minaret of a mosque, was visible. An imposing rectangular building in the center of the town could be a place of worship, he thought, and the domed structure in an annex to the town, on the opposite bank of the larger river, could have been a synagogue. But in fact, there was nothing to indicate the century or even whether they were in times BC or AD. Danny couldn't help wondering why he had been brought to this unidentifiable place. Surely there were no new painting techniques to be unearthed here.

In a field by the smaller river a small circular tent had been pitched. It had brocade trimmings around the entrance flap. A horse and a number of mules were tethered to the pegs.

At the foot of the hill stood a row of long stone buildings like brick kilns from which rose mushrooms of smoke. As they watched, the smoke from the kilns grew thicker. There was certainly more smoke than kiln ovens could account for, and it wasn't issuing from the chimney. Then a cry went up from the area. Before the cry had time to find an echo, flames were belching from the kilns, and people were running towards them. Soon it seemed that the entire population of the town, many still in nightshirts, were running across the bridge in collective panic.

Amid the chaos a line formed between the kilns and the river. Buckets were passed from hand to hand, but the water made little impression on the flames. Soon they were spurting up like a scarlet and orange fountain, almost as high as the tall chimney. In no time the fire had spread to the other buildings in the row.

A young man in a fine green gown, edged with fur and belted at the waist, emerged from the tent in the field. Behind him were fellows who had the manner and dress of servants. Some of these servants began to untether the animals in a panic, while others started to dismantle the tent, but the young man stopped them. He re-entered the tent and emerged again almost immediately holding what looked like a small, brightly colored, oval shield in one hand and a piece of cloth in the other. He spoke to the servants, who then ran before him and forged a way through the crowd.

The young man walked slowly and reverently, with his head bowed.

When he reached the front of the building the young man seemed to have no fear of the flames. He walked directly up to where they could almost lick him. The crowd ceased their noise and fell back in awe. The young man appeared to physically swell with authority and, raising the oval object and the cloth high above his head, he gave a command, which Danny could not hear distinctly. Not so much as a murmur came from the crowd. Even the animals tied to the tent supports, who had been bellowing in agitation, grew quiet. They raised their heads expectantly, as if waiting for a summons.

It was difficult to determine exactly when, but the flames had stopped, and the smoke was petering out into a hazy veil. It took some moments for the people to realize what had happened. They stood stunned, holding buckets of water, more bamboozled than the animals. Shortly, however, the shout went up. Then they dropped their buckets and besieged the young man, shouting questions at him and wrestling each other to touch his gown.

Danny and Zelia were also sparked by the excitement of the moment. They ran, skipped, skidded, slipped down the hill. Danny had forgotten, until he tripped on the hem of it, that he had put on the blue cowl in the elevator. The rosary with the large cross he held firmly in his hand. He called to Zelia to hold on a moment, but she didn't seem to hear him. She was running towards the young man and, could Danny have seen her face, he would have been astonished at the sheer intensity of the expression it wore. And her eyes were as excited as silver flames.

By the time she reached level ground the young man had

broken away from the townspeople and was standing next to a well, which was raised somewhat above the ground. He was holding the oval shield close to his chest while his servants formed a cordon round him, urging the people back.

". . . I was drawing a picture of him for my master," he was saying. "Here, on this palette. It's a relief sketch on wax, hardened by the marrow from ox bones. I did fifteen, maybe twenty sketches while he was talking to the people. But never could I create a likeness—well, a likeness, yes, but no more than a skull is like a living human face.

"His head had the carriage of a king and his eyes—those eyes were sometimes the eyes of a doe, sometimes of a lion. I could not capture that and put it onto my wax. No talent could capture that. It would be like trying to put the sun into a bottle.

"When he had finished talking to the people, he beckoned me to come over to him and he took the picture from my hand. I apologized that it was so bad and told him that my master, the King of Edessa, had commanded me to do the portrait and take it back to him. My master must stay all the time on his couch because an evil is living in his legs and he is unable to walk. Then I bowed low and told him that my master had entrusted me with a letter and gifts for him. "He has heard of your power," I said, "and begs you to come and cure him."

"He took the gifts, saying that my master's good intentions were pleasing to him. He did not touch the gifts himself, but told his servants to share them among the poorest of the people who had been listening to him. Then he took the letter, which was rolled in this goat's-wool cloth and bound with a cord. He opened it, read the letter, took a chalk from the folds of his robe, wrote something on the parchment, folded it and gave it back to me."

Danny had caught up with Zelia and they were standing among the crowd, listening to the words of the princely young man. An old woman next to Zelia happened to glance at her. She started tut-tutting with stern indignation and, fishing around among her many layers of black clothing, brought forth a mantle which she flung over Zelia's head as if to say, "Cover yourself like a respectable woman!" The corners of the mantle fell almost to her ankles.

"A water-bearer who had been among his listeners was still crouched nearby. He asked for water and the boy poured some into his hands, which he lifted up and used to bathe his face. He used this cloth to dab his face dry. Some of the water had splashed onto my picture so when he handed the cloth back to me I patted the wax with it to absorb the water and when I removed it the picture had become like a mirror-image of him. Not a line of mine had been altered nor another added, but it glowed with something of his own life. I fell to my knees in front of him. There was nothing else I could do, or wanted to. He didn't say anything, but placed his hand, still damp, on my head for a moment, and it was as if the grime of a lifetime was suddenly rinsed away.

"I wanted more than anything to stay and be his servant, but he told me to return to my master in Edessa, so I leapt up and held the picture aloft where all the people could see it, then immediately I packed the caravan and started on the homeward journey. That was two days ago. Last night we made camp here and when this fire started this morning, I felt again the touch of his hand upon my head and knew that the fire could not withstand his power which he would channel through the picture."

The people wanted to carry the young man into the town, but he was dismissive of their enthusiasm to the point of appearing rude.

"It's not me you should be thanking," he said as he strode towards his tent. "That is wasted energy indeed. Go south and see for yourselves the man whom even the birds are singing about."

Danny and Zelia moved among the dispersing crowds. Danny was curious about a number of things, the chief of which was the matter of language. The young man had spoken Greek to the people and they had understood him. Danny wasn't sure how he knew it was Greek, but he did, and he had no trouble in understanding it. More surprising was that he also understood the people when they spoke among themselves. He had no idea what their language was, and they spoke it with an odd accent which was dry and gnarled as if they had thistles in their throats when they spoke.

Although the people seemed to ignore Zelia they looked at Danny with puzzled expressions. Clearly he was not from those parts. He was taller than anyone there, their eyes said, taller than a human needs to be, and his features and manner were different, altogether different from anyone they had ever seen.

"What's your master's name?" demanded a well-dressed and well-fed citizen, thrusting his face as close to Danny's as he could (he was standing on tiptoe) and quite bristling with defiance.

Danny answered, "I don't have a master." He was speaking their language with an ease that was almost eerie.

"You fool in Roman clothes. This man here, the drawer of portraits. What's his name?"

Danny said, "I don't know. I am not with him."

"Foreigners!" snorted the man, walking away and pushing his wife ahead of him.

"Danny," said Zelia urgently, leaning forward so that she could whisper in his ear. "Please don't ask questions, just do as I say. Go to the young man's tent and ask to look at the oval picture—clearly, I can't enter a man's tent here. Study it well. I think I know what it is, but I want to be sure."

"Why . . . ?"

"Do hurry! It is the very essence of my secret."

Danny crossed to the young man's tent, and asked a servant who was feeding the mules if he could speak with his master. The servant entered the tent, then came out again to motion him in. For all its being imposing on the outside, the tent gave no indication of luxury within. A few mats were rolled up near the entrance along with a bag or two. In the center of the space some palm, or maybe rhubarb leaves were spread on the earth with a broken round of bread lying among its own crumbs in a fold of the leaves with a honey-comb in a dish beside it. Fruit, figs, dates and pomegranate lay at the base of a stone jar. Flies traced spheres above the leaves. There was no chair or cushion to sit on.

The young man, who was squatting on the ground lacing leather boots, looked at Danny with a slight frown, but bowed his head graciously. Danny returned the bow and said, "Forgive my interruption, but I would be most honored if you would allow me to look more closely at the portrait." The young man took it from a satchel on the ground beside him and held it out to Danny, whom he clearly thought to be of some superior caste.

The base was a piece of wood, very light, maybe balsa, about 30cm at its longest point and 20 at its widest. The wood was covered with a thick, clouded, white wax, which, now that it had hardened, had the texture, though not the weight, of marble. The portrait had been furrowed into the wax, when soft, with black ink. In places the lines were no more than a scratch while others were almost a quarter of a centimeter deep.

Pigments, rich and brilliant, yet at the same time subtle and delicate, had been applied with a brush of very few and very fine hairs.

The drawing itself had a quality that only the rash would attempt to describe, or even to retain as a mental image. Danny felt that if it were his, he would never tire of gazing at it. Its beauty made conventional beauty look like a rag doll in a nursery cupboard. And yet it was a beauty that was veiled; behind the veil lay a promise of even greater beauty, beauty unimaginable, beauty that would blind greedy eyes and give sight to the reverent.

"You speak Greek," said the young man as Danny handed back the picture. "But it is not chewed up Greek such as the people speak in these parts. Where are you from?"

"Lower Hutt," Danny said. His mind was still dazzled by the picture. The young man's eyebrows formed a question mark. "It's south of here." This was a bit weak, but it was the only explanation he could think to offer.

"Ah!" The young man was satisfied. "Are you traveling north? You may join our small caravan. We will be traveling quickly. My master will be anxious for news."

"Your master! King Abgarus of Edessa?"

"Indeed. You have visited our city?"

"No!" He'd like to have told him that his city still existed in the 21st century, that it was now in the eastern part of the Turkish Republic, now called Urfa, and, most important to Danny, that Zelia, who was waiting outside, came from that very city, albeit a few hundred generations later.

"You are most gracious." Danny bowed. "But I have duties here. I shan't bother you longer, but one last question. What did the man whose portrait you painted write with the chalk on the back of your master's letter before he returned it to you?"

"I do not know," he said. "The message is for the master, not for the servant."

"Of course. I am impertinent. Forgive me." Danny bowed. As he did so, the rosary slipped from his fingers. The young man stooped and picked it up. As he was handing it back, he saw the figure of the body nailed to the cross and stiffened perceptibly. Then he flung it to the ground and took a step back.

"What sort of evil jewelry is this? Some perverse Roman god? You have dishonored my hospitality. Please take it and leave my tent. Guards!"

Danny picked up the rosary, then opened his mouth to explain, but two men were already lifting him off the ground. They carried him outside and across the field to where a clump of people were still gathered, talking about the fire and the way it had been miraculously extinguished. They dumped him in the dust at the feet of these people and one of the men said, "An idolater! A death worshipper! Look!" He kicked Danny's hand and the crowd all saw the figure of the man nailed to the wood. They recoiled in instant horror. Then they spat at him, and one or two stepped forward and kicked him in the head and around the body.

Zelia ran up and courageously interposed herself between Danny and his attackers. They continued to scream heavy abuse at him, but suddenly the elevator appeared right alongside them. He managed to roll into it, and Zelia followed. She clanged the door shut, while Danny reached up and pulled the knob.

During the descent Danny sat on the floor of the elevator holding his head in his hands and groaning.

"Tell me about it," said Zelia.

"You saw it: they tried to beat me up."

"No, I mean the picture, the oval picture."

"It was a portrait. Jesus, I think. Very powerful. There's really no describing it."

Zelia clutched at her own throat as women do when confronted with matters of great moment. "It was the Mandylion." Her voice was strained yet excited. "My family have been the custodians of the Mandylion for almost two thousand years. Now it is somewhere in New Zealand. That is why I am here—to recover it."

# 23

## The Mandylion

ONCE OUT of the tunnel—Danny thankful that the demons had not made their presence felt—they returned the lamp and the crucifix to the conservatory. Then they made their way up a path that skirted the back of the convent and rejoined the stream on the far side of the hill. If Ferhat Ferhat were still around, he would never have stumbled on that route. By the old Kirkland house they cut across to Waterloo and down Knight's Road to Zelia's place.

On the way she confided her secret—the secret of the Mandylion. Its provenance—the circumstances under which it had been painted and endorsed by Christ himself—they had had just learned from the lips of the painter himself.

She told how the Mandylion had been in the custody of her family in Edessa, or Urfa, as it was now called, ever since, preserved with great reverence in the vaults beneath their ancient farmstead and only brought out on very special occasions for veneration in the churches.

"Once in the 10th century," she said, "it was taken to Constantinople, but through a complicated set of events, it was returned to us and we kept it until the late 1890's.

"In 1894 the local Bey, Orhanpasha, launched a sudden and terrible anti-Armenian offensive (in effect, it included all Christians) at the instigation of the Sultan, Abdulhamid, who was falling deeper and deeper into satanic despotism. Would you believe, he wouldn't allow electricity into the Ottoman Empire because he mistook the word *Dynamo* for *Dynamite.*

"Within a single day Orhanpasha, who called himself the *Sword of Gabriel,* had rounded up half the male Christians. He had many of them publicly shot and their bodies fed to pigs. Thereafter he was shooting one man an hour until the Mandylion was delivered into his hands. You see, he had the notion that the Mandylion was the chief Christian idol and that in eliminating it, he would eliminate Christianity.

Meanwhile my great Uncle Zeki had been smuggled silently out of the country with the real Mandylion. When he was safely abroad, an imitation was presented to Orhanpasha, who had it burned in the courtyard of the Abder Rahman Medressi. When the Sultan heard of this, he mistakenly understood that it was his own image that had been burned, and executioners were immediately dispatched to Edessa. Orhanpasha was locked in a circular iron cage, which was dragged into the mountains by a team of oxen. There the *Sword of Gabriel* was left to be fought over by wolves and jackals and hovering buzzards."

"I don't think I'd much care to live in your neighborhood," said Danny.

"Uncle Zeki joined a ship called the *Silas Fish,* which took him first to the United States and then to New Zealand. He had last written from Wellington in New Zealand, saying that he had developed a strange malady. He didn't consider it serious, but that if anything should happen to him, the Mandylion was safe.

"Nothing was heard from him till after the First World War when a letter arrived from the British Consulate in Antakya saying that Zeki had died of pneumonia in the Home of Compassion in Wellington in 1894 and that it wasn't till now that his kin had been traced. The deceased's personal effects, the letter added, had been shipped to Antakya and would be released on the payment of £7.3.9d cartage.

"In the parcel that arrived in Urfa was an envelope containing seven cards, each a different color. On one side the cards had haphazard, inked lines. On the other was writing in a medley of languages—Syriac Aramaic, Turkish, though written in Arabic script, English, and some in a tongue which they eventually identified as Maori. (Not a lot of Maori was spoken in Mesopotamia in those days, Zelia's grandfather had joked.) It was all a great mystery, yet the family knew that, once deciphered, the hiding place of the Mandylion would be revealed."

They were both so absorbed in the narrative that they almost passed Zelia's house.

"Where are these cards?" Danny asked as he opened the wicket gate to let her through.

"I'll show you."

As Danny bathed his bruised head with a wet towel, she lay the seven colored cards out on the kitchen table. So here was Uncle Zeki's simple but baffling key to the whereabouts of one of the greatest sacramentals of Christendom. Danny lowered the towel and screwed up his nose and eyes. "That's moon language!" he said.

Zelia translated: "NAVIGATOR ENGAGE (THE DOOR) STRAIGHTAWAY DISENGAGE or CONNECTING DISCONNECT THE (CURTAIN OF) JAVELINS TO MAINTAIN MASTERY or MAKE THE SPEARS SEAL AND BREAK THE SEAL CONTROLLING . . .

There are an infinite number of possible combinations, but that's the gist of the message."

"Verbal chaos," said Danny. Then, suddenly inspired, he added. "Maybe it's a form of crossword."

"Mmmm! But when Uncle Zeki wrote the message, crosswords hadn't been invented. Anyway, the letters he wrote to Edessa before he died show that he was a simple, kindly man with a great sense of fun. Even though it was necessary for him to communicate in the manner of a Delphic Oracle, he would still keep it simple to confound thieves whose tangled minds would be sniffing everywhere for runic symbols and intrigues."

Zelia reshuffled the cards and laid them out again. "Seven. Each a different color. The primary colors, in pastel, fading with time but still recognizable. On one side words in a fricassee of languages—but that's a family joke. Traditionally we Mazloums have always been linguists. It has been part of our family pride, and income.

"On the obverse side of each card, some curved lines, like strands of hair on a collar after a haircut. But they don't seem to mean anything. They aren't even doodles."

Danny asked, "Where did he live in New Zealand, your Uncle Zeki?"

"He spent all his time here in the Hutt Valley. None of his letters speak of visiting any other area. Clearly he wrote the cards when he knew he was dying, so we must assume that he has hidden the Mandylion hereabouts. We do know that he worked as a coachman for a private family. Oh yes, and there was the prophecy, the prophecy as old as the family, which said that *the Mandylion face would appear one day in a far temple, like a city rising from the water.* That's all we know. And we knew that in 1919."

Danny suddenly felt the weight of his tiredness and his head ached. He glanced at his watch and realized his mother would be worried about him. Zelia assured him that she would be perfectly safe alone in the house. Her neighbors, the Kerrigans, were a fine family and easily alerted in case of trouble, she said.

"I'll see you at the convent in the morning, then, now that we'll be working together." Danny said. Then he added, "I know someone we can ask about these cards."

"Who? Mother Madeleine?"

"No, Juliana of Norwich."

# 24

## A Dame in the Convent

THE SUMMER holiday usually stretched ahead like a lazy path but not this year, not for Danny anyway. And on top of his other responsibilities, each day the mailbag was stuffed more tightly with unwanted correspondence than the day before. It was taking almost an hour to sort out the convent's own, personal mail before the unsolicited stuff could be opened and answered.

"But the office in Hill Street is the advertised address for entrants," Danny complained to Sister Paula. "Why don't they deliver it all there? Most of it is simply addressed to Mother Madeleine, New Zealand, anyway."

"The price of fame," Sister Paula said. "The Post Office must deliver to the addressee. It's the law. But it is the people who call who trouble us most. They all want to see Madeleine. Yesterday the bell didn't stop ringing. From tomorrow we're having a security guard on the Nae Nae Road Gate to keep unannounced visitors at bay. It's positively gruesome what a whiff of money will do."

"The Convent office is full of letters," said Mother Madeleine, appearing suddenly in a doorway. "And now they are even sending canvases here from Buenos Aires. Are the Sisters to drown in an avalanche of paper while you pass the time of day? Eh!"

Danny and Zelia spent all day on the mail, indeed until it was time to collect Angela from the Center, but he made little impression on the morass of it that spilled out of the office and down the corridor towards the laundry. At lunchtime he suggested that they simply dump the letters, but Mother Madeleine insisted that each one must be answered, "for the sake of good manners and consideration of others." This exasperated Danny, who confided to Zelia that if 99% of the correspondents had any consideration for others, they wouldn't have written in the first place.

When Zelia saw the extent of the work, she persuaded Sister Eileen to bring some of the equipment from the school office to the convent. There she took over the printer and ran off hundreds of cards, thanking people for their interest in the *Lampadephoria* and referring them to an Internet site for further information. Actual entries were sent on to the offices in Hill Street. All they had to do then was physically open the letters and transcribe the addresses of inquirers onto the cards. By mid-afternoon postage had already reached the $NZ 2,000 mark.

Only one letter differed from all the others. The envelope was embossed with a shield, supported by a lion and a unicorn, with the words Buckingham Palace rising out of the paper beneath them. Zelia gave it to Mother Madeleine, who opened it and laughed out loud. She let the letter flutter down to the floor as she stumbled into a chair. "Goodness me!" she cried, her great body heaving with merriment. "89 years old, 70 of them a nun, and now they want to call me Dame!"

Danny picked up the letter and read it. It was from the office of the Private Secretary of Her Majesty the Queen, no less. *Her Majesty would be pleased to confer the title of Dame of the British Empire on Mother Madeleine Atuahera in recognition of her outstanding artistic accomplishments . . .*

"Are you going to accept, Sister?" he asked.

"That's not up to me," she said between dabbing her eyes and bursting into fresh torrents of merriment. "That must go through my superiors."

"What will we have to call you—Dame Mother Madeleine or Mother Dame Madeleine or just Dame Mother or Dame Madeleine? What's the protocol?"

Mother Madeleine had no answer, and anyway the bell rang for Vespers. She stood up and climbed the staircase towards the chapel, still laughing as if at the greatest joke in Christendom. In choir her sniffs mingled with the antiphon, and tears of mirth still rolled down her fat, old, brown wonderfully innocent face.

# 25

## The Calm
## and the Storm

 WHEN THE Sisters went into Vespers, Danny beckoned to Zelia and together they made their way down the zigzagging hill path to the conservatory. The lamp was behind the statue but, oddly, the rosary with its large crucifix was not there. Danny was sure he had returned it along with the lamp the night before. But perhaps he was mistaken. Perhaps it was still in the elevator.

"Let's hope this machine takes us to the Lady Juliana's parlor. By the way, as we are both talking pretty fantastic these days, did I mention that there is this angel who I hang out with sometimes and once, when I asked him his name, he told me that he was the Guardian of the Mandylion?"

Zelia opened her mouth to say 125 things at once, as women do, but they had reached the mouth of the tunnel and Danny said, "Shhh!" urgently, taking her hand. There was no sign of the rosary in the elevator, but they closed the doors anyway and Danny started pumping.

The elevator took over two minutes to reach its destination. Two minutes can be longer than two hours or two days when you are standing locked in a small area, apprehensive and approaching the unknown. Danny was suddenly conscious that the fingers of his left hand were entwined with the fingers of

Zelia's right hand. He wasn't aware of how this had started, of who had initiated it, but it made his spirit soar.

In the hand not occupied with Zelia's he held the halogen lamp, its beam pointed at the floor because it was so bright. He was about to say something, anything just to break the silence, when the elevator jarred to a halt.

Even as the gate began to slide open Danny knew where they were. The clean, fresh odor of lemon and beeswax, the golden shafts of tranquillity that soothed the breathing and stilled the blood, greeted them like smiling children.

The Lady Juliana was standing beside a small oak table writing on what looked like the inner side of a dried animal skin stretched taut in a rectangular form. The frame was secured to a sort of low easel, which sat on the table.

Her pen was a feather sharpened to a nib at its root, and the inkwell was a pot-bellied, narrow-necked bottle on a brass stand with an elbow, which swiveled so that the bottle waited on the writing hand. The writing was small, like the footprints of a tiny insect. Danny calculated that a whole book could probably be squeezed onto the one pelt with writing like that. That would keep books short, he reasoned, because if they got too long a writer would have to go out and kill another animal and skin and cure it, by which time he might well have lost his enthusiasm for the book.

The Lady Juliana smiled at Danny and Zelia when they entered, a glad and merry and sweet smile which made them feel that no visitors could have been more welcome. She put down her pen and drew chairs up to the table and they sat with her. No words were spoken, but it didn't matter. It was so good just to be there that words might spoil the altogether precious ambience.

The serving girl with the headdress like the Sydney Opera House brought in a hot drink in cups with two handles. The drink was the same ginger and honey he had tasted on his first visit. A small bird with yellow and red feathers chirped thinly in a cane cage, otherwise there was no sound to break the pellucid silence until a bell rang in the church beyond the grille.

The Lady Juliana stood and Danny and Zelia did the same. She took their hands in hers and said, "Think deeply on what has passed between us, my children." She crossed to the inglenook and took a carved wooden box from the mantel shelf. "Here, they will help you concentrate when you speak with heaven. We receive such priceless gifts and so few bother to pass the time of day in return." She gave them each a string of beads, like a rosary and with a cross, but without the path leading to the circle of five tens. "Go now and on some future visit, perhaps, I shall take you to her."

Then the elevator was there and they stepped, reluctantly, inside. Even as the doors closed the Lady Juliana was already kneeling at the grille, which was opened now and giving onto the chancel of the small stone church where a priest was setting up a monstrance with the Blessed Sacrament in the center, on the flat surface on the top of the tabernacle.

"Who was she?" asked an amazed Zelia as the elevator began its descent through time.

"The Lady Juliana. I told you about her, remember?" Danny threw up his hands, shrugged his shoulders and twisted his face a little to indicate that that was the limit of his information on the subject. "Oh . . . we forgot to ask her about the Mandylion. That's what we went to see her for."

"She says things without speaking. Sound, deep things. I could have stayed with her forever."

"You sure feel you've left something behind when you take leave of her. She told me to work hard on my painting and not to come back to the elevator for a while. But she didn't say anything about the Mandylion."

"Nor to me, either. Not directly, anyway. But I think she told me that something pretty frightening was going to happen to me because of the Mandylion, but to be patient and to trust in the Lord Jesus whose face the Mandylion portrays. Danny, do you find it's getting hot in here?"

At that point the elevator rocked violently.

Zelia screamed and fell back on Danny, toppling him so that they both fell to the floor and the halogen lamp went out.

There was a hissing, whistling sound, like steam from a kettle, but ominous, and it was growing louder by the second. Danny and Zelia clutched at each other in the grip of that terrible fear which drains the blood and panics the mind.

Then, as unheralded as a car smash, the thing was at their throats, thrusting its face, a face like that of a young man, long and strangely lean, close to theirs. There was nothing they could compare it with. The color of it was red, like a newly baked tile, and yellow with black spots like freckles, like the molds on ripe bananas, uglier than a tile. The creature's hair was red as rust, not cut short in front, with side-locks hanging to his temples. He was grinning at them with a vicious look, showing white teeth so big that he seemed all the uglier. His body and his hands were misshapen but he held them by the throat and wanted to stop their breath, and kill them, but somehow he could not.

Smoke was curling into the elevator through the bars and with it came great heat and a foul stench.

Danny was so terrified he couldn't move a muscle of his body. Every physical faculty had seized up. He couldn't even move his eyelids to close them.

After what seemed a great age the elevator bumped to a halt against the fenders, and the steel grid doors folded open. The ghastly, grinning tile-face rose into the air, snorted with concentrated malice, and whooshed out of the elevator to the mouth of the cave where he was joined by a dozen others just like him, sneering and leering, and scaly of flesh.

The smoke and the stink increased, but at least with the creature gone from their throats Danny and Zelia had regained the use of their limbs.

"The cross! Where's the cross?" Danny managed to gasp as he felt frantically around the floor amid the smoke.

"We didn't bring it. We couldn't find it. Don't you remember?

"NEVER!" Screamed the devils that were multiplying by the moment. "THE FACE WILL NEVER BE SEEN! NEVER!"

The noise swelled in pitch and volume. It was as if a thousand trains were roaring into the station at the same time, as if a thousand mothers were screaming for their murdered children. The smoke was acrid and burned their eyes. The stench caused their stomachs to retch and they both threw up on the glazed walls of the tunnel.

"The rosaries! Let's hold up the rosaries the Lady Juliana gave us!" They fumbled for the beads and managed to hold them aloft while at the same time trying to steady themselves and protect their eyes and mouths and noses from the smoke, which stung, like acid gas. The devils became agitated at the sight of the rosaries and let out such a volley of foul language that Danny hoped Zelia didn't know the meanings of the words—indeed, he didn't know all of them himself.

While they were clearly enraged by the rosaries, the devils weren't dispersed. They rallied and their numbers increased so that the tunnel seemed like a madhouse on the boil.

Though still trembling with fear Danny whispered, "They're pathetic, really!"

Zelia shouted boldly, "How many of you does it take to frighten a couple of school kids?" This seemed to infuriate them more, so she said, "Let's recite a Hail Mary!" They started the prayer in unison, but the flames licked the words off their tongues.

Just as the fiendish frenzy reached its climax, in which, for an instant, Danny and Zelia felt they were being plunged into the very oubliette of hell itself, a light appeared in the opening of the tunnel like a steady beacon in an ocean of ferocious night. Straightaway the demons disappeared, not into the ether, but they, their flames, their smoke, their stench, their cacophony, started to spin round and round until it was sucked into a vortex which became a dot, like a full stop without a sentence, and then vanished.

A crucifix was held aloft in the mouth of the tunnel, beneath the oil-lamp that hung from an iron beam, and the hand holding it, with the circle of the beads hanging beneath, was Raphael's. "Ah! Here you are!" he said as if they were car keys or a pair of glasses he had momentarily mislaid. "You forgot this. The way you were talking I thought it might be important."

"What . . . ? Where . . . ?"

"I was in the conservatory when you came in. Behind the yuccas. I've been crashing there this week. Comfy little nest, and no one to put the pressure on or stir up a fuss. I've rigged myself up a little kitchen. Nothing fancy, just the basics." He approached them and held his hand out towards Zelia. "The name's Raphael. We've met before. In the street, I seem to recall," he said with an easy, educated charm. "You both look as if you've met with the Minotaur *and* the Medusa. Come and have a cup of tea."

# 26

===

## *Falling in Love*

THE SUMMER days leading up to Christmas flowed past like a stream that has few stones or debris to break the surface, like unwelcome attentions from the toothy Levantine. Zelia was now managing the mail by herself, which gave Danny time to paint.

One afternoon after lunch Zelia walked around the back path with Danny and came into the studio. They had just received letters from the Ministry of Education, telling them that they had passed their School Certificate exams—a particular feat for Zelia, who had only joined the class at the tail end of the syllabus—and were in a jubilant frame of mind.

Zelia hadn't been into Danny's studio very often before, and she had never seen the Weka-Feather Cloak. It was usually behind the mirrored door when not in use. But this afternoon it was lying over a chair where Raphael had dropped it in the morning. Zelia gasped. She touched it gingerly and ran her fingers down its smooth, silky feathers. It was the most beautiful garment she had ever seen, she said. So primitive, yet so noble. Was it reserved for Maori kings, she asked, like crowns and sceptres were the exclusive right of Western kings? Danny said that, er, he didn't really know, he'd never read up much on Maori history, but he supposed it was a king's thing. "Ask

Mother Madeleine, she's a proper Maori. I think it belonged to her tribe."

"It's rather heavy." Zelia had lifted the cloak to feel its weight. "What exactly is a weka?"

"A harmless little wood hen, not much bigger than a sparrow. It can't even fly."

Zelia put the cloak around her own shoulders and fastened the flaxen cord across her breast. "What do you think?" she laughed. Danny looked at the canvas on the easel. He knew exactly what he thought. But no, it would be too much work, too ambitious. He hadn't the experience. A Kiwi Christ and a Kiwi Mary standing over the two islands like a Kiwi cradle. He refused to think of it. His temple painting and the Raphael Christ were as much as he could handle for the moment.

Zelia removed the cloak and Danny took it into the oblong room and secured it around the tailor's dummy.

"At least Raphael is putting in a lot of hours for me this week," said Danny. "I sort of told Sister Paula that Raphael might be bunking down in the conservatory. She didn't seem to mind, particularly, she said, as he was so poor that he hadn't got shoes to cover his feet. Then I told her that I was using him as a model for a Christ painting. That threw her a bit." Danny chuckled at the recollection. "But her attitude does give a sort of legitimacy to Raphael's presence around the convent grounds."

Raphael was always a good subject for discussion between them. Danny told how, when the young eccentric was modeling, he couldn't keep still for long, particularly as he had to stand with his arms out-stretched. So when Raphael could bear the position no longer, Danny would switch to his Temple painting, at which point Raphael would produce his own easel and canvas and paints and begin to copy Danny's Christ in the

Weka-Feather Cloak, line for line, size for size, color for color.
His was awful.

⚬⚬⚬⚬⚬⚬⚬⚬ ◎ ⚬⚬⚬⚬⚬⚬⚬⚬

*Listen, Ange! You remember I've often told you about the Kiwi
Christ . . . what! Yeah, I know Zelia's the bee's knees, but let me tell
you . . . What! You think I'm falling in love with her, do you! You've
been watching too much television at the Center. I think 'falling in
love' is a phrase invented by Hollywood so that lonely spinsters would
buy cinema tickets.*

*O.K., yeah she does bowl me over. You're a perceptive little sleuth,
aren't you! But you see, Ange, the best thing is that I reckon she feels
the same way about me. Well, almost the same. Or something like the
same. But it couldn't be exactly the same, could it? I mean, she's so
much more mature than I am, so much more at ease with herself.*

*But listen. . . . I knew there was a Kiwi Christ there somewhere,
Ange, but it was always hidden. I could never grasp it. It was like
knowing someone you'd never met, never even heard of, and then suddenly he is there in front of you, warm and glowing and nigh perfect.
It's uncanny! Well it's coming together, Ange, I'm working on the background and it's really coming together . . .*

*Zelia has told me a lot more about the Mandylion. How do I know
what it means? She hasn't told me yet. Yeah, sure, it is a funny word.
She says that when it's written down it looks as if it rhymes with
dandelion, but when it's spoken it rhymes with pavilion. When she
mentions it she makes you think it is the greatest treasure of the
Orient. Is Turkey part of the Orient?*

*And this afternoon, Ange, a weird thing happened. Zelia and
Raphael had gone into town to do some shopping for Sister Paula,
and who should arrive at the convent but Sir William Kydd, the great
art authority who has just arrived from England to oversee the
Lampadephoria. He was all over Mother Madeleine, but I don't think*

*she liked him much. When he started going on about how great she was, she laughed out loud and said how right he was, but she couldn't stop because she had potatoes to peel and walked away.*

*Sister Eileen showed him the painting in the chapel and the furniture in the Blue Room and he sort of sniffed at everything like a tracking hound. Museums and galleries and universities are clamoring for him, or so the papers say, and he comes to the convent at Aniwaniwa to enthuse over love seats and stained-glass nymphs. That's fishy, Ange, wouldn't you say?*

*And, even fishier, was that Ferhat Ferhat drove the car he came in. Ferhat didn't see me because I was peering through Mother Madeleine's studio window. But I'm sure it was him.*

*No, Ange. I'm not taking you to the convent. It's too far to wheel the chair, and we wouldn't get any work done because you'd want to be in on everything.*

---

Christmas Eve was on a Monday. The three of them worked all afternoon on the chapel. With Sister Paula and Sister Clare, they dusted every picture and every statue, they removed all the pews and polished them, and the floor, with bees-wax. Then they cleaned every frame of the stained-glass windows with a colorless spray from a bottle and a machine like a hairdryer. One of the Columban Fathers from St. Columban's Grove was to say Midnight Mass for the Sisters and the Magos and Zelia had been invited.

Around 3 o'clock a van arrived, and Mother Madeleine called to Danny from her studio. Within moments Zelia saw him emerge from Mother Madeleine's studio carrying his temple canvas, which he put in the back of the van.

"What's going on?" Zelia asked as the driver slammed the back door to, leapt into the cab seat and drove off.

Danny was thoughtful. "It was my temple canvas," he said. "Mother Madeleine told me she wanted it. Just like that. I could hardly say no."

"Where is she sending it?"

"To be assessed, she said. Parts of it are still wet but I guess she knows what she's doing."

"Perhaps she's got a buyer for it, and she's going to surprise you with a whole pillowcase full of money."

"Perhaps!" said Danny with minimum enthusiasm.

At that point Raphael wandered up the steps from the conservatory and announced that he was going into Wellington. Nothing else, just that he was going into Wellington, and that he'd be back around six, and he insisted that they were to be there. He gave no reason. Just then Sister Paula called to them from an upper window to come and help shift some furniture.

When they were out of sight Raphael rang a taxi from a small mobile phone he had in his jeans pocket, and hastened round the back way to Danny's studio. When the taxi arrived, he emerged with a large canvas which he only just managed to fit into the back seat before being driven hastily away.

# 27

===

# *The Heir Apparent Appears*

IN THE Generalissimo's multi-billion office complex in London his private secretarial department announced over the intercom, "Mr. von Blumenkohl. Sir William Kydd is on the line."

"Put the oily Arab through," The Generalissimo bawled. He psyched himself up to bawl some more, but thought better of it. Indeed, when Sir William's emotionless, icy voice saluted him over the wires he adopted a tone oilier than any Arab you could name.

"Sir William. Good of you to call. Your reports are on my desk each morning. Excellent work, excellent. You've got yourself on the judges' panel for this quiz thing . . . ?"

"*Reredos Lampadephoria . . .*"

"Ray-wierdo-lampa thing. Yeah! Of course, of course! Very adroit of you, if I may say. Very clever. And you'll pay off one of the finalists to transfer his rights to my boy—good, good. The only problem is—where *is* my boy?"

The Generalissimo's face betrayed bull-like determination and feverish cunning, physical expressions which could not communicate themselves to a listener twelve thousand miles away—any listener, that is, except Abu Kyed, a.k.a. Sir William Kydd, whose determination and cunning outweighed Odo von Blumenkohl's on any scale of ruthlessness.

149

"Where indeed?" echoed Sir William.

"I've heard a rumor . . ." The Generalissimo looked as if he might eat the telephone in his fury. Neither man spoke for fully thirty seconds. "Are you still there?"

"Indeed, I am." Sir William affirmed. "A rumor, you were saying."

"There is a strong rumor that the boy's actually in New Zealand, even as we speak."

Sir William Kydd did some very quick thinking. This information was entirely new to him. His own contacts had tracked the boy to California and he hourly expected to issue the order to have him abducted and brought direct to Wellington. "In New Zealand?" Sir William repeated in his zipped-up voice.

"As we speak!" The Generalissimo repeated.

At that moment Ferhat Ferhat burst into the room waving a sheet of paper. "You'll never believe . . ." he gasped. Sir William held up an imperious finger. This finger imposed instant silence. But it didn't stop Ferhat Ferhat from waving the paper excitedly. Sir William took it from his henchman's hand and absorbed its information at a glance.

Sir William's tone suddenly became all honey. "But of course he is, Odo. The dear boy has been here for some time. We thought it better not to tell you. The deadline for submission is . . . or rather was, two hours ago. He's been locked away in a veritable fever of creative activity and we agreed to let nothing, absolutely nothing, disturb him. However, you'll be glad to learn, that this very day he has submitted his work to the selection committee, a work, I might add, of notable merit and one which, I can quite confidently predict, will rank among the finalists."

The Generalissimo's response was unintelligible. Sir William listened to it with consummate patience for many seconds, then said, "Absolutely, my dear Odo, absolutely!" and hung up.

"He has actually entered a painting under his own name?" said Sir William, as much to himself as to Ferhat Ferhat. "And it's been given the double tick of secretarial approbation? My curiosity, Boris Abladavich," the knight's tone was as dry and as brittle as his soul, "sprouts wings!"

"That's the final list, just faxed through from the Cathedral office."

"Most considerate of the young rebel," Sir William creaked. "He has done half our work for us. So he must be here, in Wellington. Abladavich, or whatever your name is: contact every hotel, every restaurant in town. We will find that boy tonight."

# 28

## *The Nabob's Picnic*

SHARP AT 6 o'clock a green and silver Rolls Royce (1965) purred up the drive and swung sedately into the space in front of the convent. Danny and Zelia, who were deep in conversation as they waited for Raphael, glanced up idly, but their eyes stayed to focus with amazement on the vehicle.

A transfigured Raphael swung himself out onto the gravel feet first, but feet that were shod now in beaten leather shoes, and instead of frayed jeans and shirt in tropical colours, he was wearing a suit of ivory linen with an open ivory silk shirt. His fair hair was cut short and he was freshly shaved. The watch beneath the cuff was gold and the gold ring on his finger flashed a blue sapphire.

"Merry Christmas!" Raphael said diffidently. He looked with uncertainty at Danny but soon seemed reassured. Clearly they hadn't been into the studio since he last saw them.

"What are you two? Bethlehem innkeepers or something? I expect a bit of a welcome after all the trouble I've taken to provide transport. And to fetch your nearest and dearest." He tapped on the back window. From the rear seat Danny's mother waved from behind a newspaper, and Angela smiled and made uncoordinated hand movements. "And to book a table for our happy little party at 'The Nabob's Picnic.'"

Danny and Zelia took some moments to adjust to the new Raphael. "What's The Nabob's Picnic?" Danny asked.

Raphael stood before them with the confidence of a born aristocrat. "You couldn't be expected to know," he said, mocking his own new image. "The Nabob's Picnic is the most exclusive establishment in the Southern Hemisphere. Indeed, it is so exclusive that practically nobody who isn't anybody knows about it. I mean anybody, except those who are nobody, knows somebody who knows somebody who has heard of it. But nobody ranking lower than an earl is permitted to dine there. Even the waiters are baronets. At least!" Even Raphael's voice had undergone a transformation.

"Where does this Rolls come from, Raphael? Where did you find that get-up? Who is going to pay for this posh restaurant? We haven't got enough money."

Raphael held up his hand to fend off a distasteful concept. He was their host. Questions were vulgar.

The entrance to The Nabob's Picnic belied the splendors within. From the street on the hills behind Oriental Bay a brown, wooden door in a red brick façade sneered at passing traffic like a pert and bitter spinster. But once your knock was answered, once you had been scrutinized and pronounced pukka, you passed along a narrow corridor which gave onto a dining room as elegant as a mountain lake. The great semi-circular wall was sheer glass from floor to ceiling and it seemed to hang over the splendid inlet that was Wellington harbor. The tables were old and solid kauri and each seat was carved from kauri and had a high arched back and winged arm rests like an episcopal deck chair. There were no pictures, no decorations, just an indefinable stamp of taste and discretion, which conditioned the air more pertinently than any machine in a basement could hope to.

Most of the tables were occupied when they entered. One or two people even looked up and smiled and one elderly couple, probably Americans, who had diamonds for shirt buttons said, "Why Claude, great to see you, just great! What brings you here?" as he passed.

"I always dine here when I'm down this way," said Claude with the sigh of a blasé *bon vivant*. "It's the *only* place south of the Equator."

The *maitre d'hotel* removed one of the seats from the table and steered Angela's wheelchair into position himself, as if she was some sort of queen who couldn't be allowed to rise from her throne for such a commonplace maneuver.

The menu was in every language except English or Maori, but Raphael translated. They all ordered toheroa soup followed by sole and seaweed, except for Zelia, who wanted a full plate of oysters because she had tasted one once, in Beirut, and had thought that if the angels had bodies they would eat oysters every single day of the celestial year.

In spite of not having had time to change out of the floral patterned cotton dress she had been wearing, Danny's Mum developed a dignity in the rarified air of The Nabob's Picnic, which was, in an unaffected way, regal. And Angela managed, mostly, to carve her own fish and separate the flesh from the bones. Danny took a very humble but delicious pride in both of them, a pride, which was enhanced when he saw that Zelia, too, was impressed by the natural courtliness of their manner.

Raphael pointed out the rich and the famous, and even called "Merry Christmas!" to many of them. Danny and the womenfolk could believe they were rich and were prepared to believe they were famous, though they had never heard of any of them themselves. What surprised them was that Raphael not only knew all these people, but that he clearly thought that

Zelia and Danny and his family were more important than any of them.

It was when the evening was at its most glorious that Danny saw reflected in the vast glass window before him, as if it were a rear vision mirror, the urbane figure of Sir William Kydd enter the dining room with Ferhat Ferhat smiling mirthlessly in his wake. They had already caught sight of Raphael's group and were drawing back into the shadows of a coat tree. Once secreted there they conferred anxiously.

Soon Ferhat Ferhat slipped back into the shadows of the corridor while Sir William stepped into the limelight of The Nabob's Picnic.

Sir William's progress among the tables was something of a triumphal march. All the parties present knew him, or wanted to, and they all greeted him. A popular movie star couldn't have wished for more concentrated acclamation. He acknowledged the tributes with a cool courtesy and a set smile, while steering a direct course for Raphael's table.

Raphael half rose to greet him, but Sir William appeared not to see the young man. He stepped past him to where Zelia was sitting, stooped, bowed, picked up her left hand and lightly kissed it, saying, as he did so, something full of knightly deference in a language so obscure that it wasn't yet represented on the menu of The Nabob's Picnic.

Zelia made no reply but her face blanched and she sat rigid in her seat.

Only after this ceremony did Sir William turn to the table's host. "Claude," he said, with an inclination of the head, which might have passed for affability in a television costume drama, "We've never met, but your father is my oldest and, dare I say it?, dearest friend. Indeed, I have just come from speaking with him. He is concerned about you, dear boy, concerned. But, come come, we mustn't be alarmed. I have put his mind at rest. Presumptuous of me, you are no doubt thinking, ah, but you see"—and here he lowered his voice so that his words were only heard by those at Raphael's table—"I have been privy to the final list of entrants for the *Reredos.*"

"Claude! Claude!" Danny whispered to his mother. "I knew I'd seen his face before. In every second magazine I've ever picked up. He's not Raphael da Vinci at all; he's Claude von Blumenkohl, the Poor Little Rich Boy!"

"He has charm and exquisite manners," said Brigid Mago. "You could learn a thing or two from him."

Claude (the game's up, so let's call him by his real name), stammered something appropriately polite and insincere and sat down to attend to the food before him.

"It would be a great honor to be allowed to join you," Sir William pronounced the words in a way that it would be foolhardy to counter. He turned to Zelia. "And not least because of the presence of the charming Miss Mazloum whose family, shall we say, shares the same interests as my own. We are neighbors, in fact. A sudden strange noise issued from inside Zelia's throat and Danny's expression sagged. A waiter fetched a chair for the Anglicized Levantine.

Claude, sensing Danny and Zelia's discomfort, said that he really mustn't inconvenience himself because they had almost finished their dinner and were on the point of leaving. Sir William insisted it was no inconvenience at all and they were to have a measure of champagne with him. He motioned to the waiter and asked, so softly that the assembled diners in The Nabob's Picnic had to strain to catch the words, for a bottle of '25 to be brought to the table.

Zelia's hand, which was uncommonly cold and shaking, found Danny's under the table. She squeezed his fingers and when their eyes met, her distress doubled his own. Danny's mother sensed that something was wrong and looked to Claude to resolve the situation.

But it was Angela who took matters in hand. Her arms started to windmill. Her right hand swooped down to her plate and picked up her second sole, as yet untouched. Holding the fish by its tail she slapped Sir William twice across the face with it, then brought it down smack on the top of his bald pate where she abandoned it.

Hard on the heels of this incident Claude, barely concealing his amusement behind a suave gesture of diplomacy and his compliments for the Festive Season, ushered his party out of the restaurant and into the waiting Rolls Royce.

Sir William remained at the table, struggling to salvage his dignity while the waiters sponged his head. But it was a lost cause. He rumbled with rage and fury like a costive volcano. Eventually he rose and negotiated a track between the tables of the goggling eyes as if he had been made of a taut, stiff fiber.

When Ferhat Ferhat emerged from the shadows Sir William spat, "Follow her!"

"The idiot?" Ferhat Ferhat asked.

Sir William seethed with an anger that would have alarmed the Titans. "The Mazloum girl, you cretin. Find out where she lives and comb the house for anything that might relate to the whereabouts of the Mandylion."

"And the boy?" Ferhat Ferhat grinned with the prospect of eliminating Danny. "Shall I . . . ?"

"Emphatically not! That would arouse curiosity. Terrorize him, just."

The drive back to the Hutt Valley was the best part of the evening. Nobody but Claude knew exactly what had happened at The Nabob's Picnic, but somehow they all thought it was very funny and laughed at the mystery of it and then laughed at themselves laughing.

"It was a lucky day when I crashed into your harbor," Claude said between bouts of laughter. "Actually, I was on my way to Chile."

It was still early when they arrived at the Magos'. Brigid Mago said they were going to Midnight Mass at the convent and invited Claude to come with them. Claude said he didn't know anything about Mass, midnight or otherwise, but decided that he would go because Mother Madeleine would be there. Claude drove them to the convent.

There was still an hour or so before Mass. Mrs. Mago suggested they take a look at Danny's studio. Claude suddenly remembered that he had another appointment and was back into the car and gone before the others had time to protest.

They didn't have long to wait to discover why, for in the studio Danny's *Kiwi Christ* had been taken from its easel and Claude's awful copy had replaced it.

# 29

## *Midnight Mass*

MIDNIGHT MASS with the family and the Sisters and a few neighbors of the convent was so rich and beautiful that Danny almost forgot the disappearance of his painting. He remembered when they were home again in Hinau Street, having been driven there by one of the neighbors after tea and biscuits around a crib with the Sisters.

They were having yet more tea in the Mago kitchen, prior to Danny's walking Zelia to her house in Knight's Road, when Danny suddenly said, "Confoundationalism!" Danny never swore, but there were occasions when he was driven to invent words to express the vigor of certain convictions. "Do you realize Claude has actually stolen my painting?"

The women were sympathetic, and his Mum went so far as to say that the Lady Juliana portrait was better than many a painter manages to do in a lifetime, so he shouldn't be too over-wrought. That was consoling, but he went on to say that he couldn't imagine how Raphael or Claude or whatever his name was thought he could get away with it.

As they walked to her house Zelia said, "I can't believe Raphael and Claude are the same person. Has he got a dual personality, do you think? Like Jekyll and Hyde or Eve of the Three Faces—that was an American film they showed on the Turkish television, and all the high school girls pretended they were Eve for weeks after. Some of them did some unbelieve-able things. When they were found out they would say, 'Oh, but that wasn't me, that was Eve.'"

"I guess if you're as rich as he seems to be, you can afford to be a bit eccentric." Danny laughed in spite of himself. "Imagine having a suite in the poshest hotel in town and sleep-ing in the conservatory in Aniwaniwa."

"What does his father do, anyhow? This von Blumenkohl?" Zelia asked. "I've heard the name but always thought it was a big company like Mitsubishi or I.C.I. He must be kept awfully busy if he is one man."

"He's the archetypal business man. He owns a bit of every-thing. That restaurant tonight, he probably owns the building, the chef and all the napkins. If you bet on a horse he proba-bly owns three of the legs, the saddle and the nose. Odo von Blumenkohl! Don't you read the papers?"

"Not much!" said Zelia.

"Well, he owns them."

"Poor man," Zelia muttered in an abstract, unthinking sort of way.

"Why do you say 'poor man'?"

"Oh, I don't know. It just slipped out. I was thinking, you know, of when we visited the Lady Juliana. It made money and people-importance so inconsequential, like a baby's rattle."

Danny understood that completely. The recollection of their experience was too profound to talk about. There had been a silence in that realm, a silence which took over where music left off, a silence which provided what music could but dimly herald, yet never ever attain.

They spoke no more as they walked along Pohutukawa Street and turned into Knight's Road. With the first block of infinity opening its vistas above them, and the Milky Way like jasmine on a pergola, and the same moon which gazed unblinkingly at Eden, Golgotha and the arrival of Aotearoa's founding four canoes hanging there, luminous, reliable and unblinking still. Zelia was still standing on her small porch looking up at the beautiful sky when Danny turned for a last look at her on his way back home. Even the disappearance of his two paintings couldn't mar the joy he felt. He sighed deeply. What a day! And there would be many more—many, many more.

When Zelia finally turned to the house, she was surprised to see her front door ajar. She cautiously pushed open the door and reached in a hand to flip on the lights.

Inside everything, furniture, linen, cutlery, ornaments had been taken from their places and scattered as if by a petulant giant. Even books had been torn in half and their pages scattered.

She stood stunned and unbelieving before advancing through the living room, turning on lights as she went. A noise in the kitchen stopped her with a shock. Suddenly, a gorilla of a man appeared from the kitchen. Another stepped out of the bathroom.

"Police officers," they said flashing cards that could have been season tickets to the zoo for all Zelia could see of them.

"Are you Zelia Mazloum, Turkish national, resident in this country under permit number 63952777D, issued by the Consulate in Ankara last year and endorsed by the Embassy in Rome?"

"Who are you . . . how did you . . . ?" She felt weak, vulnerable and powerless. What had they been doing in the house with all the lights off? Waiting in ambush? Waiting to see if she was alone? She felt angry and faint at the same time. Very angry and very faint.

"Is this your scarf?" Yet another gorilla emerged from the bathroom holding Zelia's yellow scarf.

"Yes. That's the one that got caught in . . ."

Another gorilla, more overweight than the rest, materialized from behind them and proceeded to attach metal handcuffs to Zelia's wrists. "I am arresting you for the murder of Qetik Mamoulian, whose strangled corpse was discovered this evening in a shallow grave on the banks of the Hutt River." He then reeled off her statutory rights as if they were a nursery rhyme.

Zelia was too stunned to think. The men brusquely surrounded and hustled her to the door.

She was half carried, half pushed to a car parked half a block away, and thrown into the back seat. She wished desperately now that Danny had come all the way with her to the front door. Well, she would call him from the police station.

As the car sped through the silence of the Christmas night Zelia tasted blood in her mouth. Only then did she realize she had been biting her lower lip to stop herself from crying. Whatever happened she must not cry.

# 30

## *Angela Models*

 ON THE morning after Boxing Day—it said *December 27, St. John* on Mother Madeleine's board—Danny went to the convent. He had more than half expected to hear from Zelia during the last two days. He had even tried to call her to see if she'd like to come over to the Magos' for a simple Christmas supper, but there had been no answer at her house. She was still on his mind as he was parking his bicycle by the studio and Mother Madeleine called to him. Again she asked him to sit with her. In spite of her great size the old Maori nun looked particularly frail and vulnerable sitting in the Morris chair. She seemed to have lost the will to paint along with her vitality.

"Have you finished it, Mother?" he asked, nodding his head towards the canvas on the easel which, in true conformity with Mother Madeleine's horror of seeing her work in progress, was turned towards the far wall.

"Almost," she said. "Towards the end of the week. Hey, I've been thinking. I'm going to paint your sister."

"Angela! But she's in a wheelchair."

"You mean we mustn't paint people in wheelchairs?"

"No! What I mean is, you've never seen her."

"Precisely! I want to get started this very afternoon. Go and get her now; Paula will arrange a taxi."

163

"But, Mother, this is . . . Angela has a mind of her own . . . what say . . . ?"

"Hey, Big Boy, if she objects, the taxi can take her back. Now, I'm an old woman and I don't care to spend what few moments of life I have left arguing with a young Turk."

As Danny might have guessed, Angela took to modeling with élan. At first she managed to hold herself reasonably still for minutes at a time, but soon it became apparent that Mother Madeleine wasn't the sort of painter who required rigid inertia from a sitter. Angela's tongue began to loll out of her mouth and in using the heel of her hand to push it back in and close her jaw she broke into a spasm of giggling. Mother Madeleine barely noticed this as she worked, so Angela took that to mean that giggling was part of portrait sitting. Shortly she experimented with limb moving and, as Mother Madeleine worked on with unconcerned concentration, Angela took that as a franchise to allow her limbs to rove as they wished.

Angela had only been asked to sit for an hour and a half. When the time came to call the taxi, she made it amply clear that she didn't want to go. The nuns had been popping in from the convent, bringing fruit and chocolates, making a fuss of her such as would have been unthinkable at the Day Center. So it was decided that she could stay another hour, and then another, and then it was time for Vespers before the Sisters called the taxi.

At supper that evening she fairly glowed with fervor and told her mother that if things were different she would think of becoming a nun. The next morning she got out of bed, dressed herself, said her rosary and was ready for the taxi when Danny had returned from Mass. While they were waiting, Danny talked to Angela.

*And then, Ange, there was that thing mentioned on the radio news—body found in shallow grave . . . several weeks dead . . . dead by strangulation—corpse identified as Qetik Mamoulian, mechanic, of Lower Hutt . . . police are investigating. What do you think? The name sounds Turkish. Maybe I couldn't reach Zelia because there is some kind of family problem going on, but wouldn't Zelia have mentioned any relatives living in New Zealand?*

*Yesterday during lunch break, I went by her house, but it's locked up tight and the Kerrigan family next door, who she said looked out a bit for her, must be gone on a Christmas holiday because there were three newspapers piled up on their porch. I even went to the Police Station. They said they didn't know anything about a Zelia Mazloum; told me to go home and stop playing Sherlock Holmes.*

*Angela, you can't play with those cards like you'd play with any old pack on a poker table; you've got to keep them safe. You'd think after Zelia trusted us enough to keep the cards for her, that she wouldn't go off somewhere without telling us. All right, she's a big girl and I'm not her brother. Just say a prayer, will you? I can't help feeling kind of worried. I hope she's not mad at me or something.*

---

Angela spent all day Friday in the studio. Danny was pleased to see his sister so happy and Mother Madeleine, though clearly fragile with age, so intense, so possessed by the creative force. Loyal to Danny's admonition never to let the cards out of her sight Angela had brought them in the pocket of her cardigan. Several times she took them out and shuffled them about as if she expected one of them to tell her something. Then she would slide them back into her pocket, entwine that corner of the cardigan in her hands and hold her head high like a mother kangaroo protecting her joey.

That afternoon, Danny went into Mother Madeleine's studio. Angela had fallen asleep, as she was inclined to do without notice. Mother Madeleine wasn't at her easel, but sitting in a Morris chair on a dais in front of the window which looked obliquely over the steps which led down to the stream. Her rosary beads were slipping slowly between her fingers. She looked up when he entered and smiled. "Come here, Danny, and sit with me for a while," she said. "This old nun feels tired, tired, tired. She needs a bit of youthful gaiety."

Danny crossed the room and sat on a barrel facing Mother Madeleine. He leaned his head against the window frame. "I'm sorry I can't be much help, Mother," he said. "There's a lot gone wrong lately, and I don't know how to put it right."

"Hmmphr!"

They sat in silence for a long time until at last Danny said, "I can take Angela away any time you like—I mean if you have to go to the Cathedral, Mother, you know, to judge the finalists."

"They don't need me—the winner is as good as chosen, hey!"

Danny was taken aback. "Who? Which . . . ?"

"Pass me that blanket, will you, like a good, kind boy. I feel chilly in spite of the warm weather. It's the thin blood. The blood thins up with the years. At my age I've no right to have any more than a pint or two of rose water running around the system."

"Is it that Japanese who works in enamels and oil? The one with a name like a Latin fish."

"Japanese don't have a Cathedral culture. Hey, I'd take a flutter on a Kiwi if I were a betting woman. The ten will be exhibited in the Jervois Quay Gallery, but they'll all be anonymous. People can vote for the one they like best. That's democracy, Danny. It won't make a blind bit of difference, but it's democracy. Where's the girl Zelia today?"

"I don't know. I . . . I haven't seen her for a couple of days."

Unaccountably Danny was taken aback. He wondered if he was blushing.

"Ahhh!" said the old nun knowingly. "Well, she's a fine girl, stands out from the flock. Have a bit of a tiff or something? That's good and healthy—there's no crossing the river without getting wet."

Danny looked out the window in uncomfortable silence. He turned to see that Mother Madeleine had fallen asleep, for her eyes were closed and she was breathing contentedly. However she opened her eyes and nodded at Danny in a manner which was peculiar to the Maori people and said, "If I was a good nun I'd tell you to pray and have faith in God and ..."

Danny waited. She didn't finish the sentence. Then he realized that this time she really had fallen asleep.

# 31

## *Gloom*

 THE NEXT day he again went to early Mass but found no comfort in prayer. He couldn't think of spiritual things for any more than a second. Straightaway his mind would snap back like a mousetrap on a spring to Zelia, and then to Fur Hat, then to Captain Kydd who, the papers were saying, was a good friend of Claude's father.

When he took Angela to the convent, Mother Madeleine was actually waiting for her. Sister Paula had left a list of chores in his studio, and he was glad of them. The studio, with the Weka-Feather Cloak on the tailor's dummy and dried oils and brushes and screwed up newspaper scattered around, lacked the stimulus he had grown used to associating with it. Without his two paintings and nothing but Claude's lifeless canvas—it looked more like a farmyard hen squashed flat against a wall than a Christ figure in a Weka-Feather Cloak—there was no work there for him to focus on. Only the lift held any chance of shaking him out of his gloom, but he felt a reluctance to go there—it was as if his own misery put it out of bounds, as if he had a distemper which precluded travel, at least until the distemper disappeared. And anyway it wouldn't be the same without Zelia.

Danny thought that catching up with computer work might

distract his mind from Zelia, who probably had a perfectly good reason for taking off for a few days. He wrote a short letter saying that the competition entry date had passed and that no more correspondence could be gone into and printed off enough copies to answer all the post deadline mail well into the New Year. He reproduced the letter on the e-mail format and answered all inquiries on that medium with it. After that he surfed the Internet, looking up every reference he could find to stucco and fresco and downloading all the material that seemed relevant.

His gloom began to lift a little when he found a site, which took him on a tour of the Palazzo Medici in Florence.

On the East wall of the chapel, a guide page written in English announced, was a 25-foot wide fresco by Benozzo Gozzoli. Danny chuckled to himself and clicked around on the mouse until he came to the chapel. Sure enough there was a vast *Procession of the Magi* with trees unknown to botany breaking up the days' work just as Benozzo had told him. Danny gazed at it with a strange pride that was almost possessive, as if he himself had had a part in the production of it. And then, as he remonstrated with himself for thinking such foolishness, he saw himself stamped in profile on the wall.

He clicked the little magnifying glass that honed in on a picture, and gave an audible gasp. That was he, Danny Mago, directly behind the young man on the leading horse. It was definitely him, the dark curly hair, his own style, not like those other medieval fellows, the long nose extending in a straight line from the forehead like a Roman helmet, the mouth, the downcast eyes, the clear skin. He looked for sandshoes, but in the melee of feet he couldn't make out which were his. Perhaps Benozzo didn't have a memory for feet, but as to faces he had been right, he did have a mind that stored faces. The site said that this *Procession of the Magi* was painted in 1459. Benozzo had said that he was 19 when they met. That means he must have painted that 20 years after.

The diversion had given him a measure of strength and resolution. He thought that perhaps his gloom had lifted sufficiently to allow him to go to the lift. Maybe something there, like the Lady Juliana, might help him find out what had happened to Zelia, but at that moment the Vespers bell was ringing, and it was time to get Angela home.

"Come again tomorrow," said Mother Madeleine as they left. "After Mass."

"But it's Sunday." Mother Madeleine never painted on the Day of Rest.

"I have to," she said with a peculiar certainty, which Danny was to remember poignantly before the year was out.

# 32

## *Dick Tracy*

 NEXT MORNING, on an inside page of the Sunday paper, he found a short article saying that the police wanted to interview a niece of the murder victim, Zelia Mazloum, a schoolgirl of an address in Knight's Road who, it was suggested, might have been on holiday in some other part of the country. So there was some connection between the man who'd been found and Zelia. Would Zelia have gone on holiday without saying anything about it to him or to the sisters? No! There was nothing secretive or duplicitous about Zelia.

Passing a public telephone Danny had what seemed like a brilliant idea. In the light of this new information he would try the police again. He stepped into the booth. He dialed the number of the local station, which was printed on a card on the wall. Then he held a handkerchief over his mouth, as he had seen characters do in movies when they wanted to disguise their vocal patterns.

A gruff voice answered.

Danny said, "I have some information on the case."

"What case?"

"The murder case. The fat Arab." For the moment Danny couldn't remember the name—Qetik Mamoulian—he'd seen in the newspaper. Those Arabs called themselves some pretty weird things.

171

"Who's speaking? What's your name and address?" The voice got gruffer.

"Listen, Mister, I'm calling the shots here." Danny couldn't believe he'd spoken that sentence. He looked accusingly at the handkerchief.

"Who is this?"

"Do you want the gen on this rap, Buster?"

"What number are you ringing from?"

"Seems I'm connected to a penpusher. Get me the big pig!"

"Are you the kid who came in here the other day thinking he's Dick Tracy?"

The phone went dead. Danny stuffed the handkerchief into his pocket and left the phone box. He couldn't believe that he'd done anything so ludicrous. Was he losing his marbles? He glanced furtively to right and left and then walked swiftly, ran actually, all the way to the church.

After Sunday Mass, Danny took Angela once more to the convent in a taxi and saw her settled in Mother Madeleine's studio. He had determined, after seeing if there was anything he could do for Sr. Paula, to make his way to Tera Whare, the lovely old house the newspapers had said Sir William Kydd had rented for his time in New Zealand. It had come to him in Mass that Captain Kydd, remembering Zelia's trembling aversion of him, might indeed be behind her inexplicable disappearance. In any case, Mother Madeleine wanted him to go and see the exhibition of the ten finalists. He'd lost enthusiasm for the competition but he'd go there and go to Tera Whare later.

At lunch in the studio—the nuns insisted that it was easier to serve lunch there than uproot Mother Madeleine and wheel Angela up and down stairs to the dining room—the talk was of the exorbitant sum of money offered as a prize and what wonders such a sum could do for the poor and the sick. Angela agreed, with a great show of disharmonized movement, where-upon the plain-speaking Sister Paula said to Danny, "If you had a choice between winning the competition and seeing your sister cured, which would you choose?"

Danny was confused, and angry with himself for showing that he was confused in front of all the Sisters. It wasn't fair to ask a boy a question like that. Angela's forefingers were drawing twisted circles in the air, pointing repeatedly to herself and mouthing, Me! Me! Me!

Turning as red as a traffic light he said, "Well, it doesn't signify, does it, because I haven't entered the competition?"

"But I thought you . . . Mother M. said . . ."

"Sister Paula," Mother Madeleine asked gently, and few women could be as gentle as the gigantic Mother Madeleine when talking to her sisters in Christ, "Be so good as to phone for a taxi. It's to take Danny into the gallery to see the exhibition. I'm determined you shall go, Danny, and, hey, I'm paying for the taxi, putting my money where my mouth is, as the vulgar expression has it. Sister Paula, some taxi money, please."

When the taxi arrived in Wellington, Danny told the driver to take him around to Oriental Bay. He decided he would look at Tera Whare first and the exhibition after.

---

"The kid's got his own whatsitsname into the top ten in this quiz. His own work! A picture or something he put together himself. We were always talented, the Von Blumenkohlx—that's with an X, make sure you print it right—S is for the hoi poloi. The family archives are stuffed full of dead poets, writers, fishermen, all those sort of blokes. Artists! That's the word! Beethoven was an ancestor. It's an established fact. Gainsborough. He was an uncle way back. There are hundreds of them lurking around among the branches of the family tree."

"Where are these archives, Mr. von Blumenkohl?"

"Are you being insolent, boy? Who are you? NBC? BBC?"

"CBS, sir. This is the nightly News Forum Special."

"CBS?"

"Yes sir."

"I own it. You're fired. I won't have insubordination."

"Over here, Mr. Odo, sir. DDT Berlin. Could you just confirm for our viewers that your son Claude is among the finalists in the *New Zealand Reredos Lampadephoria* entirely on his own merits."

"Absolutely, Berlin! Absolutely! I myself didn't know where the boy was these past six months. Now I realize that he was pumping the wells of creativity. Did I say that? I like it! You can all quote me on that one, gentlemen. My boy Claude has pumped the wells of creativity. I repeat it. Pumped the wells!"

"Will you be going out to New Zealand if he wins, Generalissimo?"

"*If* he wins? Which are you?"

"NBS!"

"The Axis! Watch it, sonny. *If* he wins? That kind of concept is foreign to my way of thinking. That's why I've got feelers out for an NBS takeover and why your job's in jeopardy. I'm flying out there tomorrow because he's *going* to win. And why's he going to win? Because he's a von Blumenkohl. That's why! Because he's my boy! That's the message I'm giving to the world."

As the press conference wound up, Odo overheard a reporter say, "I knew he was a monster and a bully, but I hadn't realized he was a fool too." This observation hadn't been intended for Odo's ears, which may be the reason they had such a profound effect. For the first time in his life his self-confidence wavered; the novelty of not being absolutely and indisputably perfect appalled him at first, but gradually arrested his interest, and even had a mollifying effect. His sleep that night was not undisturbed, and in the morning he had lost several grams according to his zinc and alabaster bathroom scales.

***

Danny walked up the hill behind Oriental Bay to Tera Whare. There were several cars parked along the driveway, but even such signs of activity failed to dispel the sinister aura that the place presented to him. The answers to many of his questions lay here, he felt. But what did he have to do to discover them? It was all so frustrating!

The front gate was unlocked. He slipped through and disappeared immediately into the foliage to the left. Making a path between flax and fern and summer lilies, he came to the edge of a lawn at the side of the sprawling house. The wall there was stone with high mullioned windows, and jutting out from its near corner was the turret.

Even against a cloudless summer sky, as blue as a swimming pool, the turret looked sinister. From his vantage it could have been a gigantic stemless goblet held aloft to toast the gods. The narrow arrow-slit insets were barred on the exterior face, and white gauze curtains lay limply beyond their inner windows.

It seemed that a figure moved between the windows, so he ducked and ran across the lawn to the back of the house, which was dark with afternoon shadow. There were no outbuildings on this side, only a shed in a kitchen garden that sloped down to pine trees. The shuttered doors of a coal cellar were well chained and padlocked. Next to it was a woodpile with a canvas cover. He ducked beneath what he assumed were kitchen windows, but strode nonchalantly past the porch and back door. It was open. Inside he could make out a hallway with coats on pegs and gumboots against the wall. There was nothing anywhere that could give him a foothold into any sort of investigation. In a book or a movie he would at least have found a handkerchief with a Z sewn into its corner in pink and lemon cotton thread by this time. Surely.

The north side was irregular and one part arched into an alley, beyond which was a courtyard. Then came a length of shuttered windows and stone steps running up the side of the wall to the roof. Danny stood at the bottom, daring himself to ascend when the fingers of a large hand clamped themselves around the nape of his neck.

"Gottcha!"

Danny's nervous system turned to jelly, liquid, gas. His life flashed, clear and vivid before his eyes. He was fishing for the right words to commend his soul to the Trinity in the care of the Blessed Virgin when his captor swung him round, embraced him in a great bear hug and kissed him noisily on the crown of the head. "Danny boy! You never said you were a burglar. We could have worked together."

It was Claude. He was dressed in tennis whites and held a racquet in the hand that hadn't gripped Danny's neck.

"I was . . . well, I was looking for . . ."

"For your old friend Raphael to ask why he hasn't been to see you all week. I could kick myself, Danny. Come and have some tea on the lawn. I've been so busy. You probably know that the press cottoned on to that painting of mine. My *Weka-Feather Christ* was among the ten finalists for the Reredos. Well, they haven't left me a moment to myself. Radios, newspapers, television crews in the middle of the night. After this I could sleep soundly in a barrel going over Niagara."

"Actually," said Danny. "I was looking for Zelia. And it was my painting you took, not yours."

"No. Yours is the *In the Temple Killing the Lamb*. You can't have two designs selected for the finals."

"I didn't . . . Mother Madeleine!" Suddenly it was all clear to him. "She entered my Jerusalem! That's why she wants me to see the exhibition." He was disconcerted, then pleased, then more than a little proud, all in the space of five seconds. *And among the finalists!*

They'd turned by the conservatory in front of the house and were heading across the lawn. Some men and women were seated at the white tables. Sir William Kydd's was the only face Danny recognized.

Claude put his arm around Danny and directed him toward the buffet table, saying, "Zelia! How is she? I guess that sweet kid must be angry as thunder with me, eh! I'll come out now, Danny. We'll have some tea, then we'll drive straight out to the Hutt Valley and I'll make my apologies."

"Your *Weka-Feather Virgin* is still in the studio at Aniwaniwa."

"I've got my car in the drive. We'll just take tea first 'cause I promised. Then we'll go and see Zelia."

Sir William Kydd, who had barely acknowledged Danny's existence before, actually extended his hand when Danny joined the company, and allowed it to be shaken. "And what fair wind brings you to Tera Whare?" he asked.

"He came to see me," said Claude. "We go back a long way, Danny and me, a long way."

"All of a month," said Danny.

Sir William addressed the ladies taking tea. "The Chairperson of the *Reredos* Committee, the famous Maori, Dame Mother Madeleine herself, spoke to me of this young man only the other day. She feels he is the most promising young artist in New Zealand." He raised his voice a quaver and his eyebrows followed. "The Great White Hope," he said, puckering his lips as if to restrain a smile. The ladies tittered. Danny felt like smacking him in the mouth.

"*I* have Maori blood," Danny said. "My mother's mother's family were Ngati Tawa."

"Really!" exclaimed Sir William in a voice as delicate as gossamer. "One would never know it."

Danny didn't answer immediately. He let the silence stretch time taut. Then he said. "Well, we are not all what we seem, are we? Some of the most evil villains in history have dined with kings and worn kid gloves."

It was out of his mouth before he'd weighed the "kid" against the "Kydd." When the connection hit him it seemed so apposite that he laughed. Danny's whole torso vibrated with laughter. Sir William looked at him stonily and the ladies with apprehensive puzzlement, but this only made Danny's laughter more uninhibited. He himself could scarcely believe that he, a by-word in social timidity and self-effacement, was indulging in such unilateral merriment.

But it was funny. It *was* very funny. Hypocrisy, viewed objectively, was one of the funniest things in the world.

Danny, chuckling, sniffing and dabbing his eyes with his sleeve, walked away from the group with no more concern for them than if they had been a clump of trees. At the gate he half turned back to see if Claude was following, but he was not. However, his eye caught the arrow-slits in the haunted turret, and again he saw a figure there. This time it wasn't moving. It stood quite still in one of the shadowy recesses, the face and figure framed by the white gauze curtains. Danny's laughter died on his lips. It might have been a ghost, he had no way of telling, but if it was a ghost it was a mighty familiar one. If it was a ghost he would bet everything he held dear that it was the ghost of Zelia.

# 33

## *The Rainbow Revealed*

 DANNY WALKED back into town. He walked past the crowds outside the Gallery at Jervois Quay where the ten contending works of art for the *Reredos Lampadephoria* prize were being exhibited. He didn't give a thought to either the building, or to his own work on show there, because his mind was wholly absorbed in the rescuing of Zelia.

He had no doubt but that the girl in the arrow-slit was Zelia. If he had questioned the matter at first, it was because of the suddenness, the shock of coming face to face with the unexpected. But once he had left the grounds of Tera Whare he knew for sure. The certainty increased along with the problem of what he must do to get her out of there.

It was as the Hutt Valley train pulled out of Wellington station that the full horror of Zelia's situation stood stark before his mind. They would kill her. Whether they got the information they wanted from her or not, they would kill her. She knew too much about Sir William Kydd, and his status in the art world, indeed in any world, would be in jeopardy as long as Zelia lived to tell of the base character behind the suave, polished exterior.

In the train he thought that, back at the convent, he could at least tell Mother Madeleine about this bizarre discovery, and just maybe, given her wisdom and experience, she might come up with a workable strategy for getting Zelia out of the haunted turret. It tortured Danny to think what they might be doing to her in there. Images of thumbscrews and spiked coffins floated around the corridors of his mind. Racks to stretch the body. Red-hot coals. The water torture. Bastinado. It was all too terrible. He had to do something, but what?

That should have occupied his whole mind, but on the way from the station to the convent, a part of the mystery of Uncle Zeki's cards was unraveled to him. The meaning behind that jumble of languages was as clear as fresh spring water. It had to do with the elevator. With the door of the elevator. All that connecting and disconnecting . . . Uncle Zeki had been coachman for the family who had originally built the house before it became a convent. Yes! It was so obvious. The Mandylion was somewhere there, in the convent, and one could get to it by way of the elevator.

He didn't go to the studio—he went directly to the tunnel and entered the elevator. He closed the door. Then he opened it again. CONNECT AND DISCONNECT. He repeated the action twice quickly. The elevator started to move.

It wasn't like the usual ascent, which always had an air of the unreal. The elevator was rising noisily like any old fashioned elevator. It chugged up about ten meters, then stopped. Danny looked cautiously at the blank wall in front of the grille. He touched it. It was slimy with damp. He shook the grille. It rattled. He jumped up and down. Nothing happened.

Danny took to pumping the handle, of opening the elevator gates and slamming them closed. The mechanism was dead and gave no indication of intending to come to life.

He didn't allow himself to panic. He stood erect and thought the situation through.

There seemed to be no resolve so he thought it through again. No way around. He was stuck. There was no way out. He could shout for all he was worth; there was no one to hear him. After all the excitement it seemed a very shoddy, unnecessary end. And what would Angela do without him? And his mother? And Zelia . . . ?

Death would be slow because there was plenty of oxygen. Starvation probably. That could take a couple of months. No— less, with dehydration. Nine, ten days. He didn't want to die, but if he were meant to he'd accept it. There was a lot to look forward to. The angel, the Lady Juliana, the . . .

This was stupid speculation.

Wait a minute. There was a trap door in the roof. It was too dark to see it, but he knew it was there. He took deep breaths, then leapt up. His hand didn't even touch the roof. He tried again. And again. It was futile. In a burst of frustration he beat his fists against the wall of the lift cage to the left. The upper part rattled, but a metal bar that he hadn't noted before held the structure firm in the center. He ran his hand along it. At the end was a trigger-shaped catch. It was stiff, but he wrenched at it, and the bar separated at a toothed joint, like two octopuses whose tentacles have been interlocked, pulling away from each other.

Danny tugged at the grille, which easily swung back. At the same time the wall in front folded out on hinges to reveal a tailor's dummy.

It was the room behind the mirror door, which usually housed the Weka-Feather Cloak. He'd never looked closely at that wall to the left of the mirror before but it didn't take an Homeric imagination to guess that the central section of the paneled wall could be a door. It even had a handle in the form of a knob. An old clothes brush hung from it on a length of twine.

Danny laughed. It wasn't a loud laugh, it was more of a mocking chuckle because the joke was on him. JAVELINS

AND TEETH CONNECTING AND DISCONNECT-
ING—those polyglot words on the rainbow cards—ENGAGE
—that was it—ENGAGE AND DISENGAGE. That was a signal for the machine to stop at this secret cupboard which
housed the Weka . . . Of course! The Mandylion was secreted
in the eel-skin lining of the Weka-feather cloak. It was all so
simple once you knew it.

He closed the lift door and the door of the cupboard. The
mirror door was open. He walked past his easel. Claude's
ghastly copy of his *Kiwi Christ* stood askew on the pegs. He
barely noticed it. He was looking for the Cloak. It wasn't in
any of the obvious places. It was only used for two feasts in
the chapel and neither of them was imminent.

Please God, Claude hadn't taken that along with his painting. If that was the case it could be in the hands of the wily
Kydd by now. Danny almost panicked. He didn't knock on the
door of Mother Madeleine's studio, but burst through into the
room in a sort of a frenzy.

Mother Madeleine and Angela were the only people there.
They both looked at him in a curious way that had nothing
to do with his wild entrance. Angela's limbs were still, but her
mouth was twisting in an effort to create a smile that conveyed
pleasure and surprise—and a measure of triumph. The face of
the old Maori nun was grinning and something of Miss Paekakariki Beach, 1935, had returned and was dancing in her eyes.
Between them, on the barrel, lay the Weka-Feather Cloak, its
eel-skin lining slit along a horizontal stitch and hanging like an
open sack. Mother Madeleine's easel was turned away from her
podium and was facing into the center of the studio. Angela's
portrait was covered with a length of oil cloth, but resting on
the pegs was a thin, hide envelope, a deep red, and glowing with
age, quite large, the size of a tabloid newspaper, its edges held
together all round by a zigzagging cord like wide shoe lacing.

Clearly something was up, so for the moment Danny held back the urgency of his own news and attended to theirs.

"Go on!" Mother Madeleine nodded to Angela. "It's your discovery. You tell him."

Angela whirled her arm to beckon him to her. She wheeled her chair to a cleared table top and took the cards from her cardigan pocket. "Aniwaniwa!" she mouthed and threw her arm up to describe a great arc in the air. "Aniwaniwa!" She splayed the cards and painted the arc with them. "Aniwaniwa! Aniwaniwa!" Danny bit his lower lip as if ashamed of his ignorance. "I'm sorry, Ange. I don't know what Aniwaniwa means except that it's the name for this particular stretch of the Waiwhetu Stream, and the area around here."

"Aniwaniwa! Aniwaniwa!" Angela had dropped the colored cards on the table and was poking at them individually with her forefinger. Her shoulders heaved with frustration. Still poking, she hit out at Danny with her left hand. "Aniwaniwa!"

"How could a pakeha understand, hey?" Mother Madeleine saved the day. "It's a Maori word for a rainbow, Big Boy. The cards are the colors of the rainbow."

This fact established, Angela fairly shimmied with excitement. She pushed both her hands outwards as if keeping crowds back and then proceeded to lay the cards on the table with their color and legend side down. It was as if she was assembling a jigsaw puzzle, which, in a way, she was, for when she had them in the order she wanted, the seemingly haphazard lines on the plain side of the cards, the strands of hair on the collar, formed a bird. The lines in the back of the bird where the four corners met even spelt out its species—WEKA—the small flightless wood hen, common in the New Zealand bush and only notable for its soft, downy feathers which were used to make the ceremonial cloaks for Maori chiefs.

Aniwaniwa! That was what Angela's curious body language

was saying. Weka! The Weka-Feather Cloak in Aniwaniwa! Great Uncle Zeki had hidden the Mandylion in the lining of the Weka-Feather Cloak.

Danny didn't feign surprise, but neither did he tell them that he had just, a moment before, figured out the puzzle for himself. His eyes moved to the hide, wine-red envelope on the easel. "Have you looked at it?" he asked in a reverent whisper.

"Looked at it!" Mother Madeleine's chuckle broke the tension of the moment. "Hey, boy! We unlaced that bundle three times, didn't we, Angela? And threaded it up again. It was worth having lived all these years just for a sight of it."

"May I?" Danny moved in front of the easel and gingerly unlaced the zigzag binding on the ancient leather. Inside was a thin silver reliquary, chased and bejeweled at the corners. The door of the reliquary was secured by a simple catch on the side.

He disconnected the catch and lifted the door and there it was, just as he had seen it in the tent of the Edessan emissary two thousand years before. Gold filigree had been worked around its perimeter and small rubies, emeralds and sapphires set among the gold, but the picture itself was the same. Even more now it seemed to live. The eyes of the Sacred Face settled on him as if they had found him in a crowd after much searching. They brought such moisture to his own eyes that the picture became a blur.

He turned away, ashamed lest his sister and the old nun should see his emotion. But they had impressions of their own, quite independent of him.

Mother Madeleine said, as much to herself as to Danny and Angela, "If that's the face of my Lord etched on a bit of old wax, whatever will it be like in glory, burning with love, brighter than a thousand suns? What do you think, hey, Big Boy? What do you think?"

# 34

===

# *It Couldn't Be True,*
# *Of Course*

 IT WASN'T till Danny and Angela were home that Danny had a chance to do something about Zelia. On a desperate impulse he told his mother over the dinner table that Zelia wasn't on holiday as he had thought, but, he was pretty sure, was being held captive in the turret of Tera Whare. Then he held his breath. He really expected her to mutter, "Yes, yes, darling, now eat up," or some such platitude, as parents do. But instead, she lay her newspaper on her lap with a sort of deliberate finality and attended to what he said with such seriousness that he was constrained to continue. He told her about Sir William Kydd, and Ferhat Ferhat. And to explain all this he had to tell about the Mandylion and, well, everything really, except the elevator. For all her motherly loyalty even Brigid Mago might be inclined to call the emergency services for a straight jacket if he launched into an explanation of that phenomenon.

But it was Angela, at the other end of the table, who asked a question.

"What, Ange? Claude! I don't know. I just can't figure out about Claude. The way he acted this afternoon I couldn't believe that he knew Zelia was in the turret. Not even the best actor in the world would go about trying to deceive like that. It was too unstudied. Yet why didn't he come with me when

185

I left? Does he know that Kydd and Fur Hat are crooked as coat hangers? I've got a lot of figuring out to do—a lot of figuring out on a dozen different fronts."

Their mother said, "Yes! I suppose we all must, now that you've confided in us. But our main concern must be for Zelia, and in the meantime I wouldn't waste my energy on trying to understand Claude. He doesn't necessarily think like the rest of us. I think he was brought up with too much money and no love. That's against nature on both counts. He is used to having what he wants, when he wants it. Yet he is not "spoiled" in the sense of having an insufferable ego. He is not grasping. If he'd been raised in a different environment he might have been a winsome ascetic. He probably thinks that since he posed for the painting, it is as much his as yours."

"But he stole it."

"Yes, dear, I know, but, you see, if anyone else took your picture they'd be thieving. But when a person like Claude takes something he assumes he has a right to it."

"Why?"

"Well, because everything he has wanted, except parental love apparently, has been his, automatically, and because he modeled for it and, the awkward one, because there is a psychology at work which tells him that everything he does will be the best in the end for all concerned. That's the way limitless money, and no adult influence to the contrary, have trained him to think."

Danny said, "Have you taken a psychology course without telling me, Mum?"

But Brigid Mago was in full flow now, and not to be stopped. "Furthermore, he plans only for the moment. The consequences of his actions don't occur to him. We mustn't mistrust him. He may be on the side of the angels, but, oh dear, it is all a bit complicated. The fact that he left his father's influence and branched out on his own was a positive grasp for self-expression, for independence. He seems to have done a splendid job, from what I can piece together. It was as if a Dallas cowboy moved into the Hottentot homelands and worked at passing himself off as a Hottentot. The Texan in Claude couldn't help but surface every now and then and the Hottentots couldn't help but notice.

"Take your father, for instance," she waved her hand to indicate the paintings of New Zealand flora which adorned the walls. . . .

When he helped Angela get to bed, Danny told her, *"Ange, I'm going back up to the convent. I don't like the idea of the Mandylion just sitting in Mother M's studio. I wouldn't put it past Captain Kydd and Fur Hat to come after me now, and if they went there and found that. . . . It doesn't bear thinking about, Ange. When we finally get Zelia out of the tower at Tera Whare she won't thank us if we haven't seen to it that the Mandylion is safe."*

At the top of Knight's Road he stopped off at the dairy to buy a packet of chewing gum. He felt a foreboding, a dread that he couldn't shake off. He had a sudden, overwhelming and unprecedented desire for chewing gum. Not to chew at that moment, but as a sort of security. Chewing gum presented itself as something inconsequential and reasonably familiar to cling to if the foreboding and dread became what they promised— a gargantuan horror.

He bought a packet of twenty-four sticks of spearmint and, as he passed his money across the counter, the ubiquitous television caught his attention. Caught? Too light a word! It sprang at him like a huge and sinister jack-in-the-box. The newscaster announced that *the world-renowned New Zealand artist, Dame Mother Madeleine Atuaheira, had just passed away at the convent of her Order in Aniwaniwa, in the Hutt Valley. Messages of condolence were already pouring in from. . . .*

Danny found it difficult to control the bicycle. He tried to steady it; to keep his eyes clear and his mind concentrated, but it wobbled all over the road.

It wasn't true, of course. There had been a mistake. He had been with her only three, four hours ago. She was painting Angela. She couldn't be dead. She couldn't be dead; she was New Zealand. They had only just found the Mandylion. Everything would be all right once he got there. It was a foolish misunderstanding.

Already there were cars parked the length of the drive to the convent and an inordinate number of people were gathered there—forty, maybe fifty or even sixty people. And more were arriving all the time. The porch of the studio was already waist deep in flowers. Sister Eileen stood in front of the closed door talking to people, accepting flowers and passing them to Sister Clare. Inside Sister Paula was hanging black drapes across the windows.

He wheeled his bike around the back of the convent and left it outside the laundry. The old nun with no teeth and watery blue eyes sat in her wheelchair by a tub of blue hydrangeas fingering her rosary. She looked up as Danny passed. "We always argued over who'd be the first to go," she said softly. "She was more worthy than I in everything; she was the only one who didn't know it."

He took the path around the back of the studio and entered by the door that gave on to the area that he used as his own. Everything looked different; or rather, the same, but reconstructed on another plane. He knocked on the door of Mother Madeleine's studio and stepped in. A space had been cleared in the center of the room and Mother Madeleine's body lay on a wheeled ambulance trolley in the old habit of her Order, full veil and wimple, copious pleated skirts, crucifix at the breast and large rosary beads at the side. She looked smaller in death but her body still filled the trolley.

Sister Paula was on a ladder, sliding the drapes over the tops of the curtain rails. She said, "It was all so sudden. After you and your sister had gone off in the taxi I came to take her to the chapel for Rosary. She said she'd say the rosary in heaven and then her whole body went limp. Her eyes were still open and she had that smile . . . forgive me, Danny. I'm really crying for joy. It's all so sudden."

She indicated a bolt of material and Danny passed the free end up and handed her the scissors. "I can't imagine where all these people have appeared from. They want to pay their respects, but we can't have them all in here, and the chapel is too small. We've phoned the Mother Provincial and she's ringing the Cardinal. I think they'll take her into the old Cathedral if she must remain a celebrity after death. People can file through there and look at her and say a prayer. Look, there are television vans pulling up in front of the convent now. Where will it all stop?"

Danny took a step to the side and peered through the window. There was, indeed, a television van with supporting vehicles. Some men were already erecting lights and others were toting cameras on their shoulders. An ambulance swept up, flashing its importance with a revolving overhead beam. Behind it came a convoy of cars. Several clerics stepped out of one while the others disgorged the *Reredos* selection committee. Among them were Sir William Kydd and his secretary, Boris Abladabvich a.k.a. Ferhat Ferhat.

A coffin was taken from an undertaker's van and Sir William and the clerics made a way for it through the crowds. They were coming towards the studio.

Danny threw the Weka-Feather Cloak around his shoulders and said urgently to Sister Paula, "These men mustn't see these things, Sister. Mother M. wouldn't want it. Trust me. I'll explain later." With a single movement he swept up the canvas on the easel and the folio containing the Mandylion and hurried towards his little back studio. As he reached it, Sister Eileen had opened the main studio door, and a priest and Sir William were on the threshold.

Had they seen him retreating? Probably! They had that five-second advantage over him. And people slipping through doorways in Weka-Feather Cloaks aren't candidates for anonymity. One way or the other he wasn't taking chances.

Danny placed the portrait on his own easel and tucked the Mandylion beneath his arm. He was turning for the door when the oilcloth slipped from the frame. His eye took in the picture briefly. He must have made a mistake. It wasn't Angela's picture as he'd thought. It was a painting of a girl, full of charm and beauty, standing beneath a pohutukawa full of crimson needles, looking into a convent garden. The nuns inside were dressed in full brown habits with black veils and soft white linen at the neck. Cloistered sisters of Mount Carmel. They were laughing in the sunlight. He replaced the oilcloth. It was too late to retrieve Angela's portrait now. He wouldn't take the elevator. The Mandylion was too precious to risk losing in some time and territory haphazardly chanced upon.

Danny closed the door quietly behind him and made off through the bush, along the track that led down to the conservatory. A dull, uniform buzz of voices wafted over the tops of the trees from the crowds assembled to pay tribute to Mother Madeleine, yet as he got nearer to the stream, Danny became aware of other voices, distinct from the crowd. He stopped and listened. They were behind him, coming nearer, urgent, maybe angry voices. Branches were snapping, leaves underfoot rustled as they were kicked and scattered.

He skirted the conservatory and turned along the revetment. There was no light here at all, but familiarity helped him to find the steps. Inside the tunnel he felt his way along the wall to the lift and stood there by the gate, his back to the tiles, clutching the Mandylion to his chest and breathing in as if air was gold dust and his lungs were saddlebags, holding it there, then breathing out in a minor ecstasy of relief. This exercise calmed him and, when he was calm, helped to pass the time.

Danny stood there for a long while. The fact was, he couldn't make up his mind what to do. Of course, the voices might have been bored younger members of the mourners, exploring the bush as they waited for their elders. But if it was Captain Kydd and Fur Hat Squared or their henchmen following him, they could well still be there, hanging around the conservatory. Or they might have returned to the convent and be waiting for him still. Or they might have gone off to his home and be lurking in the undergrowth, alert for his step on the garden path. Whichever way he looked at it, he was better off in the damp, dank-smelling tunnel leaning against the cold tiles.

He waited on like that for well over an hour, probably two, breathing systematically for ten minutes, then saying a decade of the rosary, then breathing again, then praying again. When he'd finished the glorious mysteries, he began to reconsider the advantages of travelling somewhere in the lift. Time spent in the places the elevator took one to didn't count as time in real life, but at least a journey would be a diversion, and it was possible that he could go to the parlor of the Lady Juliana. She might give him some ideas on how to rescue Zelia. If he put the Mandylion back inside the lining of the cloak . . . like that . . . and secured the cloak about his chest with the flax-fiber cord . . . there! That was it! He probably looked like a diminutive, furry archbishop. Oh well! He just hoped that the lift wouldn't put him down anywhere in the 20th or 21st century. You could pass a Weka-Feather Cloak off almost anywhere in history up till 1900. After that you'd be in danger of being lynched as an oddball.

Danny reached both hands out in the total darkness and inched along until they touched the metal grille of the gates. He found the handle on the side, which he had seen before but never used. He forced it down and the elevator, which was still up on the studio level, slowly descended.

With a concentrated movement he pulled the gates back. The darkness was so intense that he couldn't see even a hint of a reflection in the mirror on the wall of the lift cage in front of him. He was thinking of the colossal difficulties that blind people must face every hour of their lives when, obscurely at first, an image did appear in the mirror, well behind him towards the mouth of the tunnel. It was an orb, a part of the darkness, but a different shade, and it was moving rapidly towards him.

An awful dread stung Danny as the ghastly thing bore down on him. It was like a torrent of writhing tentacles, each crackling with fire fueled by a venom spurting from its suppurating pores. Danny was hurled onto the floor of the lift cage and the grille was wrenched shut. Then all the pandemonium of hell was concentrated in that small space. Foul screams, blasphemies, obscenities and demented howls such as could never know joy or friendship. Green fumes seeped into the cage with the odor, familiar now, but no less gross and nauseating.

Then the vile visage, uglier than anything imaginable, appeared so close to Danny that he felt the burning of it on his skin. "THE FACE WILL NEVER BE SEEN!" It shrieked with malice that could have killed.

He doesn't know I've got it! was the thought that crossed Danny's fear-stunned yet still conscious mind. Clearly it has been the Mandylion that the demon has been referring to all along, and he doesn't know that I've got it here in the lining of the cloak.

He thought that if he could put his hand back and draw it out of the cloak the fiends would scatter, but fear had paralyzed his body. He was unable even to move his hand into his pocket to take out his beads with their large cross.

There were hundreds of the fiends and each moment more would materialize, all screaming with the fury of despair. Danny lay in a heap on the ground, immobilized by dread. His one conscious thought was to reach his rosary or the Mandylion, but it was impossible. He couldn't even summon the thought to ask for heaven's help.

Horde upon horde of these loathsome scorpions of hate appeared, but their numbers didn't fill the cage. They were not of a spatial substance. They could be more easily counted by degrees, like fever, like flame, than by numbers. An instinct in Danny marveled that he didn't die, that the intensity of their evil didn't snuff the light out of his body like a candle flame in a typhoon.

Then, on a sudden, the floor of the lift wasn't there. Instead, a vast, dark, dreadful pit gaped beneath him. The steeply slopping sides were of mud, wet and slimy. He was sliding down and clawing at the sides, but there was no solid surface to grip. Each time he dug a handhold with his fingers, the clump would break away and he would slide further into the crater. The vile beings cavorted obscenely around the brim and their demonic din grew to a pitch that threatened to burst his ear drums, and in their perverse glee they took to throwing stones and balls of mud at him.

Danny reached a point of fear and horror beyond which a

created being could not proceed. With a gasp of anguish he ceased to claw at the mud and yielded to gravity.

His descent into the abyss was swift.

The horror of it all short-circuited his nervous system and his every sense and faculty went blank.

# 35

=====

## *In the Haunted Turret*

 ZELIA WASN'T certain where she was being held, but was reasonably sure that it was in the so-called haunted turret of Tera Whare, the house on Mount Victoria where she had heard Sir William was staying. The shape of the room, the view over the harbor from one of the long, thin windows, and of a part of the drive from another, all more or less confirmed her reckoning. And, of course, the fact that Abu Kyed, a.k.a. Sir William Kydd, visited her two or three times every day.

She had not been ill-treated. On the contrary, the apartment in the turret was as well appointed as the best rooms in a five-star-hotel. An elderly lady who smiled at her in a kindly way delivered excellent meals. She didn't seem to speak English, this lady, and she was watched carefully by two of the hefty fellows, the bogus policemen who had abducted Zelia on Christmas Eve. They stood glowering insolently at the door as the elderly lady served the food. Zelia was grateful that this lady was there because her presence precluded abuse, or worse, from the hefties who looked yobbish enough to perpetrate any indignity.

Sir William Kydd always played the gentleman when he visited Zelia. Any stranger looking through the keyhole might be forgiven for thinking that a nobleman was visiting his queen. His deference to her was absolute, on the surface anyway. In the most polished manner he made it plain that he intended to take possession of the Mandylion. He further expanded to impress upon her that she was welcome to co-operate by sharing what knowledge she had of its where-abouts, or to be . . . well . . . persuaded, and, if necessary, my dear young lady, liquidated.

That would be regrettable, of course, and by no one more than him, but the fate of the world depended on who had cus-tody of the Mandylion—the forces he represented or—she must forgive him—a dying clan in a Mesopotamian backwa-ter.

Naturally she needed time to consider. Sir William was pre-pared to be as generous as circumstances would allow. He would not pressurize her until his work in New Zealand was finished, that was, until after the winner of the *Reredos Lampadephoria* had been announced on the morning of New Year's Eve. Tomorrow in fact.

Very late on Sunday evening, when he returned from the convent where he had represented the Lampadephoria Committee at the sudden passing of Mother Madeleine, Sir William Kydd entered the turret. He told Zelia that the win-ner of the *Lampadephoria* would be officially announced by the Cardinal during the consecration of the Cathedral. Later a grand reception was planned on a great motor yacht, the *M. V. Montezuma,* for Claude von Blu . . . er . . . the winner. Workmen were already moving furniture, victuals and cutlery from Tera Whare to the *M. V. Montezuma* in preparation for what was to be the most lavish and spectacular social event in New Zealand history.

Odo Von Blumenkohl's jet was putting down at Wellington International in the morning and the Generalissimo himself was coming directly to the ship by helicopter.

There was no reason, no reason at all, why Zelia shouldn't

be a part of that, indeed why she shouldn't be the hostess on Claude's arm. All she had to do was share her information. So simple.

"Is Raphael . . . Claude . . . is he in on this with you?" Zelia asked with a note of bitterness.

"My dear young lady," for a moment Sir William Kydd let his mask slip. "I wouldn't trust that buffoon with a hand of aces." Straightaway he tried to laugh the claim off, but Zelia was relieved that Claude had no part in Kydd's evil scheming.

"Better a buffoon," she said, "than Beelzebub."

"You have far too much intelligence to believe such nonsense. I am quite confident that intelligence will prevail . . . but should you force me to dispose of you then, O dear, it would distress me so much to be put to it, but I would be forced to arrange the same choice for your family in Urfa. Such a waste, dear Miss Mazloum. Such a needless waste . . . all for a silly picture which has proved, over many centuries, of having its own way of finding a path back to its legitimate custodian."

Zelia had lived each minute of each hour of her confinement in the company of just such ghastly threats. At times some gremlin in her own psyche almost convinced her to give over Uncle Zeki's colored cards. If she, with all her prayer and study, couldn't figure out what they meant, what greater chance would the hell-bent Captain Kydd have? That was how her gremlin taunted. Then she was glad she didn't have them. The thought of what Kydd's thugs might do to Angela or Danny stiffened her resolve more than once. However, she had been close to the breaking point when she had seen Danny on the drive that day. The angle of that arrow-slit didn't allow a view of the lawn but she could see the section of the drive near the gate. The window apertures were sectioned with glass on the inside surface, and barred with iron on the exterior face. This precluded any possibility of her cries being heard, but on this occasion she was so surprised that she could only stand limp and stare anyway. By the time she had roused herself to wave he had gone.

Yet they had grasped a moment of recognition. She was convinced of that, and it restored her courage. That courage came flooding back till she felt like a blood twin of Joan of Arc, brave and resolute and quite without thought of herself.

She must keep that courage. Cost what it might she must keep that courage. She said, quite simply, "If you kill me you will find it too difficult to get rid of my body. Danny knows I'm here, and he'll have told others."

Sir William stepped across the room to face a large canvas above a mantle shelf on the wall of the octagonal living room. It was a portrait of a young man dressed in mid 19th century style, with thick sideburns on his jowls and a mischievous slant to his eye. "On the contrary, my dear. Your body will be found quite publicly on the ground down there," he pointed beyond the window. "The most natural thing in the world. The gentleman depicted in this portrait here is one Edward Jerningham Wakefield. Now, Edward Jerningham Wakefield built this house and along with it, clever fellow, built up the rumor that this turret was haunted. It was a ploy to keep robbers at bay, considerably cheaper and more reliable than insurance, and so entrenched did Mr. Wakefield's little fiction become that it is believed to this day. So what more natural than an innocent girl, tormented by the disgraceful propositions of a degenerate school fellow, should seek refuge with an older compatriot, my humble self, and firm family friend, only to be harried by ghosts and, in her agitated state, to fling herself from the parapets. Oh, there is a door to the roof over there," he added. "It will be unlocked for the occasion."

Zelia almost lost her cool. She said, "If Edward Jerningham whatever-his-name-was knew of the evil uses his harmless ruse was being put to, he'd let the full weight of his outrage fall upon you."

"My dear Zelia . . ." Sir William started urbanely enough, but before the full sentence had passed his lips the portrait lifted itself off the wall and came crashing down, splitting itself over him so that only his grotesquely puzzled head and shoulders showed through the punctured canvas.

Zelia laughed in wide-eyed wonder. "And that flower vase, too," she added.

The vase rose to obey, and the crack of skull against porcelain was painful to hear. Gladioli, shards and water fell about Sir William's living bust.

"And then he'd kick you out the door!" she suggested, tempting amazement.

The indignity of being bustled by the unseen, while ensconced in a vast ornate gilded plaster frame, and dripping with plants, not to mention their shattered container, was magnified when visited upon a man of Sir William Kydd's social stature.

Zelia, however, was too astounded to take unlimited delight in his humiliation, and when the door finally slammed shut behind the knight, who lay sprawled inelegantly beneath a disapproving oil of the Duke of Wellington, she felt so scared that she half wished him back. But then a gladiolus slowly rose from the ground and placed itself gently in her hand that she held cupped in front of her.

It was so simple a gesture that her fears melted immediately; they gave place to an exquisite joy, which turned her eyes as luminous and blue as aquamarine.

* * *

When Danny's mind crept back to consciousness, he was once more in the arms of the angel. Beneath them the dawn, still racing ahead like the waters of a tide, revealed the first landfall of the southern island, a labyrinth of waterways, a vast Venice, submerged mountains, a land sculpted by ice to represent Beauty and Loneliness in an eternal embrace. Mists of virgin wool padded the valleys.

"What about Zelia?" Danny asked the angel, but he might just as well have asked a passing cloud.

High, rocky hills, a bay, a city as neat as a cottage garden, a sun-soaked alluvial land of fruit orchards, tobacco fields, hops, and sweet berries, rich and abundant. To the north a bay of beaches, gold and green and silver, met the ocean and gave way to an endless shingle breakwater of menacing solitude.

They veered south, down the western coast, which was a vast drainage plain for the citadels of snow-layered rock that formed the spine of the land. Now they were low over patchwork farms, paying homage to another of the intense wells of light, now breezing through a flock of oystercatchers on the wing, now soaring up the face of sheer black rock, high above pillows of cloud, now along unexplored valleys of beech and pine, now following the course of glaciers nibbling inexorably at mountains.

After the wilderness of snow and rock they rose over the fjord land, swooping here and there to skim the surface of a lake or careering along one of the innumerable alleyways of water. The mass of land appeared so vast to Danny that it seemed to him that they had covered half the globe's surface instead of just the base of a not particularly large island in the South Pacific.

Above the small, southernmost city, Danny saw the third island of the chain away to the south, the full stop at the end of the signature, the last outpost before forbidding Antarctica.

Rolling sheep country, rivers, roads, ships out on the ocean like fragile twigs, coffee percolating in suburban homes, hens laying, the relentless, non-stop banal talk, the endless, endless blasphemies and obscenities, the soul-dead people, the frightened people, the people who knew but weren't telling, the people who were telling but didn't know, the baffled, the lonely, the truly happy, they were all part of the land and the rock and the fern and the snow.

As they moved up the eastern littoral over a sedate old grey city at the end of a fjord and moved inland, Danny experienced an overwhelming surge of love for the land. Yet at the same time there was sadness, a sadness at the compliancy of people who allowed themselves to be fed with the evil of the few whose hearts pumped hellfire and liquid lies. Sometimes he had to avert his eyes from his own land because the pain was intolerable.

Once Danny told the angel that he had seen enough, but there was no telling angels anything. The only reaction of that glorious being was to move faster up over the wide flatlands between the alps and the sea and to dive in on the largest city in the south.

The flowers of eucharistic light were intense here, but so too was a veneer, like a leprous skin, which covered most things that affected people's opinions and prejudices and directed what they did. The angel swept low over one or two places where the skin was blessedly thin, but generally its very prevalence had been the cause of his not noticing it before. Several radio stations were generating slick, gimmicky talk that vied with the sunrise as the nation's bright and early face. Television was already swamping minds refreshed by sleep with a panic of fashions, with sly smiles and lies to turn hearts from thoughts of peace. Presses were churning out thick pages of inanities, disguised as news and considered comment. Parents were betraying their trust, disposing of inconvenient children, killing them in the cradle of the womb before they had learned to breathe.

Precious few sought relationship with their God; the spirit of prayer was as rare as a selfless smile.

Mountains, towns, hills, rivers, valleys, roads, people, he saw most of them thick with the diseased skin now as they passed above the upper eastern seaboard of the island. The sudden realization of this defect, this national obsession for the material, for the trivial, for the fascination of being deceived by creatures, didn't lessen the love he felt for his country, it simply made the ache greater. He longed to do something, but was pragmatic enough, even though young, to know that it would take most of his energies trying to prevent himself from falling into the same trap. Because the trap didn't seem like a trap when it snared you, and the deeper you fell into it, the brighter its colors became, and the sweeter its candy.

"Why are so many people wooden?" he asked. "Why have so many no sense of beauty and mystery and joy?"

The angel spoke with magisterial pity. "New Zealand is fast falling from grace," he said. "Your country is in danger of breaking every bone in its soul."

"Couldn't you thaw out for a minute and help me to rescue Zelia from the turret . . . ?"

The angel made no response.

"I didn't think so! How about giving Angela a chance for a normal life . . . ?"

"You show me everything that ever happened in New Zealand, except what I want to see, let me listen to every word ever spoken except the ones I want to hear. I don't suppose I could have a more obliging angel next time?"

"Believe, pray, yield. Absorb what you are shown. All will come together for your great task," said the angel.

Then they were hovering high above Wellington Harbor.

He saw his own home as the angel glided down and circled the rim of the flat, closely populated valley to the north. His mother was still asleep, but Angela was out of bed and sitting in her wooden chair, as opposed to her wheelchair, telling her beads as she did every morning on rising. Her limbs were remarkably still as she sat alone, concentrating on her prayer.

There was Holy Trinity School, and over there Sts. Peter and Paul's church. To the east the narrow stream wound out of the gorse of the high hills and curled around the area named after that stretch of it, Aniwaniwa. St Martin de Porres Convent, gold and rose-grey in the early sunlight, stood like a Delphic temple on its plateau. The Sisters were praying in the chapel. Mother Madeleine's body wasn't there. It was on the other side of the valley in a mortuary attached to the hospital. Already arrangements were being made to transfer it to the new Cathedral in the city where it could lie in state, as it were, for the people to pay their last respects to their great countrywoman who had never lost the common touch.

Danny took the opportunity to study the elevator shaft. It actually terminated on the roof of the studio but, looking through the veils of time, it was clear that earlier on in the 20th century, before the property had been a convent, there had been a covered walkway from the top of the elevator shaft across to the first floor of the main house. On summer evenings it had been customary for the family and guests to take the elevator down to the conservatory and stroll along the bank of the Waiwhetu Stream. Now the top of the elevator casing looked like the trunk of a dead tree perched on the side of the roof, invisible from below.

A fissure into the future arrested his attention and he applied his eye to it for a moment. There was a dining room, large and well furnished. It was a New Year's Eve. A number of people were at table—men, their wives and the young adults of the house. The host was a man of some importance in the community. He looked shrewd but honest, clever but kindly—a judge, perhaps. One of the men was a dramatic actor with an international reputation, and the fine looking one was a priest—no, a bishop. Surely the purple shirtfront and the pectoral cross denoted a bishop. And the small abstracted-looking one with the darkly beautiful wife—hey, that was Zelia! And himself. Was the bishop really Pascal? And was the host, and judge, Myers? And Duffy, an actor? Spotted Duffy! But the sight drifted off, like a picture passed in a gallery, and gave way to 100,000 more.

The eye of the harbor, with the city clinging happily to its hills, wore a mantle of loveliness and dignity that Danny had never associated with it before. It was true that familiarity blunted vision. Here was a bride of cities in full train, quite unappreciated by those who lived in the folds of her gown.

Of the larger of the islands in the great oval harbor Danny saw many things, hints of many secrets and once, long before the arrival of the English pakeha, Masses celebrated by Spanish priests from a galleon not noticeably bigger than a large lorry. There was much that was fascinating there, but Danny's main attention was diverted to something of paramount interest. Zelia's voice spoke from the turret of Tera Whare over on Mt. Victoria. And the person she was speaking to was the suave villain, Sir William Kydd.

Danny strained to the spot and tugged at the angel. The angel let him go, or rather went with him, but the angel made it clear that this was not the hour appointed for rescue. There was work to be done first. All matters were allotted their fixtures in the divine organization of things. To tamper with them and substitute one's own agenda made for enormous and quite unnecessary complications.

Zelia stood with her back to the arrow-slit windows as

Danny and the angel wafted invisibly into the room. Sir William stood just inside the door. He was pulling on his gloves.

". . . That would be regrettable, of course, and by no one more than me, but the fate of the world, my dear girl, depends on who has custody of the Mandylion. . . ."

Danny heard the conversation through with growing indignation. He felt impelled to lash out at the cunning Kydd, but the angel's will held him bound until Kydd, striking a superior pose beneath the picture of Edward Jerningham Wakefield, tried even the angelic patience and yielded Danny a dive back into time and with a short leash of liberty.

Danny, still wearing the Weka-Feather Cloak, but invisible to the occupants of the room, leapt through the air to the picture. With a single movement he lifted it from its hook and brought it crashing down around the ears of Sir William Kydd.

"And the flower vase, too," cried an astonished but delighted Zelia. Danny picked up the vase and brought it down on the art expert's head with a healthy violence.

"And then he'd kick you out the door!" Danny had no conscience about his unfair advantage. He pushed and kicked and bullied the man and the frame until both he and it lay askew on the boards of the gallery without, directly under the disapproving eye of the Iron Duke who had given his name to the City.

On closing the door behind the battered knight he took the key from the outside of the lock and turned it from the inside. But his triumph turned to alarm when he saw Zelia's pleasure in her enemy's thrashing suddenly give way to a fear that the turret might well be haunted and that once more she was alone in it. Danny was suddenly frantic to know how to alleviate her mounting terror when, noticing a large flower from the smashed bowl lying on the carpet, he picked it up and lay it in her hands which she held in front of her.

"When can I get her out of here?" he asked the angel.

"Presently," came the wordless reply. "Keep the key to the door and you can free her presently."

The angel, with Danny once more in his arms, wafted gently over Wellington. Then, in a flash, Danny, though still outside Time, was standing in the sanctuary of the new Cathedral, which was dedicated to the Holy Face.

Danny stood there, in the sanctuary, wearing the Weka–Feather Cloak and rubbing his eyes with the heels of his hands to make sure that what they saw was not an illusion.

# 36

## Our Lady
## of the Voyage Home

 "MASTER DANIEL, where in Tartarus have you been?" It was young Benozzo Gozzoli, his mass of hair pinned up with paint brushes like a Japanese Mikado, and his originally blue cowl a fright of paints. He was striding towards Danny, clearly delighted to see him, but at the same time bent on efficiency, because behind him many boys and friars were working industriously, the same he had met and spent time with in the Florentine cloister.

The sanctuary of the new Cathedral, as yet unconsecrated, was as cluttered as a building site. Barrels, vats, troughs were strewn around the steps and along the walls. A fire in a portable stove was melting raw pigments and boiling dyes. A pyramid of silver sand spilled over into the nave. The boys had erected a system of cane scaffolding against the face of the reredos wall, a structure so rickety that it wouldn't tax the powers of a very minor prophet to predict that the chirp of a skylark might send it toppling. Yet the minor prophet would be wrong because the friars were moving up and down its ladders and along its horizontals with ease; and the boys were engaged in acrobatics when required to move from one level to the next, and negotiated its topmost stages with no apparent fear of collapse.

Benozzo grasped Danny's thin shoulders and kissed him noisily on each cheek. "Are you going to carnival as some sort of crazy bird?" he laughed, fingering the Weka-Feather Cloak. Then he said, with a certain urgency, "We've been ready since cockcrow. Have you got the design?"

Fra Giovanni and his brother Fra Benedetto, who had been kneeling quietly in prayer near the sacristy door, rose and came forward. They smiled at Danny and bowed modestly. Danny inclined his head but didn't answer. His mouth hung open and he was staring at Fra Giovanni. Whether the angel was communicating the information to him or something had tapped the arsenal of universal knowledge he didn't know. But it was. He was certain of it. The grave, gentle friar, aware of Danny's sudden confusion, smiled again and in a sweet gesture, untranslatable, touched him lightly on the arm.

Danny said, "Are you really Fra Angelico?"

"No. I'm known as Fra Giovanni," he said simply. "There is no Fra Angelico in our community." He looked to his brother for confirmation. Fra Benedetto shook his head. It was clear that neither of them had heard of an Angelico; but Danny knew that it was so, that this was the man history was to know as Fra Angelico.

"Have you got the Mandylion?" Fra Giovanni asked. "We were told that you would have the Mandylion."

Danny took the cloak from his shoulders and laid it on the altar. He reached into the eel-skin lining and took out the laced envelope.

"That's it?" exclaimed Benozzo, clearly disappointed. Danny undid the binding and withdrew the reliquary. From the reliquary he took the sacred portrait. There was an audible intake of breath. Those who were near drew closer and those on the scaffolding swung to the ground and gathered to gaze in wonder. Fra Giovanni blessed himself and bowed low. No one praised it. No one spoke. Words couldn't communicate here; here words could only obtrude and obstruct.

Fra Giovanni nodded to Benozzo and Benozzo gave the order to prepare the plaster. The lime kegs stacked against the sanctuary walls were jimmied open by some of the young men. Others fetched deep pails full of water, Danny wasn't sure from where. Some scooped sand into the troughs, some lime, some water. Others mixed. There was an admirable sense of timing and precision about the activity. Each man knew exactly what he had to do to maintain the mechanical efficacy of the whole, and he did it.

Fra Giovanni and Fra Benedetto motioned Danny to follow them into the sacristy. Several of the friars and young men were there. They had discovered a large box full of octavo sheets and another with ball felt pens, both of which miracles of technology they had mastered, but were still wondering over. Danny placed the Mandylion on a makeshift drawing board, which was already covered with sketches.

Fra Giovanni took an octavo sheet to represent the reredos wall. In the center of the upper half he quickly sketched the face of the Mandylion and stood back. Should it stand alone, he asked, or should the rest of the wall be filled with representations—symbols, scenes and saints?

Now Danny knew why he had been granted the privilege of the flights over his islands with the angel. All that he'd seen and heard he was to condense into a surround, a pedestal, as it were, for a reproduction of the Mandylion face. But how was he, Danny Mago, 16, going to do that, even with the help of one of the best and most saintly painters that 2000 years of Christian art had produced? He was totally inadequate. Never in his life had he felt a greater need for prayer.

"New Zealand things," Danny said feebly.

"Certainly," the unquestioning acquiescence of the friars was a charming fruit of religious obedience. But even so, questions had to be asked. "New Zealand things? Exactly what are they?"

There was no time for dithering. He'd have to start somewhere. "Kiwis, ferns, tikis—you know—like Dad's!" On reflection they probably didn't. Captain Cook hadn't been born yet. Neither had Christopher Columbus, if it came to that. Danny took a sheaf of paper and sketched a ponga fern, a kauri tree, a tui perched on a kowai branch, a waterfall he'd seen that morning in the fjords. Fox Glacier, Pelorus Jack, a King Country pa, the pen couldn't keep pace with his drawings, which passed from hand to wondering hand as he sketched more. The almost perfect cone of Mt. Taranaki, a sheep dip ("That will symbolize the Sacrament of Confession," he said; they all smiled dutifully, but no one had a notion what he was talking about), White Island, a weta—everything his artist father had left on the walls of their family home—a yacht, a Chinese gooseberry, a pounamu, a pohutukawa, the Basin Reserve.

When Benozzo came into the sacristy, he took over part of the desk to draw faces, but Danny was emboldened enough to shake his head at Benozzo's faces and to draw faces of his own—old Maori women with tattooed chins, wise chiefs, heavily tattooed warriors. He drew Mother Madeleine and a sheep shearer and a rugby scrum. He drew a lighthouse keeper, a young mother, and a lorry driver. He drew the faces of the silent people bowed deep in communion with the Eucharistic presence just as he had seen them so vividly throughout the land moments before. He drew the blasphemers, the drunks, the fornicators, the unloved babies in the womb.

Benozzo wasn't offended. Instead he tried to copy the face of one of Danny's Maori in haka mode, but both the Maori features, and the concept of a face-pulling war dance was too foreign to his experience. "Are they Moors?" Benozzo asked.

A boy came into the sacristy to announce that the upper half of the wall would be ready to work on in a quarter of the clock. There was no panic. It was as if the entire operation was being controlled by a force outside themselves, a benign force, all-powerful but self-effacing, in need of nothing, yet dependent on their co-operation, talent and industry.

Each sketch was scrutinized, maybe revised a little, numbered and allotted a place on a scheme sheet. For the moment it was necessary, given the time it took this mix of plaster to dry, the attention of all concerned was on the upper wall. The face on the Mandylion was to be reproduced as far as the mouth. Around it they would paint aspects representative of nature's bounty—the birds, the waterfall, the native bush. Fra Giovanni and Fra Benedetto would concentrate on the face. Benozzo and an assistant would sketch in the upper north side, while Zanobi and another friar would concentrate on the south. Danny was to move among the three groups working with each of them, checking on the authenticity of the native species, which the artists had never seen for themselves. Fra Giovanni modestly referred to Danny as the *supervisor,* a title that he declined without fuss. He hadn't known what a fresco was until they'd told him, he said.

When the plaster was ready, work started in silence and continued that way with no word spoken but the bare essentials.

The lining and the drawing of the fresco plaster was undertaken with astonishing rapidity. The boys stood by like living lecterns, holding the Mandylion for Fra Giovanni and Fra Benedetto, and Danny's sketches for the background artists, while others bore trays of charcoal pencils, cloths, knives, quills, ink and feather brushes.

Before long the boys were swapping their trays for pigments and mixing palettes, and it was now that Danny started work in earnest. With the help of the Florentines' expertise he managed to produce a dozen or so different greens and browns from the powders and cake-stones of pigments which gave vibrant life to the native bush, until one could almost swear that breezes were rustling through them and that leaves and fern fronds were shaking silver. Benozzo's waterfall was no still-life; it fell in torrents onto a ledge, then cascaded to a deep pool on the forest floor, which never ceased to churn up bubbles like blue marble. Furthermore, Benozzo painted the moa on its banks and identified himself with it to such a measure that, with its determined beak and wide investigative eyes, it looked remarkably like Benozzo himself.

Danny was reluctant to interrupt the work of Fra Giovanni and Fra Benedetto. Indeed, at times he found himself standing by, staring at their concentrated dedication as they transferred the magnificence that was the Mandylion, perfection by perfection, from the petrified wax to the wet plaster. He would have been content to spend all his time watching the brothers work at this admirable fusion of genius and grace, but they persuaded him to assist them, asking his advice about the color of the eyes, the shape of the nose, the texture of the beard.

"The most important thing, Master Daniel," Fra Giovanni had said just before the work started, "is the mouth. It is also the most difficult because we must paint it in two parts—half blind, so to speak. Look at the Mandylion. There is a quality in the expression of the mouth that has no counterpart in any work of art or iconography that I know of. The mouth there is more human, more poignantly loving than paint can demonstrate. There is such an expression of selflessness in it—like a mother searching for her child in a crowd. And even if we manage to reproduce the upper lip exactly as it is on the wax, and do the same with the lower lip when the next plaster is applied, there is no guarantee that that divine longing of the Savior will be captured."

When they finally came to the painting of the upper lip, Danny was watching eagerly to see how they would approach it. Would they hesitate, study from different angles, discuss? So far they had worked on every aspect of the portrait as if they had been planning it in millimeter by millimeter detail for many weeks. Could they do the same with that problematic, infinitely expressive mouth? To Danny's surprise, when they were, so to speak, cornered by the mouth, when everything else that could be done had been done, they neither attacked it nor balked at it. They laid their brushes on the palettes carried by the boys and knelt down there on the cane staging and immersed themselves in prayer.

After five minutes they were back on their feet, quietly painting the mouth of Christ as it appeared on the Mandylion. And after another twenty minutes they set aside their brushes. The upper half of the mural was finished. The work had taken exactly five hours and 17 minutes.

Danny sat and rested on the sanctuary steps while the boys disappeared through an open doorway that was certainly no aperture included in the design of the new Wellington Cathedral. It was surrounded with cherubs carved out of porphyry and it tended to vanish when it wasn't in use. Danny wasn't sure, but on the one occasion when he strained to get a glimpse of what was beyond it, he thought he saw the courtyard where he'd been in a snow fight and where he'd lost his crucifix and been terrorized by the devil.

Presently the boys returned with baskets full of fingers of fresh-baked bread and a sort of shortcake and tiny meat pies, which could be eaten three, four, five at a time. They brought jugs of wine too, a rich wine, red as ruby, and glass goblets to drink it from, and cheeses and melons and tree tomatoes. They faced the wall as they ate and drank, expressed satisfaction with what they had already done and discussed and sketched and exchanged ideas about the decoration of the lower half. Danny's contribution to the meal was 23 sticks of spearmint chewing gum. It was all he had, and he felt somewhat mean about so paltry an offering, but the Florentines were agog at the taste, the texture, the sheer elasticity of the confection. They couldn't have been more impressed had he taken them all for lunch to The Nabob's Picnic and picked up the tab himself.

Eventually a pattern was decided upon. At the base center would be an altar corresponding to the actual altar. Around it a herd of sheep would be grazing. On the altar table would be a sacrificial lamb. Danny sketched this as near as he could to the lamb as he remembered it from the Temple in Jerusalem and from the painting he had later made of that awful but riveting scene.

Between the lamb and the Mandylion face would be a chalice with a Host raised above it. The faces and symbols, Maori, Pakeha and communally New Zealand, would adorn the sides and blend in at the join with what was already painted in the first phase.

Both the friars and the boys expressed agreement with the design that was finally submitted for general inspection, but that enthusiasm, that spark of a light in the eye and the excitement it generated, was wanting.

"There is no Blessed Virgin," said Fra Giovanni, pin-pointing the problem at last. "The picture will never be complete without her and yet . . ." The humble friar waved his hands helplessly in the air. ". . . and yet where can we place her without upsetting the balance of the picture."

The Mandylion face was, in a sense, too overwhelming, too dominant to share the space with any other figures except the decorative. A small representation of the Virgin would consign the Mother of God to a mere face in the crowd and that would never do. A larger one, on the other hand, would be ungainly. Had they considered the matter in the first place, an Immaculate Conception to one side at the top of the picture would have been suitable, but it was too late for that now. There was no revision in fresco work.

The problem seemed insoluble. The plasterers had already started their mix and were applying it to the lower portion of the wall when another door, a metal one, appeared to the south of the chancel and a girl of about 17 stepped out. The boys, and even the friars, gaped in stunned wonder as the door faded away. But it wasn't the door they were gaping at. It was the girl. She had long fair hair and skin as flawless as a raindrop. She wore a calf-length floral skirt with a simple cream blouse and a pink cardigan. She stood in the sanctuary quite unabashed by the men in strange garbs and with their hair piled up on the tops of their heads. She smiled, giggled almost, but didn't move from where she stood.

Danny had seen her before. He knew the face from . . . where . . . ? He had seen it recently. But where . . . ?

Fra Giovanni whispered, "What a perfect model for the Virgin."

"Surely God has sent this young one to us for that purpose," said his brother.

Benozzo moved forward. With the brushes in his hair and a face suddenly tormented by angst and suffering, he looked like a young stag brought to its knees by the hunter's arrows.

"Where have you come from?" he asked, as if these were his last words and he only awaited an answer to expire.

She really did giggle then, though charmingly, without any hint of ridicule. But she didn't answer. She seemed to look to Danny for support.

In a sudden mental storm Danny realized two things.

The first was that this girl was the one whose portrait Mother Madeleine had painted, the portrait he had taken the night before from her studio in mistake for Angela's. It was odd that he had never seen the girl in the nun's studio, as he had been there every day, but so many odd things were happening all the time that one more or one less made no waves.

The other sudden realization was that, yes, of course they could incorporate a good-sized image of the Blessed Virgin into the mural. They could do away with the goal posts and geysers and greenstone stuff in the lower north corner and have, say, a grotto like Lourdes, or a tree like Fatima. Or perhaps a composite. His mind was in a turmoil. He must devise something definite, and very soon, as the plasterers were quickly covering the wall.

Danny bowed his head and said a short prayer to the Virgin. In effect he asked her to design her part of the picture herself. Whatever gave the greatest glory to God, he added. It wouldn't be worth doing at all if glory was aimed elsewhere.

The Weka-Feather Cloak still lay on the altar. Danny beckoned to the girl and she came forward. She walked slowly and with a curious dignity. On the steps she stumbled ever so slightly and straightaway a dozen pairs of hands offered themselves to steady her. She welcomed them and giggled.

"Would you mind modeling for us for a moment," he said. He wasn't sure what language he had spoken in, so he repeated the sentence in English and added, "Please!"

"Sure!" said the girl. Then, lightly touching Benozzo's face, she chuckled like a little girl who has seen her first kitten. "You must be Benozzo, the Florentine," she said. Her voice was like the splash of molten diamonds. The boys stood electrified, apart from Benozzo, who, though likewise electrified, was on his knees. Danny placed the Cloak over her shoulders and made to secure the flaxen twine at the front, but Benozzo got there before him.

If she was standing like that . . . like a Lourdes statue, Danny thought—but no! No, it wouldn't do to have her facing the congregation. Every other face, every other object had the Mandylion as its center of focus. Perhaps the Blessed Virgin could be represented in profile. Danny moved the girl's chin. Her lips tightened as she attempted to suppress a laugh. That was better, but it reduced the Mother of God to one of the multitude. That wasn't fitting. Danny couldn't have expounded the theology behind it, he just knew it wasn't fitting.

Benozzo suggested the girl place her left hand high on her chest. She did so, but only after looking to Danny for confirmation.

"Zanobi's good at this sort of thing," Fra Benedetto remarked, and the unassuming, compact little fellow came forward and took over the director's job from Benozzo. He suggested that a rock could be jutting out from the side of the picture and that the Virgin could be standing on it, pointing perhaps, or raising her hand towards the face of Christ. With blushing diffidence Zanobi took the girl's hand and helped her to step onto some boxes, and from them onto the altar.

Every artist reached for sketching paper. Zanobi tilted the model's head this way and that. With a modesty that might have been amusing if it hadn't been so innocent, he moved her arms and her legs. But no stance gelled; no stance caught the role of Mary, pre-eminent among the people, leading them to gaze on the face of God.

Zanobi reached down and took one of the boxes. He placed it before the girl's feet and asked her to step on it. As she did so she stumbled, turned fully towards the reredos wall and held her hands out, palms down, one each side of the Weka-Feather

Cloak as if grasping for support. With a single will every man around the altar, friar and boy, surged forward to assist. They were falling on each other and lifting their hands high to grasp hers.

The minds of Fra Giovanni and Danny Mago clicked simultaneously, like two cameras. The arrangement, the choreography, was perfect.

"Freeze it!" Danny snapped, borrowing an expression of his school's PE teacher. "Everybody hold it! Don't move a millimeter!" Danny sketched. Fra Giovanni sketched. Fra Benedetto sketched. Several others who had not been close enough to the altar to have been part of the tableau sketched. They all sketched vigorously until the plasterers announced that the wall was almost ready to take the initial line drawings.

The models all relaxed in unison with a long, loud sigh. The girl stepped down with the help of those nearest to her. She removed the cloak from about her shoulders and placed it on the altar table. Benozzo was for standing by her, but Fra Benedetto roped him into allotting sketches and areas to the friars and boys to limn. Meanwhile Danny and Fra Giovanni and Zanobi worked on the sketches of Our Lady.

"We are trying to do five weeks' work in as many minutes here," said Zanobi.

"This project is heaven's own work, Master Strozzi," said Fra Giovanni in his kindly way. "We are only the brushes." He compared his own sketch with those of the others. They were all much the same. "This figure seems perfect," he said. "Simple and elegant. We will be ridiculed for painting the Virgin from the back, but these hands say more than a face ever could, no matter how well executed. I feel very sure, my brothers, that this idea comes from Our Blessed Mother herself."

"The figure is perfect, master, yes, but the rock is wrong." This was a bold statement for the young, self-deprecating

Zanobi to make to the great Fra Giovanni, but the friar studied the composition for a moment, then agreed. "It is, perhaps, too bulky, too earthbound."

"There should be a suggestion of movement forward, towards the Christ, the Virgin leading, all else following . . ."

"On a horse, like the French Maid of Orleans . . ."

"Or better, a cloud . . ."

The girl was a little to the side of the group, standing on tip toe, stretching to see the sketches over their shoulders, merry with her tinkling chuckle. Suddenly she tapped Danny on the shoulder. When he looked at her she put her hand to her mouth to stifle her giggles.

"What is it?" Danny asked, almost giggling himself, as if it was infectious.

"Te Arawa! Te Awanui!" Now her hands were together, curving out in front of her as if she was describing an elephant's trunk. "The canoes, the Maori canoes!"

Danny gasped with the sheer appropriateness of the idea. Yes! The Virgin, clothed with the Weka-Feather Cloak, facing Christwards at the prow of a Maori canoe, her hands stretched down, and all her children reaching up to them from the sea. He didn't even pause to acknowledge gratitude to the source. His pencil was waltzing on the paper, sweeping up a curved prow in bold lines and describing it to Fra Giovanni as he sketched.

Some hours later, when the canoes were already lined onto the plaster and Danny and some puzzled but keen Florentines were well on the way to finishing the painting of their exotic bodywork, his eyes searched the room for the girl. The Cloak and the Mandylion had been placed neatly on the altar top, and the girl was seated with the plasterers by the lime barrels, chatting happily. When Danny caught her eye, she stood up and smiled broadly and threw a signal in his direction. He couldn't quite get its meaning at first and then, as the girl seemed to fade into the wall, almost like a mirage, he cottoned on to what she was telling him. *The bees' knees,* she was signaling. The thumb and forefinger made an *O* and she winked with her left eye. The picture, the Florentines, everything was the bees' knees. Within a moment this splendid creature had disappeared from sight. It was Angela. A delightful, healthy, ethereal, but fully animated Angela.

Danny had no time to think this through because almost immediately the angel appeared and beckoned him. The Florentines were adding the finishing touches to the mural. It would be pointless to say goodbye. Whatever friendship had been forged between them had been fixed in the fresco. He'd have liked a few moments to stand back and look at the work, to watch the effect of the sun's rays from the Cathedral's myriad light-reflecting surfaces, to figure out Angela's part in it, but the angel was not disposed to indulge Danny's vanity. He had just enough time, as he was whisked away, to pick up the Cloak and the Mandylion.

"Does Our Lady like the painting?" he asked the angel as they soared above the city.

Knowing the angel, he didn't expect an answer, but in fact there was a response. The words formed very clearly in his consciousness. They were: It is to be called *Our Lady of the Voyage Home.*

# 37

≡

# *Dumped*
# *Unceremoniously*

DANNY THOUGHT about this. *Our Lady of the Voyage Home.* He liked it. There was poetry in there somewhere. Now his mind was beginning to encompass a pattern, a pattern that linked most of the events of the past months, a pattern, which no one, apart from an angel, could have guessed at, much less devised. Now he could appreciate the reason for the flights over New Zealand, for the places he had been taken to in the elevator—the Mandylion painter's tent, the Jerusalem Temple, St. Marco's in Florence. These all had a significance now, they were all connected with reproducing the authentic Face of Christ, of enshrining His features in lands still undiscovered when He had come to claim the earth.

"I wonder if you'd be kind enough to explain to me about Angela?" he asked. "Where did she come from? Has she been—you know—cured? Was she produced especially to model for *Our Lady of the Voyage Home?* I'd be ever so grateful if you'd explain to me what's going on . . ." He might just as well not have spoken for all the reaction he got from the angel. That superbly disinterested being simply plunged towards the lights on the hill below and dumped Danny unceremoniously among the shrubbery in the grounds of Tera Whare.

Lights were on in the ground floor of Tera Whare, and

Danny could hear voices and the sound of energetic move-ment. Staying well in the shadow of the foliage, he moved nearer the house. Two vans, one large and the other smaller, stood with their cargo doors open to the terrace, which led out from the vast sun-room. Drivers were dozing at the wheels. Men in overalls, supervised by Kydd's bully boys, were carrying furniture from the house to the large van.

One of the bully boys, last seen as the gorilla posing as a policeman while ransacking Zelia's house a few nights before, told the workmen gruffly that that was all of the heavy stuff and that now they were to bring the food from the kitchen. The bully boys themselves led the way.

One of the overalled men said, "The food's for the small van, chaps," as they followed. The voice was awfully like Myers' silly English accent, Danny thought, as he slipped up the steps and flitted across the sunroom. Among the bizarre ornaments in that museum of a room was a stuffed double-humped camel. Slung between the humps was a fine silk saddlebag woven in a classic Persian design. Without so much as pausing, Danny whipped it off the back of the beast and tucked it beneath his arm with the folded Cloak.

He took the main stairs two at a time and turned left along the landing. At the end was the corridor with the large por-trait of the Duke of Wellington. He took the key from his pocket and turned it in the lock of the door opposite.

"Danny!" Zelia gasped.

"Zelia—quickly! We've got to get out of here!" Already he was removing the laced red envelope containing the Mandylion reliquary from the lining of the cloak and sliding it into the saddlebag. Then he was folding the Cloak and wedging it in alongside.

Zelia was surprised and puzzled and confused. "What have you got there? Why have you brought the Cloak here?"

"It's the Mandylion. I'll explain later."

"You know, I had a dream about the cards. The message was so simple. The Mandylion was hidden in the Cloak all the time and . . ."

"Zelia . . . we've got to hurry!"

They were halfway down the staircase when the workmen filed across the sun-room carrying caterers' trays. Danny and Zelia flattened themselves against the stairwell wall, and when the men had deposited their load and trailed back to the kitchen, the kidnapped and her rescuer made a noiseless dash into the outer darkness.

The back doors of the larger van were still open and they reached the same decision together. They climbed over a stack of deck chairs and sat together on a divan shrouded in a dust cover. Even if the workmen discovered them at the other end, Danny mused, they could pass themselves off as New Year revelers.

"Pascal, you come in this one with me. Duffy, follow us in the catering van." The doors banged to, and there was a muffled leave-taking of the bully boys before the engine fired up and the van moved off.

"That was Myers! Spotted Duffy, and Pascal! It has to be! They must have got a holiday job as removal men. Let's just hope they don't see us."

As the convoy rolled down Mt. Victoria, Danny told Zelia about the Mandylion now in the camel's saddlebag; about Angela cracking the code, and her and Mother Madeleine opening up the lining of the Cloak. Curiously, with Danny's revelation when on the train, and Zelia's dream, they all seemed to have become aware of its whereabouts at the same time.

There in the dark van, Zelia clutched the bag to herself with an intense and reverent pressure. Unbeknown to Danny several tears coursed down her cheeks, tears two thousand years in the making, tears that couldn't explain their own provenance, tears composed of past fears and present joys and prayers for future security. They were tears of gratitude for the pride her parents would have in her, and not only her parents but also perhaps many future generations—even until the end of time. Danny barely had time to tell of Mother Madeleine's death when the van pulled to a stop, and the doors were opened and men were moving the furniture. Danny peered between the piano and the folded deck chairs. Yes, it was Myers and those blokes. But there were others too, men and women who had clearly come from the sleek ship beyond and were carrying the stuff from the van up the short gangway.

They could never make a dash for it—but maybe if they didn't look at anybody, and kept their heads down. . . .

They placed the camel's saddle-bag on the covered divan and carried it out between them, following the piano when the space was cleared. They stayed behind the piano up the gangway and onto the foredeck where they set it down beneath an awning. No one gave them a glance.

# Aboard Ship

 THEY WERE about to return to the gangway with a view to getting on the far side of the vans and ambling off like passersby when the gruesome and unmistakable frame of Ferhat Ferhat, his outsized teeth already gnawing at the fresh crust of dawn, appeared from a companionway. Danny and Zelia made a rapid descent to a lower deck and vanished into the housing.

A long alleyway stretched ahead of them with three well-spaced doors on either side. The first of these, on the port side, was open, so they slid into the cabin beyond and closed the door behind them. Two rectangular port windows with brass lugs let in the early light, and they could see that the space was a compact day-room with chairs around a central table. A desk was fixed to the bulkhead beneath one of the windows. On the desk was a telephone and a brochure from the *Lampadephoria* finalists' exhibition at the Jervois Quay Gallery. It was open at a photo of Danny's painting of the *Kiwi Christ*. The figure $10,000,000 had been scribbled across it in a red felt pen.

Leading off this day-room was a bedroom with a large bed, a closet, two more port windows with a dressing table between them. A bathroom separated the two rooms. They decided to stay in the bedroom and hide in the closet if anyone entered the cabin.

The port windows—squares of glass thick enough to withstand an ocean's fury, framed in brass and secured with threaded bolts called lugs—on this deck were level with the quay. Danny and Zelia saw the last of the goods taken aboard and the vans drive off. Myers and Duffy and Pascal weren't in the vans, so Danny assumed that they must still be on the ship.

Soon they drew the curtains and Zelia reverently took the envelope with the reliquary out of the camel bag and silently studied the Mandylion.

When she had returned the precious cargo to the camel bag, Danny told of all that had happened since she had been abducted. Zelia was particularly moved by the account of Mother Madeleine's death and amused to learn that it was Danny himself who had broken the portrait of Edward Jerningham Wakefield over Kydd's head and hustled him out the door. Angela's appearance to model for Our Lady delighted, intrigued and puzzled her; but it was the appearance of the Florentines in the Cathedral that affected her most deeply. "The face will rise again in a far temple, like a city rising from the water," she kept repeating softly. "It's the prophecy, Danny. It has come true. Everything is fitting into place now. All the haphazard things like the Mandylion being taken from Urfa, Uncle Zeki's coming to New Zealand just because that is where the first ship he found happened to be going. Then his dying and leaving it hidden here for a hundred years, my being sent out to find it, being in the same class as you—these things are all part of God's jigsaw puzzle.

"Even the counter-forces represented by Kydd, they are all essential to the pattern. He is actually Abu Kyed, you know, an Edessanean whose family have hated, opposed and fought mine since the Roman Empire still straddled the world. I was beginning to suspect it was him, and then he told me himself in the turret, smirking in his hateful way."

They talked and dozed and talked some more until the port windows behind the curtain were awash with the morning sun. Danny looked at his watch. It was 7:45. The dedication of the Cathedral was to start at 9. After the Mass the Cardinal was to announce which of the finalists' work was to adorn the vast area behind the altar.

The Cardinal had already made it clear that he would not allow the presentation of the prize money inside the Cathedral, though he had agreed to this being done on the steps outside, after the Mass. This information Danny had had from Mother Madeleine, but now that she was dead, he thought, it was more than likely that the hierarchy would want her body to lie in state, as it were, in the new Cathedral, so there was no telling exactly what course the periphery cere-monies might take.

"But," Zelia observed, "once they find the wall already painted, they mightn't even present the prize." Danny had for-gotten to reckon on the effect that that phenomenon might have.

Zelia parted the curtains a crack to check that the quayside was clear. She quickly beckoned to Danny. Two shiny limos were drawn up at the bottom of the gangway. One was full of bully boys. Kydd was seated in the back of the other, accom-panied by a woman dressed as if for a horse race meeting instead of the dedication of a Cathedral, gesticulating in his superior way to someone on board. Ferhat Ferhat, apparently the person being addressed, came down the gangway, got into the limo with William Kydd, and they were all straightaway driven off.

Danny and Zelia turned from the window as the vehicles retreated and agreed that there was nothing now to impede their departure. Sitting on the bed they discussed their itiner-ary and further agreed to avoid the Cathedral. The plan was to get the Mandylion on a plane out of the country straight-away—to Ankara, if possible. The problem was her passport. Had Kydd's men taken it when they ransacked her house? If not, maybe the police had it as they were looking for her. Perhaps the best thing was to go to the police first. But they might want to keep her. Especially if she told them that Kydd and Ferhat Ferhat were the murderers. Well then, Danny would have to take the Mandylion to Urfa. But he didn't have a passport either. To get one would take at least a week. They would have to lie low somewhere in the meantime. Everything was terribly complicated when you began to think about it.

And then they were conscious of the sunlight being blocked from the port window. Three heads took up most of the space. The three were gazing at Danny and Zelia with uncontrived surprise and curiosity.

"Duffy, do my eyes behold . . . ?"

". . . a mirage, Myers? I believe they do. I truly believe they do behold a mirage . . ."

". . . like *The Flying Dutchman,* like *The Beast from 20,000 Fathoms* . . ."

"What weird tales the sea has to tell, my friends."

"A marine Mago, enmeshed with mermaid . . ."

Danny said, "Listen, you blokes. There are serious things going on here. Please spare us the funnies. I'll explain it all later, but in the meantime you've got to help us get off this ship."

"Oh, goodness me! Pascal, did you hear that? Serious matters are afoot—serious Mago matters . . ."

They were disturbed by a car pulling up on the quay. Danny and Zelia stood out of sight with their backs against the bulkhead. They heard Myers and company say that they would collect the luggage, and then heard them leap straight over the bulwark onto the quay. Almost straightaway steps were heard coming down the companionway outside the cabin. Zelia took the folio with the zigzag stitching containing the Mandylion off the bed. In a panic she slid back the front panel of the closet, propped the folio up against the wall and closed it again. Danny, still craning to see if he could see who was coming up the gangway, assumed she was slipping the Mandylion back into the Cloak, which they had brought aboard in the camel bag. He turned now and grabbed the bag with one hand and Zelia's hand with his other. They heard the dayroom door open and then saw the bedroom door swing towards them.

"Claude!" said Danny.

"Have you two been waiting for me? I'd have rushed if I'd known. I was at yet another New Year bash at The Nabob. It still hasn't finished. They'll all come on here afterwards. Put them down there. . . ." Claude turned to Myers and Co., who had appeared, carrying light luggage and fishing tackle. "Say!" He turned back to Danny and Zelia. "I've got to go to the Cathedral. Do come with me. I beg you. I want to give it a miss, but I can't really. Then we'll come straight back here to celebrate and catch up on these past days."

"OK!" said Danny. He had no intention of returning with Claude, but accompanying him would get them off the ship without effort.

Myers and Co. gazed with jaw-sagging wonder upon the familiarity between their fellow pupils and the rich, famous and talented von Blumenkohl *wunderkind*.

As they turned to move out of the cabin, Danny turned to Myers and Co. and said, "Sorry . . ." Claude, misunderstanding Danny's motives, whispered something about forgetting to tip them and pressed a wad of notes into Danny's hand. Danny gave his classmates fifty dollars each and didn't smile once.

Buoyed up by the experience, Danny turned jauntily to Claude as they walked down the gangway, "I must say, you don't look very happy. Don't you know that you've won the

*Lampadephoria?*" He was tempted to add, "with my painting" but what was the use?

"It's Mother Madeleine's death," said Claude dramatically. "So tragic, so very tragic."

"She *was* 89," said Danny. He emphasized the "was."

"Incredibly tragic," said Claude.

"It wasn't tragic in the least," said Danny. "It was as natural as switching off the lights in the theatre before the curtain goes up."

Zelia showed signs of being agitated during the drive to the Cathedral, though she said nothing. For his part, Danny was so relieved to be off the boat and so preoccupied with wondering about the unearthly fresco, the Mandylion, Kydd and Fur Hat and a dozen other things that he didn't notice her agitation.

# 39

## *Battle in the Cathedral*

 WHEN THEY finally made it into the Cathedral —the press recognition of Claude assured them an open aisle to the door—Danny stopped, stunned.

Claude walked with casual, yet audacious, aplomb up the length of the nave and joined Kydd at the sanctuary steps. Zelia whispered that they would have to get away as soon as they could because the Mandylion was still on the ship. Without thinking, Danny handed her the camel bag containing the cloak; she hesitated a moment, then went forward to a pew.

Danny stood where he was, as stunned as Lot's wife.

Everything had been a dream. A fantasy. Perhaps he was going mad.

It seemed that the Mass had already finished. The Cardinal was rising from his throne.

There was no fresco on the wall. No re-creation of the Mandylion. No *Our Lady of the Voyage Home*.

The Kydd party conferred *sub voce* with the Cardinal and his immediate clerics. Pleasantries were exchanged.

What was true and what wasn't? Was there a Mandylion at all? Was the elevator just a concoction of his fevered brain? It was due to all this art, maybe! Art had turned his head. He should have stuck with being half-back in the rugby team like everybody else.

It was at this point that sight was given to the eyes of Danny's spirit, and he could see what was really happening above the heads of the people. Beneath, above and around the altar, phalanx upon phalanx of angels prostrated themselves in an ecstasy of joyful adoration. It was as if the clouds between earth and heaven had been lifted and oceans of resplendent light had tumbled forth to inebriate the world.

At the same time, along with Kydd and the envelope he held aloft for the benefit of the television cameras, a mob of demons had arrived, scaly, pointed, rust-colored demons, incredibly ugly, screeching with arrogance and tormented with hate. And there, in the great vault of the ten thousand prisms, a little rehearsal for Armageddon took place. It wasn't a battle such as the battles of men, where one soldier kills another until the victors take over the territory of the vanquished. It was more like a mighty, all-encompassing tug-o-war with the demons as agitated as a big, black, billy-can on the boil, and the angels holding out against them with a patience as loud as cannon fire and a forbearance as sharp as a sword.

There was no doubting which power would triumph in the end, but you couldn't tell the demons that. Such evil as theirs is blinded by its own fury and it flays on, not because of res-olute courage, but through stark, mind-numbing stupidity. They kicked up quite a dust and tugged heavily on the patience of the angels.

In the tangible world the Cardinal was preparing to take the envelope from Sir William Kydd and move outside to declare the winner.

Danny wanted to get out of the building, but the crowds had closed up again like the Red Sea over the Pharaoh's Army. He stood alone at the back of the nave, while behind him the crowds not in the pews were being kept back from surging into the aisle by men dressed as Knights of Columbus. The pressure from the multitudes congregated on the steps of the Cathedral and the precinct beyond was enormous. One of the Knights managed to pluck at his sleeve and point him to one of the pews, where a girl alongside Zelia was gesticulating awkwardly at him to come and join her.

It was Angela, but not the Angela who had modeled for Mother Madeleine's portrait and for *Our Lady of the Voyage Home*. Yet it was an Angela standing on her own feet without need of a chair. An Angela who could look at him without her eyes becoming crossed. Zelia had her hand on Angela's shoulder and was looking curiously at Danny.

Few things could be more disparate, more suggestive of insanity, than standing in awe before a battle for the soul of a Cathedral, a city, a nation, and being distracted by a sister whom one has seen that very morning as whole and as healthy as a spring lamb and now, twisting with distorted limbs again, waving an invitation to sit beside her. At the same time a very small boy—-4, maybe 5—emerged from between the legs of the Knights of Columbus, toting a red pistol. Unimpeded by anything like inhibition, the child aimed at Danny and pulled the trigger. His aim was faultless but, alas, the ammunition in his weapon had been expended. An unenthusiastic emission of water appeared and trickled to the ground. The assassin made a rush for Danny's feet. Danny, whose attention was already divided, leaned down and whisked the boy up into his arms. To assuage the child's belligerence he took the pistol from his hand, immersed it in the font and recharged it with Holy Water.

The battle above was reaching a climax. The angels stood together like a great snow-covered mountain, and the demons threw themselves upon it like wave after wave of swarming scorpions. All the angels looked for was a show of support from poor, blind humankind.

On an impulse, Danny, emboldened by the sudden wailing of the child, who was also pounding small fists on the side of his head, raised the weapon aloft and drew back the trigger. The jet of water that emerged from the barrel had all the force of a fireman's hose and caused instant havoc among the ranks of Satan's malevolent militia. It was like plunging a firebrand into a hornet's nest, like spraying them with sulfuric acid. Some devils simply frizzled to a cinder like bacon in a frying pan that is too hot, others screamed and clawed each other in their stampede for an exit. No army was ever so cowardly in retreat.

Of course, the congregation saw nothing of this. Most were in the pews between Danny and the sanctuary and were unaware of anything untoward taking place behind them. Only a few at the back saw a youth that was shooting a water pistol in the air to amuse a toddler. Several even made tch-tch noises to express quite appropriate disapproval of the time and place chosen for such levity.

Danny had returned the weapon to the boy and was handing him back to his mother, who had attracted his attention across the barrier, when a peculiar sense of startlement, static like an electrical fire, ran through the whole congregation.

Then, as the last of the demons was catapulted back into the pit, a murmur started up among the congregation, a murmur like a parliament of geese, and it was growing louder by the moment. The Cardinal stopped in the center of the sanctuary. He turned towards the altar and the reredos wall.

Then Danny was aware that Angela was reaching out and pulling him into the pew. His mother was there too, she was crying and trying to kiss him. The girl was giggling and clinging to his arm. Zelia was still clearly distracted.

How long did madness last, Danny wondered. Would he be

mad forever, or was this just a temporary strain? There were sure to be drugs? Would they lock him away? Would he be allowed out for Mother Madeleine's funeral? It was hard on his mother, Angela being like she was, and now him, loopy as a dingbat.

"We thought you'd be here." his mother was saying. "Poor Mother Madeleine! I never met her but I felt I knew her like a kindly aunt!"

Angela had coiled an arm around his neck and was kissing his cheek. "I can walk a little bit. Look!" She stood in the pew, all by herself, lifting her knees up and down, one after the other. "I had this wonderful dream!" she told him in their language, which was half sound, half limb and facial movement. "I'll tell you about it later." She jerked her head up and down as if to put a stamp of affirmation on the truth of what she had to tell. Then she added, "But it wasn't a dream at all, was it? You know it wasn't a dream."

The murmur around them had swiftly become a hectic chatter, and was now a roar. People were standing up and stumbling into the aisles. Many were getting up onto the pew benches and straining their heads towards the reredos wall, because something was happening there, something unbelievable was happening to the wall, something was emerging into it, onto it, through it, images, a face, the face of Christ, it was surfacing slowly and with great majesty, like a city rising from the water.

The Cardinal never did get round to opening the envelope. He raised his arms and intoned the *Te Deum* and the clergy, and the people, and the angels, who knew the words, took up the tune. The rest of the congregation fell back into a reverent, awed silence.

Long, long after the hymn was finished, the Cardinal stood up. Like everyone else he found it difficult to take his eyes off the magnificent fresco, which now covered the entire back wall

of the Cathedral, its colors shimmering in the morning sunlight, filtering through the thousands of transparent facets that
made up the other walls and roof of the edifice.

It was essentially a New Zealand picture. Very few representations in it were exclusively New Zealand, but collectively
the work couldn't represent anything else. Among the faces and
the foliage Mary, from the prow of the canoe, was pointing
the way, leading the way to the face of Christ. The whole fresco
was so achingly beautiful that many of the faithful, and even
more who weren't, wept for the joy of looking at it.

Eventually the Cardinal turned and asked the people to
leave quietly, which, astonishingly, they proceeded to do. A
group of the Knights wheeled out the catafalque carrying
Mother Madeleine's body in an open coffin. They placed it in
the center of the central nave, facing the altar. Around it they
set six candlesticks with lighted candles, whose flames too,
though tiny in the vast Cathedral, were nonetheless reflected
in the hundreds of oblique glass surfaces of the structure, a continual, dancing echo of light.

In the sudden stillness and silence that followed the setting
up of the catafalque, Danny took the Weka-Feather Cloak from
the camel bag, folded it over his arm, took his sister's hand and
stepped with her into the center of the aisle. Then, with his
head bowed and with a gait of ceremonial reverence, he walked
with her down the length of the nave. Beside him Angela hobbled crookedly, but with a dignity that commanded the attention of the entire congregation.

They passed the coffin and entered the sanctuary. Danny
genuflected before the tabernacle, bowed towards the Cardinal,
then, standing directly below the figure of Our Lady of the
Voyage Home, he held up the Cloak by the corners of its neck
so that all eyes present could see that the Weka-Feather Cloak
in his hands was the same as the Weka-Feather Cloak around

the shoulders of the Virgin Mother at the prow of the canoe. Then he placed it around the shoulders of Angela snuggling beside him.

Danny held the cloak around Angela's shoulders for quite a long time, but there was no sound or movement from anywhere in the Cathedral. He was aware of Kydd, only a yard or two away, staring at him with vicious contempt, and Claude, with dismay, amusement, and even admiration. But he took little notice of them. He was doing something quite out of character, but something he was compelled to do by a source outside himself. That angel perhaps! The Custodian of the Mandylion. Was he the power behind this exhibition?

Eventually Danny removed the cloak from his sister's back. Holding it before him he moved out of the sanctuary and stopped by the coffin. With a single movement he spread the Cloak over the body of Mother Madeleine so that only her big, brown, smiling, dead face showed between it and her wimple.

Danny and Angela made their way quietly back to the pew. Her arm was linked in his, yet she walked all by herself. True, her gait was ungainly, but she required no outside support and the glory of the achievement showed in the angle at which she held her head.

The Cardinal, clearly moved by Danny's action, walked around the coffin and out of his church. The people followed him in a slow-moving procession. (Later, the Knights organized an orderly line of worshippers and respect-payers and curiosity seekers, and if you look at the records of the time, you'll see that almost a hundred thousand people had filed past before the funeral Mass for Mother Madeleine, and that before the summer was over, the number of people who came to gaze in wonder at the apparently miraculous fresco totaled more than the entire population of New Zealand and Australia put together.)

# 40

## *Back Aboard*
## *the* M.V. Montezuma

 KYDD AND his party walked behind the Cardinal. As he passed the Mago party, Kydd glared at Zelia, obviously surprised and furious to see her at liberty. He whispered something to Ferhat Ferhat, who, with a sly smile, in turn whispered to the bully boys.

When the Cathedral was more or less empty—only two nuns were left kneeling in prayer in the pews alongside the coffin—Zelia, who had been looking at the retreating Sir William Kydd with apprehension mingled with disdain, pulled Danny over to the nearest side-altar area. He slumped against the wall and his eyes closed with exhaustion. After a moment or two color began to return to his drained cheeks. He felt that he had been relieved of the threat of insanity and that he could once again return to his customary thoughts, actions and reactions. But there was something. Something important. He shook his head as if to energize the mechanism there, and opened his eyes. Angela was shyly handing back to Zelia the stack of colored cards. That was what he was straining to recall, something Zelia had said about the Mandylion as they entered the Cathedral. Where was the Mandylion? In the cloak covering Mother Madeleine's body, he thought, not having seen Zelia slip it into the cabin closet before they had left the ship.

Maybe that is as safe a place as any. He began to juggle the matter over in his mind, but was distracted by Angela, who was now standing in front of him, her hands on his arm. Her eyes were sparkling with gratitude. They told him that she knew why he had taken her with him into the sanctuary.

"It *was* you who modeled for *Our Lady of the Voyage Home,* wasn't it? How . . . ?" He was smiling happily, even through his own confusion. "Tell me. I don't care if it is believable or not. All the rules that govern the universe have been shattered these past few days . . ."

Angela pulled at the sleeve of their mother to tell the story as Angela had told it to her that morning.

"Well," said Mrs. Mago, lowering her voice so that it wouldn't resound in the vast and now mostly empty Cathedral. "Last night, after you put Angela to bed, she said she couldn't sleep. . . . After several hours she got out of bed and was sitting on the chair saying her rosary when Mother Madeleine came into the room. She says she didn't know where she came from, she was just there. Angela says she wasn't an old lady moving like an enormous slow wave any more, instead she was like a little child, a soul, swift and lively and whiter than a lily. Angela herself wrote these words on paper: *swift and lively and whiter than a lily.* She still wore her nun's clothes, she said, but they shone with a fantastic light, like the wedding gown of a princess. Someone called Juliana was with her. Mother Madeleine took Ange's hand and told her to stand up. Then she told her to look in the mirror. There was a girl there she had never known before, and she was so overwhelmed that she just stood there gaping at the girl, who gaped back. When she eventually turned round, Mother Madeleine and the Lady Juliana were both gone, but the mirror had become a doorway. She said the door was open and that she felt impelled to walk through it."

Danny and Zelia were listening intently to Brigid Mago, but she herself seemed mystified at this point. She held up her arms to indicate that that was all Angela had managed to tell her.

At this point Angela excitedly took over the telling of her experience herself. Using the private language that had been built up in the intimacy of the family she told how she had stepped through the door and was with Danny in the Cathedral. Danny watched his sister's movements, translating them in his own mind. It was as if the delightfully giggling Angela who modeled as Our Lady for the Florentines was talking.

"...And you didn't recognize me. It was a wonderful game, wondering when you'd realize it was me, but you were so intent on your work there . . . and all those strange, wonderful men . . . and getting me to model for Our Lady.

"When the door appeared again I knew I had to step back into it. I arrived back in my bedroom. Almost immediately the door wasn't there anymore, only the mirror, and I could see that I was the same crooked old marionette that I have always been, but that didn't make me sad. It didn't make me sad at all, because while I had been modeling for Mary, I had seen clearly how things would be in heaven, and it is impossible to be sad after that. Anyway, I could stand up by myself, and even walk, sort of. I woke Mother and told her everything, and we both laughed and cried and walked together. Then we rang a taxi and came here to the Cathedral because she said you would be sure to be here."

"I can't keep up with all these wonders," said Brigid Mago. Then she added, almost as a *non sequitur,* "I've only now realized that much of that painting, all the native bush anyway, is identical with your father's work. That waterfall among the ferns is the same as the painting above the fireplace. Look—

there! Do you think somehow his spirit had something to do with it?"

Angela was about to explain to her mother, in her eccentric fashion, but Danny hugged his sister and kissed her before cutting in with, "Yes, Mum. I reckon Dad must have had something do with that painting. Probably more than we'll ever know. But right now we've got to figure out what to do about saving the . . ."

He abandoned his sentence before even reaching a comma, because the two sisters who had been kneeling near the coffin were suddenly among them at the side altar. Neither the Magos nor Zelia had paid the veiled, kneeling figures enough attention to recognize Sister Eileen and Sister Paula. Now that they were close, it was clear that the sisters had been crying, but the peace in their eyes told that their tears were as much tears of the joy of holy resignation as of sorrow.

With an abrupt laugh Sister Eileen said, "She's gone, but she has certainly left a medley of mysteries in her wake. This magnificent mural," she waved her arm towards the retaining wall behind the altar. "The cloak! How did it get here? How did it get into the painting?"

"Well . . ." Danny opened his mouth to speak, but no words came. He looked like a swimmer poised to dive from the banks of the Hellespont. It was all too vast and complicated for conversational reporting.

"Why don't we all go back to Aniwaniwa and talk about it over lunch," suggested the ever-practical Sister Paula.

"Excellent idea!"

All six of them knelt for a moment's prayer, and after an obeisance towards the coffin, walked down the nave past the people queued to pay their respects (meanwhile gazing wide-eyed at the great fresco) and out into the summer sunlight.

The Cathedral precinct was still crowded with people and

THE WEKA-FEATHER CLOAK

the clergy and the Knights of Columbus were organizing the mourners and the curious. A way was made for them through to the street. On Lambton Quay they discussed transport to the Hutt Valley. Zelia insisted that Brigid Mago and Angela go with the Sisters in the Magos' Ford and that she and Danny would follow in the train. She was uncharacteristically insistent and even before anyone had answered, she was crossing the street, pulling Danny after her, which rather precluded any discussion of the matter.

"The Mandylion," she whispered nervously. "The Mandylion is still on the ship. It's in the cabin closet. We must retrieve it somehow."

"Retrieve it," Danny repeated as he shuffled to keep in step with her and thinking, absurdly, of a dog chasing a stick.

As they turned down a side street towards the docks, a car screeched to a halt on Lambton Quay, reversed rapidly, then wheeled towards them, butting its nose right up onto the pavement alongside them. They barely had time to register the maneuver before the car doors were swung open and they were being forced inside.

"Don't thank me," said an oily Ferhat Ferhat as the bully boy driver jerked the vehicle back onto the street and concentrated his weight on the accelerator. "Only too willing to oblige."

They reached the ship in a matter of moments, but instead of making for the main gangway the driver zigzagged between containers and warehouses to a nearby dock and the entire party was crowded into one of the *Montezuma's* jolly boats. From there they were taken around to the far side of the *Montezuma,* out of sight of the shore, and made to climb aboard by means of a rope ladder.

Danny and Zelia were taken to the lower deck and bundled into the same cabin they had been in before, the one allotted to Claude. Ferhat Ferhat, leering like a cat who has a mouse at its mercy, took the key from the door and locked it from the outside. He stationed a bully boy there and another on the outer deck to watch the port windows.

Celebrations were already underway on board. Journalists, national and foreign, had already sent their copy in—*Magnate's Artist Son Scoops the Millions, Claude Culls the Cash,* etc—and had arrived early to wave their invitations at the stewards, who had taken up their position at the foot of the gangway. Journalists have a universal need to get fed and to crack champagne before crowds arrive.

They dropped the lugs and opened the window—the lookout bully boy was some distance along the deck, chatting to a group of females—and on the quay beyond they could see that Sir William Kydd and Claude had arrived as they themselves were being brought round to the starboard side on the jolly boat. It was clear, too, that a press conference was about to begin.

A great number of people had collected on the quayside, people who didn't have invitations to the celebratory party aboard the *M.V. Montezuma,* but who were content to keep a critical eye on those who did. Car after car arrived to disgorge influential folk dressed for a day's cruising in Wellington Harbour and in the Sounds across the Cook Strait. Yet the talk among the people, at least that which carried from the quay to the cabin level with it, had little to do with maritime recreation, but a lot to do with the mysterious fresco on the wall of the crystal Cathedral. As there had been no official announcement about the winner of the *Reredos Lampadephoria,* and no $10,000,000 check awarded, the celebrations seemed premature, if not, indeed, flat. But the onlookers on the quay were not jealous of the guests, or malicious in their questioning of the politics of the arrangements, no matter how loudly they expressed those questions.

The Press personnel on the quay put the people's questions bluntly to Kydd and Claude. Kydd was the very epitome of diplomatic urbanity. He smiled at the press like an indulgent benefactor and explained, "His Eminence, overcome as he was by the emotion of the moment, simply neglected to make the announcement. However I can assure you, ladies, gentlemen, all, that the work of young Claude von Blumenkohl here is the committee's unanimous choice to win the *Lampadephoria*. Mr. Odo von Blumenkohl himself, who by coincidence is also the artist's father, has already touched down at Wellington International and will be arriving here on the *M.V. Montezuma's* own helicopter pad in a very short while to present the prize check on behalf of and—I stress this, and trust you gentlemen of the press will too—with the full permission and blessing of the Cardinal."

"But, Sir William, what about the fresco that appeared without human explanation on the Cathedral wall . . ."

Presenting his smiling, long-suffering face, Sir William brushed an insect from his collar. "Impudent graffiti!" he explained. "Electronic chicanery! Of no consequence. Easily erased!"

"But the Cardinal himself has been quoted as saying that it is a work of such merit as to stand comparison with anything in the Vatican."

"No further questions . . ."

Sir William strode up the gangway with the confidence of a general who has just accepted an enemy's surrender. Less than ten minutes later the crew let go the mooring ropes, and the engines, which had been on stand-bye, snorted into life. The *M.V. Montezuma,* proud as a young cockerel and raucous with revelers, swung slowly into the harbor.

At much the same time, the heads and shoulders of Myers, Duffy and Pascal appeared framed in the open window of the captives' cabin. They now wore the starched white jackets of ship waiters instead of the overalls of removal men.

"I say, Mago, this is a bit rum, isn't it, you back aboard and under guard. What are we to deduce from such a scenario? Not stowing away, are you?" They couldn't resist the spurious English accents, even here in this adult setting during the school holidays.

"Listen, you fellas, our lives are in danger. I can't explain it now, but you've got to believe me. If you'll just suspend the classroom antics for the time being and do as I ask, I guarantee you'll be national heroes in all tomorrow's papers."

"Oh bonza!" exclaimed Pascal. "I say, chaps. Wouldn't it be a hoot to be national heroes?"

"Rather ripping really . . ."

They were interrupted by the sound of determined feet descending the companionway.

With sound intuition Zelia said, "It's Kydd!"

"Everything I say from now on is false."

"Danny, whatever are you . . . ?"

"Don't question. We haven't time. Just believe . . . everything I say is a whopping great, enormous, absolutely horrendous hoax. Quick, the curtains."

Zelia hastily drew the curtain across the window box, blocking out the faces of the wide-eyed trio, as Sir William Kydd and Ferhat Ferhat unlocked the door and stepped into the room. Ferhat Ferhat shut the door and stood with his back against it.

Kydd spoke. The fever of a thwarted will was beginning to show through the studied suavity. Hate and vengeance were locked in his eyes. He spoke rapidly. "I have had enough of this nonsense. I don't know what tricks your people are playing with that wretched cartoon appearing on the back wall of the church—a holograph I suppose. Clever, but not clever enough. At the moment your lives are in my hands. I want the Mandylion and I want it now. Unless you hand it over I will dispose of you with the same efficiency as I disposed of Qetik Mamoulian."

"So you *did* kill Qetik," said Zelia softly.

"I proposed, and my trusted aide here, Boris Abladavich, disposed." Ferhat Ferhat was clearly pleased to have the master refer to him in his assumed Russian persona. To show his solidarity with the cause of Kydd, the toothy Levantine drew a pistol from somewhere inside his jacket. Neither Danny nor Zelia had ever seen a real gun close up before. It was an extremely ugly instrument—implacably, soullessly arrogant, as menacing as the demons in the elevator.

"You are evil, Abu Kyed," Zelia still spoke softly, but her words were intense and sincere. "I would rather die than have the Mandylion desecrated by so much as a glance from your foul eyes."

Danny cleared his throat and took two steps forward, distancing himself from Zelia to stand almost alongside Ferhat Ferhat.

"You speak for yourself, Zelia. I'm not playing the martyr for a handful of colored cards." Was that really Danny's voice? "Let the gentleman see them before we're all slaughtered where we stand."

With reluctant obedience, Zelia fetched the cards up from the pocket of her cardigan and handed them to Sir William. Danny gave a brief history of the cards and pointed out their encrypted peculiarities. They had only just solved the puzzle, he told Kydd. The Mandylion had been hidden all the time in the lining of the Weka-Feather Cloak.

"The Weka-Feather Cloak . . . what is the Weka-Feather Cloak?"

"It was part of the regalia of the Maori chiefs. The particular one that hid the Mandylion is now covering the body of Mother Madeleine in her coffin in the new Cathedral."

"How was the Mandylion hidden in the Cloak?"

"It was secured in an ancient silver reliquary, sprinkled with tiny jewels and lined with silk and damask. This was encased in a red envelope which was laced around the edges."

This description rang true with Kydd.

Above the ship a buzz like a bees' jamboree grew louder and louder. Ferhat Ferhat opened the door and announced that the helicopter was approaching. Kydd said that Danny was to come with them. Ferhat Ferhat pressed the butt of his pistol into the small of Danny's back. The door was locked behind them.

Myers parted the curtains of the port window. His face bore the marks of a witness to intrigue. "Wow!" He exclaimed, "This is like the movies."

Zelia asked what the guard who was supposed to be watching the windows was doing. Pascal said he was OK. He was talking to some women at the other end of the deck. He'd told Pascal that a mad dog had bitten the people in the cabin, and they were there to see that those people didn't try to fling themselves out of the window.

Duffy asked, "What can we do to help?"

"Get me a pair of pliers," said Zelia. This mission took some minutes, but Spotted Duffy returned with the tool. Zelia went into the bedroom and closed the door. Pascal had gone off to spy on Kydd and Ferhat Ferhat, and Myers was moving back and forth, between the open area for'ard and the deck housing, to report on the landing of the helicopter.

# 41

===

## *The Battle for the Mandylion*

KYDD AND Ferhat Ferhat with a captive Danny joined Claude by the helicopter pad just as the noisy, turbulent machine touched down. Even before the rotors had spun to a standstill, the great Odo von Blumenkohl had jumped to the deck. He had spotted Claude on the welcoming dais just below the elevated pad and ran to embrace him.

What Claude saw in his father's eye, in his expansive smile, in his very gait, was something he had never encountered before. It showed a human side of Odo that probably even Odo didn't know he had, and it certainly laid flat the defenses that an emotionally cold childhood had erected around Claude.

Odo kissed his son on both cheeks, then held him at arm's length to admire this reproduction of himself. "You won this thing all on your ownsome—that's the kind of boy that makes a father burst at the seams with pride."

"Well, Danny here did help," said Claude.

"Danny!" Odo swooped up the young artist's hand and jerked it vigorously. "You cheered on my boy! Consider yourself family, Danny, family."

Odo's eye fell on the preoccupied Kydd. "Sir William. Faithful agent. Good to see you. Good indeed. Did you arrange

248

all this?" His arms opened to encompass the ship, the sea, the very sun in the sky itself. "Splendid! Splendid!"

As the group moved to the glassed-off lounge area, much enhanced by the elegant Tera Whare furniture, William Kydd, whose agitation was becoming more pronounced by the minute, whispered urgently to Ferhat Ferhat, who nodded with the eagerness of a fiend who has been introduced to a new sin, and slipped off to a lower deck. Pascal, relishing his role as spy, followed at a distance of about three fathoms, which seemed appropriate for marine espionage.

Then Sir William Kydd cornered Danny. In a tense, decisive tone he said that together they would take the helicopter ashore to retrieve the Cloak. If they had not returned within two hours, Zelia would freeze to death in the meat room below decks. Ferhat Ferhat was seeing to it at that very moment.

"No sweat," said Danny, smiling sunnily. "We can be there and back in twenty minutes. Why didn't you tell me that the old Mandything was what you wanted? Though I can't think why. It's only an old bit of painted wood with some colored stones around the frame. Give me a shout when you're ready. It would never do to let the poor little Turkish girl catch cold in the meat room."

Odo was proclaiming on the glories of the visual arts. Sir William Kydd paused in the midst of his intrigues to ask curtly if he'd care to fly ashore briefly to see his son's prize-winning entry before presenting the check. Odo, who had just been handed a dry Martini, declined with uncharacteristic graciousness, saying that it would be a delight in store.

Kydd, taking Danny with him, went off to find the helicopter pilot. Claude pointed out the spot where the plane he had been a passenger in had crashed just two months before. It was that contingency that brought him to New Zealand, Claude added.

"Sheer . . . sheer . . . sheer . . ." Odo looked to the martini waiter to supply a word.

"Serendipity," that functionary suggested.

"Sheer serendipity," Odo repeated expansively and Claude marveled at this new, almost genial, father who went on to greet the more important of the guests who were converging on the lounge to meet him. Of course, Claude had no way of knowing that, under certain conditions, the fate of children can have a civilizing effect even on the most bull-headed of parents.

Pascal followed Ferhat Ferhat back to the cabin which held the captives. He didn't descend the companionway, but doubled round and took the open stairs down to the lower deck. Myers and Duffy were no longer there, and the guards had left off chatting to the female guests and were answering Ferhat Ferhat's call on their mobile phones. Through the port window he could see Zelia being led out of the cabin. Alert and in spying mode as he was, it seemed to Pascal that they turned right in the alleyway upon leaving the cabin, and not left, which would have taken them up the companionway.

Retracing his steps, and picking up a tray with a few used glasses on it en route, Pascal crept down the companionway in time to see one of Ferhat Ferhat's men opening the fire-door at the end of the alleyway. When he had it swung back on its hinges, another heavy door, the opening mechanism of which was a large steel wheel, stood immediately in front of them. A narrow alleyway ran athwartships between these two doors. One of the thugs spun the wheel till a green light above the door turned to red and the door itself opened ponderously like the access to a bank vault. Blankets of icy air, like frozen steam, billowed out to chill the alleyway. Inside, butchers' carcasses hung from meat-hooks among the mists, and boxes thick with ice crystals were piled against the walls. The accelerated hum of refrigeration machinery issued from the bowels of the room like some ghastly dirge.

Zelia had no time to consider what was happening. She was bustled inside and the doors slammed shut before she had time to register fear or to protest.

Ferhat Ferhat spun the wheel until the light above the door turned green, then, opening the glass panel on the regulating box, turned the temperature down from -4°C to -8°C.

With smirks of cruel satisfaction the men stepped back into the accommodation alleyway and closed the fire door. Ferhat Ferhat didn't notice the handsome steward with the drinks tray as he made for the companionway, nor did the bully boys as they settled down to the tedium of standing guard to ensure that no one entered or left by the fire door.

Pascal felt there was something askew here as he juggled with the unfamiliar tray, some aspect of marine architecture that didn't align with logic. Surely any ship's cook, requiring provisions from the meat room wouldn't have to negotiate guest accommodation and open a fire door to access it. The mystery taxed him as he made for the upper deck to find Myers and Duffy.

Straightaway he caught sight of them, but they were some distance away, near the steps leading to the helicopter pad. Pascal stepped onto a small bollard in an attempt to attract their attention, and, as he did so, a rather cool-looking Danny passed in front of his two schoolfellows with a fiercely determined Sir William and the helicopter pilot.

At that moment Danny seemed to drop something and he and Myers and Duffy all swooped at the same time to retrieve it. Kydd saw nothing of this because he was occupied with giving instructions to the pilot, but Pascal observed that Danny was whispering to Myers and Duffy, communicating a message of some urgency by the concentration on all three faces.

As Danny and Kydd and the pilot approached the helicopter, the two waiters dodged through the guests and motioned to Pascal who was still standing on the bollard.

After a carefully nonchalant look over his shoulder, Myers quickly whispered, "Danny says there's something we've got to find and then protect from that crook, Kydd; something Zelia has hidden in the cabin where they were held prisoner. Even worse, though, he says Kydd has had Zelia put into the . . ."

"Yes, I know where he's put Zelia. I was just coming for you. Listen, you look in the cabin. I've got an idea about Zelia." Myers and Duffy were already moving away from the debonair young waiter, who was adroitly turning in the opposite direction as if to offer his tray to a passing guest.

Their hands clutching the polished metal railings of the companionway, Myers and Duffy slid down without once touching the steps with their feet. The guards at the end of the alleyway looked at them vacantly, as they entered the cabin allotted to Claude. Once inside they hastily shut the door and started a frantic search. It did not take them long to find and remove the laced leather envelope from the cabinet. However, before they could even think about a new hiding place, a noise made them both turn toward the doorway. A fiendishly smiling Ferhat Ferhat stood in the open door with his hand extended.

*           ◎           *

The engine of the helicopter deafened the guests temporarily as it limbered up for flight, and soon the machine was swinging out to starboard and then falling away gracefully towards the stern.

Kydd sat with the pilot at the controls. Danny was standing in the small open cargo space at the rear of the cockpit, clinging with both hands to an overhead transom, staring directly down into the water beneath. When Ferhat Ferhat phoned Kydd via the mobile, all the increasingly jumpy knight could understand was, "I got it. I got it." He told the pilot to veer round and drop close to the after-rails. Then he left his seat and went back into the cargo space. Below, by the after flag-pole, hair careering wildly in the strong thrust of the whirling rotor blades, were two waiters being tightly held by bully boys and Ferhat Ferhat, now standing in their midst, holding aloft something for his inspection.

Danny said, "Oh, no! How did he get *that!*"

Kydd was frantic. "Get what? What is it? It's the Mandylion, isn't it?" Kydd grasped Danny by the neck of his shirt. "It is, isn't it?" The misery of Danny's face at the misfire of his hurried diversionary plan told Sir William all he needed to know.

"You'll have to go down for it."

Kydd had no intention of facing the discovery of Zelia's body locked in the meat room, or if she was found alive, her witness to his admission that he had killed Qetik Mamoulian. As it was, he'd be cutting it fine to get a flight out of the country before the police got wind of his criminal activities. Kydd had found the salvage hoist attachment in the cargo space, and, with the authority of the gun, was overseeing Danny securing the harness around himself. Foregoing any preliminary niceties, Kydd shoved Danny, who fell a meter or so beneath the belly of the helicopter.

Ferhat Ferhat was suddenly struggling with the waiters, who had apparently twisted free, for the possession of the reliquary envelope. Kydd took the pistol out from under his belt and fired a shot, which hit the winch casing with a metallic ping. This convinced Myers and Duffy to let go of the envelope. Ferhat Ferhat, seeing what Kydd was about, looped a boat hook through one of the lace bindings and held it up towards the helicopter. There were several meters between the envelope and Danny's grasp.

The noise of the helicopter hovering around the stern of the ship, coupled with the ping of the pistol shot, brought the guests flocking from the open decks above to see what was going on beneath the awning which covered the afterdeck.

Odo, seated in the VIP lounge, stopped a passing officer to inquire what the commotion was about. The officer said the captain had sent him to investigate, so Odo and Claude accompanied him. The officer cleared a path through the inquisitive and the curious beneath the awning. As Danny swung there, Kydd tried to work the salvage hoist's winch, but he only managed to drop Danny a further meter into space. Ferhat Ferhat had straddled the flagpole and was inching out along it till the envelope on the end of the boat hook was within Danny's reach.

After several tries—he was swinging rather widely and was battered and blinded by the upthrusts generated by the rotors—Danny managed to grasp the envelope containing the reliquary. Kydd, as if possessed by some malign spirit, suddenly screamed, in a voice that over-rode the racket made by the helicopter, "THE FACE WILL NEVER BE SEEN! THE FACE WILL NEVER BE SEEN!" Then he threw himself on the hoist, making Danny swing in even wilder arcs as he was jerked upward. Sir William threw himself on the deck of the cargo space, stretching towards the envelope with his free hand and trying to clutch the wire of Danny's hoist with the other, which still held the pistol.

Odo, who had pushed his way to the rails of the afterdeck, shouted a barrage of indignation at Kydd, demanded that he stop making a spectacle of himself and come to his senses. Odo would have said more, too, but suddenly he crumpled to the deck.

Kydd's entire concentration had been on the envelope. Stretching his arm to its utmost, he had just managed to snatch the envelope from Danny's hand as the gun discharged and the bullet hit Odo von Blumenkohl. Kydd himself slid from the cargo hold and catapulted seawards like a jettisoned sack of flour. Simultaneously Ferhat Ferhat, startled by the sound of the firearm, fell from his precarious perch on the flagpole so that both Levantines hit the water together.

Fortunately most people on the afterdeck were too stunned by the shooting of Odo to observe the fountains of reddened water as the two bodies were caught in the whirling blades of the ship's twin propellers. Danny, dangling in space, saw the awful carnage and would have been physically sick except for the realization that the envelope which held the reliquary and the Mandylion had been in Kydd's hand as he'd fallen and that now they, too, must be lost forever.

The horror of acknowledging that, in this case, evil had won the day, that the satanic prophecy that THE FACE WOULD NEVER BE SEEN had been so painfully realized before his very eyes, induced a gloom that threatened to swamp his consciousness.

The helicopter swung out starboard of the ship, then nosed back to the landing pad, to place Danny neatly on his feet and give him time to shed the harness of the safety hoist and make a dash for a lower deck before the pilot brought the machine gently onto its markings.

Just before these tragic events unfolded on the afterdeck, Pascal had been playing the sleuth. On a framed plan of the vessel in the foyer he discovered that the galley was aft of the lower accommodation alleyway. The meat room, marked as *Meat, Fruit, Veg Cold Store* on the plan, was in the athwartships alleyway beyond the fire door. That much he knew, but—and this was the happy consequence of his investigation—the main access to the alleyway was direct from the galley, the ship's kitchen. So it was to this area that Pascal made his way.

Some six or seven women, each looking like a chef with white pudding hats and white aprons, were gathered around a workbench, assembling buffet dishes from baskets of prepared food.

"Not yet!" they said dismissively to Pascal. "We'll let you know when we're ready."

Pascal made a quick reconnoiter of the galley. Apart from the deck access through which he had entered, there were three other doors. He knew from the plan in the foyer that one would be the bakery, one the dry stores and the other the alleyway with the refrigerated rooms, but which was which?

Pascal walked towards the doors, which again prompted a chorus of cooks telling him that he was off bounds and that he was to get out of the galley.

He turned and faced the women. If there was one thing the handsome Pascal had learned in his short life, it was how to employ his singularly pleasing features to advantage. And among his repertoire of smiles was his *innocent-confused-youth-in-desperate-need-of-mothering special*—a real jackpot, reserved only for the most serious of predicaments.

"Captain's orders," he said, and then smiled this never-known-to-fail smile. "He wants you to search the meat room. He has had information from ashore that someone might have been accidentally locked in there."

Cooks tumbled over one another to oblige the charming emissary of the Captain himself, and within a minute an extremely cold young woman was being ushered into the warmth of the galley. She looked like a grandmother with white hair; her arms were crossed over her upper chest as if frozen there, and her fists were clutching the corners of her cardigan. Cups of tea from a pot on the hot plate and the vigorous attentions of the cooks thawed her somewhat and she managed, with Pascal's ready assistance, to walk towards the afterdeck to discover the cause of the noise and commotion that was coming from there.

They stepped beneath the awning just in time to witness the shooting of Odo and the frenzied and inelegant behavior of Sir William Kydd, followed by the plunge to death of both him and his deplorable henchman, Ferhat Ferhat, who also liked to be known in New Zealand as Boris Abladavich, but who would probably never be remembered or spoken of by any name, by anyone, ever again. Amen.

Neither Zelia nor Pascal took more than a secondary notice of these events. Their whole concern was for Danny, suspended in mid air beneath the noisy, whirling, hovering machine. When it dipped away from the vessel and then circled to bring Danny back to the pad, they ran to the upper decks to greet him. Pascal joined Myers and Duffy in slapping his back in recognition of his bravery, and Zelia, though clearly moved by the same emotion, yet stood back a little from the group.

Danny had no need to wonder at Zelia's reticence. He was overcome with shame and sorrow. He couldn't look her in the eye. The Mandylion had been lost. Forever. And it was his fault. In the instant it took for the falling Kydd to grab it from his hand, 2000 years of concentrated care and protection of the sacred object had been negated. He, Danny Mago, had allowed the only authentic contemporary portrait of Christ to plunge with that evil obsessive into the destructive blades of the *M.V. Montezuma* as into the very pit of hell itself.

Suddenly, he was pushed to one side as ship's officers forced a path to the helicopter pad. They were followed by stretcher-bearers, and Claude, and by a man who kept shouting that he was a doctor and that everyone was to make way. The Generalissimo was still alive, but it was imperative to get him to the hospital at once. Danny's last sight of Claude was as he gently helped maneuver the stretcher into place in the same cargo platform just abandoned by Danny.

# 42

New Year's Eve Supper
at Aniwaniwa

FOR THE rest of the day grief was curtailed by chaos. After the violent deaths the mood among the passengers was to return to the quay. But the protagonists in the drama didn't manage to get ashore till evening because there was a continual procession of newspapermen, police, TV cameras, all wanting statements, opinions, details lurid or enlightening. Danny had been befriended by the Captain, who allowed him and Zelia, along with Myers and Pascal and Duffy, to be interviewed by the media in the civilized surroundings of his day room.

Late in the afternoon a message came aboard for them from the practical and efficient Sister Eileen, who had been following the news on television. She had contacted the Cardinal, who in turn had contacted the Captain through the ship's agents. And so, as that remarkable day was dying, Danny and Zelia and their school fellows found themselves in two cars heading towards Aniwaniwa. Somehow Zelia was taken in a police car by a group of friendly policemen (Danny could understand why she wouldn't want to ride with him now; indeed, he wondered whether she could ever bring herself to speak to him again), while he himself was in the other with Myers, Duffy and Pascal.

Counterbalancing the deep gloom he felt over failing Zelia,

Danny was compelled to revise his opinion of these three. Their conduct throughout the day had been so admirable, so helpful with the police, so polite with the press, so without self-aggrandizement when the cameras were focused on them, that Danny found himself looking forward to a new school term distinguished by equality and mutual respect.

"I smell a maggot," said Duffy as Danny Mago stepped into the car. "Do you smell a maggot, Myers? Pascal? A maggot?"

The boys addressed raised their heads and sniffed the air like hounds at hunt. "Some decomposing matter, certainly," said Myers.

"Decidedly off," was Pascal's contribution. "Positive putrefaction!"

They kept the badinage up all the way to Nae Nae, gasping, beseeching the driver to open all windows, and even telephoning a local radio station on Myers' mobile to ask advice on the extermination of objectionable larva. At that moment, in his gloom, Danny felt like he deserved it all.

At the convent the ribbing suddenly stopped, and the boys reverted to being the pleasant, sociable fellows they had been since Danny had given them Claude's tip in the morning. It was a psychology that puzzled Danny until some voice of intuition, or perhaps his angel hovering in the invisible world, suggested that they had never known how to treat him, that no one had ever taught them how to treat an equal whose destiny, they divined, was incomparably greater than theirs. Habit had given them a defensive limb that only time could atrophy. All he could do was put up with it until that happened.

Brigid and Angela were waiting with the Sisters on the Aniwaniwa steps along with Zelia. To Danny's greater surprise, so was Claude. He said that he had been able to leave his father, who, though still in critical condition, had stabilized.

Together they all moved towards the convent parlor. The

Sisters had been delighted with the change in Angela and were still intrigued by the fact that, when they discovered Mother Madeleine's portrait of her, its oils still wet in Danny's studio, it depicted her as being a fully able young woman. They had brought it back to the parlor, and Angela now stood silent in front of the portrait of herself, not for the first time since she and her mother had come up to be with the Sisters. There was no surprise, or anger, or resentment at the sight of the beautiful and healthy representation of herself that she saw. Indeed, the sight of it brought a smile to her contorted features, a smile of such gentleness and contentment that everyone there felt their spirits lift. As Sister Paula said later, "I had the peculiar feeling that the Blessed Virgin herself was confiding some very special secret to Angela, something that God had given to be shared just between the two of them."

The table in the convent dining room was large and circular. After Grace there were no formalities. Food was passed around and conversation was, unavoidably, on the day's events. The Sisters were still absorbing the fact that Mother Madeleine was no longer with them. They were familiar with the dramatic happenings in the Cathedral and on the *M. V. Montezuma* because there had been nothing else on the radio or the television or the lips of anyone they had come across since midday.

Presently Claude surprised Danny by saying, "I just learned today that for these past couple of months my father was plotting and scheming for me to win the Reredos and it happened . . . and yet it all happened without any reference to him whatsoever—my flight to Chile crashing here, my *Kiwi Christ* winning. . . ."

"My *Kiwi Christ*," said Danny. If this was a moment of truth, he wasn't going to let falsehoods become entrenched without a challenge.

"They say you see your whole life pass before you as you die," Claude said very soberly. "Well, I saw all my father's life as that bullet hit him, and it was far from beautiful. His selfishness, his money-grabbing, his manipulation of people, they were all there, and yet, you know, there was something else too. In the center of all there was a precious, indestructible little core of pure light, as simple and as innocent as the infant God, which survived unadulterated. Perhaps his conscience, even when wallowing in the extremes of selfishness, never quite consented to the stifling of that.

"I mostly despised him until today. Now, I can't tell you how grateful I am that maybe I'll have another chance with him. The doctors aren't sure whether he will come out of the coma or not, or if he does, how much brain damage there'll be, but I can tell you, I plan to stick with him. He's not lovable, but maybe I'm the only person alive who has any reason to love him."

The Sisters and their guests were silent, some wondering if this complete turn around of attitude was not perhaps the greatest miracle of all. After a few quiet moments Sister Paula asked him if anyone had told him how he stood as the *Lampadephoria* prize-winner, now that powers beyond human explanation seemed to have taken the decoration of the wall behind the altar into their own hands. Danny laughed, and said it hardly mattered, now that Claude probably was in line to manage one of the largest fortunes in the world. Claude surprised Danny, indeed, he surprised everybody, by admitting that the painting he had entered was actually Danny's and that he intended to make sure the rightful winner received the bag of gold, whether as a check from the brewery or from his own funds.

Danny didn't protest. "That's fair," he said. Angela thought it was terribly funny and Brigid Mago almost fainted.

Danny couldn't look Zelia in the eye. In her regard, he

couldn't have felt guiltier if her entire family had been found dead in their beds and he was proved to be responsible. This day, which was the high point of his life, even if he lived to be 90,—what with his, and Fra Angelico's and Benozzo's etc, fresco already causing a world-wide sensation, and his *Kiwi Christ* canvas actually winning the *Lampadephoria,*—on this day, when he could be excused for being giddy with glory, all he wanted to do was crawl away somewhere and weep and wait for death to knock and offer blessed relief. It had been hard for him even to look at her all evening.

Almost as if in response to his thoughts, the talk turned to the magnificent face of Christ that had appeared on the wall. The Sisters had all seen it during the afternoon when they had gone into Wellington to pay their respects to the sorely missed Mother of their community, whose body was still lying in state in the Cathedral aisle, wrapped in the Weka-Feather Cloak. Particularly uncanny, they said, was what appeared to be a representation of the same cloak covering the shoulders of Our Lady standing at the prow of the Maori canoe. Inevitably the Sisters wanted to know what Danny and Zelia had tactfully resisted divulging to the press all afternoon—what was it that the unhappy Sir William Kydd had been so anxious to get his hands on, when he was leaning from the helicopter, and had taken with him to his gory death.

Danny muttered something about it being confidential, something between Zelia's family and Kydd's. They had been neighbors in Zelia's middle-eastern town, he said, all rather personal.

The questioners accepted this, but Zelia contradicted him. She said that she wanted the Sisters to know, and that Claude and the boys deserved an explanation, as they had all been part of the unfolding of the climax. She would tell the story, if all present promised to not let it go beyond the convent walls.

And that is what she did. With one hand clutching at her throat as if she was still feeling the cold of the *Montezuma's* freezer, Zelia told the story, all of it, from the mission of the envoy of the King of Edessa, through Uncle Zeki's journey and death, right on to the discovery of the Sacred Heirloom in the lining of the Weka-Feather Cloak. She omitted nothing but the elevator.

When it came to Danny's part in losing his grip on the envelope containing the Mandylion reliquary, he flushed with shame. No one, least of all Zelia, accused him. It was clear that his motives, even when he feigned indifference, were untarnished by self-interest, that he had done his best to lead Sir William off the scent of the Mandylion, but he felt that, had his sense of decision and purpose been greater, the Mandylion could have been saved. As it was, Kydd and the demons had triumphed. The face would never be seen—well, on the Cathedral wall, yes, but not the original, not the picture that Christ himself had modeled for, which Christ himself had endorsed by passing his hand over and injecting with his own life.

Even if Zelia didn't seem as concerned about the loss of the Mandylion as he was, Danny was convinced that everything had ended in death—death and failure. He really was the maggot—putrid, abominable.

Spotted Duffy leaned across the table towards Zelia. He said, "What puzzles me is why you asked for a pair of pliers, you remember, through the porthole. What did you want pliers for?"

Zelia's eyes were almost violet, and she gave a little laugh. "The plug in the sink," she said. "I needed the pliers to disconnect the chain that attached the plug to the sink."

"Why?"

Zelia took her hand from her throat. She undid the top but-

tons of her cardigan. Then, feeling for the chain which encir-
cled her neck, she drew it over her head. The center link was
twisted through the upper part of the filigree gold work that
surrounded the piece of light, waxed, oval wood on which was
painted the face that could melt hearts with its glance.

She lay it on the table and moved it gently into a clear space.
All eyes were fixed on the portrait. Some gasped. Some sighed.
Angela emitted a cry of pure, crystalline joy. Claude made a
strange whistling sound. Sister Paula wept. No two people's
reaction was the same. Perhaps each saw something slightly
different, but one thing was certain, they all, adults, girls and
boys gazed wordlessly at the Face painted on the Mandylion
for the very long time that Zelia left it in the center of the
table. And furthermore, I suspect, it is quite possible that each
individual would have been rapturously content to have
remained there gazing at the Face all night—or, indeed, for the
rest of eternity.

As for Danny, his face was aglow as he lifted his eyes to meet
those of a radiant Zelia. He couldn't help but remember
another scene around a judge's table, a moment in a future
New Year's Eve, already viewed, though briefly, from the security of an angel's wing, and reckoned that, with the connivance
of that angel, his earthly happiness could be complete indeed.

# *Author's Note*

 ALL CHARACTERS in this book are fictitious
except the angels. Personalities such as Julian of
Norwich, Giovanni da Fiesole (Fra Angelico) and
his brother Benedetto, Benozzo Gozzoli, Zanobi
Strozzi, the emissary of the King of Edessa, the Turkish Pashas
and Sultans, and Edward Jerningham Wakefield have been
respectfully borrowed from history, and replaced.

The existence of the Mandylion, pronounced to rhyme with
pavilion, is so strong in tradition that there is a possibility that
it did, and does, exist. A number of sites throughout the world,
including the Vatican and Buckingham Palace, harbor an item
which enthusiasts claim to be the original. Be that as it may,
the Christ, whose portrait it is, dwells in all the tabernacles of
the world and may be visited at any time.

The building called here the Convent of St. Martin de Porres
is a real building, still standing on its hillside in Nae Nae in the
Hutt Valley near Wellington, the capital city of New Zealand.
The Duthie family, who had a hardware business in Wellington,
built it towards the end of the 19th century. In 1915 it was sold
to the Sisters of Mercy, who used it as an orphanage for boys
disadvantaged by the First World War. It later extended from
the hillside house to school and farmhouses in the plain below.
It was called St. Thomas' Boys' Home and continued into the mid-
fifties when the sisters sold the property and moved. The lower
school is now a built-up suburban housing estate. The splendid
old house is no longer a convent, but is now called Balgownie
House, and is being well preserved in private hands.

# Glossary

## NATIVE WORDS

**aniwaniwa** — rainbow

**Aotearoa** — original Maori name for New Zealand. It means "The land of the Long White Cloud."

**haka** — a Maori war dance and chant.

**Hawaiiki** — the Polynesian spirit world. In Maori lore all souls travelled there after death via the northernmost part of the land.

**kahikatea** — a native New Zealand tree or wood from same.

**katipo** — a venomous, black New Zealand spider with red back markings; a form of Black Widow.

**kauri** — a native New Zealand. tree or wood from same.

**kauri gum** — a commercially valuable resin from the kauri tree.

**Kiwi** — an apteryx, a native, flightless, nocturnal New Zealand bird. Also a nickname given to any person or thing from New Zealand.

**kohekohe** — a native New Zealand tree or wood from same.

**Maori** — the Polynesians who settled in New Zealand.

**Ngati** — A tribe, so Ngati Tawa would be the Tawa Tribe.

**Nae Nae** — An area on the eastern side of the Hutt Valley.

**Paekakariki** — a beach town on the west coast, north of Wellington.

**Pa** — a Maori village.

**Pakeha** — the Maori word used in New Zealand for a white man.

**paua** — a type of edible shellfish, an abalone.

**Petone** — the beach front area of the Hutt valley.

Ponga--a native fern tree.

**pohutukawa** — New Zealand evergreen tree which produces clusters of red stamens at Christmas time.

**pounamu** — greenstone, nephrite prized as a decorative pendant and as a weapon or tool head.

**pukeko** — a purplish swamp hen about the size of a pheasant.

**rimu** — A native tree.

**Te Arawa & Te Awanui** — names of two of the original canoes that are said to have brought the original Polynesian settlers to New Zealand a thousand years ago.

**Te Ati Awa** — a Maori tribe from the Wellington area.

**tiki** — an embryo-like image used as an ornament, usually made of greenstone.

**toheroa soup** — Toheroa is a shellfish which makes an exquisite soup.

**towai** — a native New Zealand tree or wood from same.

**unaunahi** — a characteristic feature of Maori woodcarving.

**weta** — an evil-looking scorpion-like insect which is, in fact, perfectly harmless.

**whare** — house. (Rhymes with 'lorry'.)

## OTHER REFERENCES

**Armageddon** — the place of the last decisive battle at the Day of Judgment, or any 'final' conflict on a great scale.

**Basin Reserve** — The Wellington Cricket ground.

**bastinado** — beating the soles of a victim's feet with a stick or cudgel.

**Columban Fathers** — a missionary congregation of priests with bases in New Zealand.

**'Eye of the fish'** — in Maori lore The North Island of New Zealand was a big fish brought up from the sea and Wellington harbor was its eye.

**Hawkes Bay** — A province on the central western part of the North Island.

**Hellespont** — A strait connecting the Aegean Sea with the Sea of Marmara in Turkey. In ancient times it was the scene of the legendary exploits of Hero and Leander. Nowadays it is more often called Dardanelles.

**houpplelandes** — tunics with long skirts worn in medieval Europe.

**Maid of Orleans** — St. Joan of Arc.

**Moor** — a Moroccan.

**Mount Cook** — New Zealand's highest mountain; it is in the Southern Alps Range.

M.V.--moving vessel.

**Pelorus Jack** — an albino dolphin which guided ships through the Pelorus Sound in the late 19th/early 20th centuries.

Pukka--authentic, first class (from Hindi language, adopted by English colonials in India).

**short-tailed bats** — the only bat of the 800+ species in the world that can both fly and run on all fours.

**White Island** — a continuously active island volcano off the east coast of the North Island.

# *What the Rosary Is About*

### *Originating in the Psalms*

To trace the history of the rosary one must go back to the Old Testament days of King David, around whose songs and hymns the Book of Psalms took shape. These psalms express to God every emotion known to man, and are the backbone of Jewish liturgy. Jesus used them. The earliest Christians, realizing that in Jesus the psalms were fulfilled, made them central to their liturgy and prayer life–all 150 of them.

On the Christian rosary–and every religion has its rosary–150 prayers are meant to be said. The beads reflect the fact that the early Christian monks were vowed to a life of reciting the 150 psalms. Many of these hermits soon knew them by heart. But if for some reason a monk was not able to recite the psalms each day, he might substitute that "perfect prayer of Jesus," the Our Father (Matthew 6:9-13). Fingering beads or knots on a rope helped them move through their prayers. For centuries, the Christian rosary was a chain of Our Fathers recited three times around on 50 beads.

### *Countering Heresy*

Then, in the 12th century, a heresy developed in the south of France. It claimed that Jesus was divine, but not fully human. Strange beliefs and practices developed from that error. As a weapon against the heresy, one St. Dominic's friars turned to the Scripture passage that most strikingly announces Christ's incarnation as man. This is the angel's greeting in the first chapter of Luke: "Hail, Mary, full of grace. . . ." It is to the Domincans that we owe the modern arrangement of five sections in the rosary, with an Our Father prayer heading each set of ten Hail Mary beads.

### Contemplating Jesus

But that was not all: each of the three rounds of 50 prayers was connected to a "mystery" of the Christian faith in Jesus. Thus, the first round of prayers became—and remains to this day—devoted to the five Joyful Mysteries. These are The Annunciation of the angel; Mary's Visit to her cousin Elizabeth; The Birth of Christ in a manger; The Presenting of Christ in the Temple; and The Finding of Jesus in the Temple. As it has been put, "In the Joyful Mysteries Mary shows us her 'baby pictures of Jesus.' "

In similar fashion the Sorrowful Mysteries (the second round of prayers) contemplate the sufferings of Jesus in his Passion; and the Glorious Mysteries, his triumph over death and sin. While Jesus is contemplated, Mary is addressed (not worshiped as has been erroneously claimed by many), and sought as our friend, living in heaven, and as that Mother whom Jesus has always honored.

### The Modern Rosary

The modern Christian rosary has a "tail" leading into the round of fifty that begins with a cross used as a starting point to recite the creed of the first Apostles, followed by a large bead, then three small beads, and another large bead. The first large bead is for an Our Father and the second is for the Glory Be prayer; these are the only places where these two prayers each have their own bead. The three small beads in between, on which are prayed three "Hail Mary's," are reminders to pray for a personal increase in faith, hope and love. What is known as the "Glory be" prayer, a tribute to the Trinity, is also incorporated into each decade, often followed by a prayer springing from the Apparitions of Mary at Fatima, Portugal. Various additions and uses have been made over the centuries, but the essence of the rosary as a call to Christian prayer and growth in faith and love has remained intact.